ROYAL MATE

EVA CHASE

BOUND TO THE FAE

Talia

This night should be a time for celebration. The arch-lords of the summer fae just welcomed one of the men I love to rule alongside them. Minutes ago, the field around me was full of dancing and laughter in honor of his coronation. And I had a promise from all three of my lovers tingling giddily through me. The air itself felt full of joy.

Now I'm backing away through the crowd with my stomach twisted and my thoughts scattered by a surge of cold horror. Not because of the arrival of the five Unseelie arch-lords with huge raven-like wings jutting from their backs, as unsettling as they are as they stare down the Seelie trio. Something much worse is happening *inside* me.

A voice—a vibrant tenor, unmistakably male and shocked—peals through the searing gap that seems to have opened down the center of my being. *Where are you going? We have to— We must speak.*

No. No, no, no. I'm incapable of anything other than that repeated but probably futile denial.

No one else can hear his words, just as no one else could sense the burning jolt that tore through me when my gaze collided with that of the youngest of the winter arch-lords. The space that opened up inside me conveys not only his voice but also a wave of inexplicable impressions: the sight of my slim, pink-haired form vanishing amid the bodies of the gathered summer fae, the flex of unfamiliar muscles and the wash of the warm breeze tickling across feathers attached to those limbs, a stutter of a pulse that's beating even harder than mine.

I don't want this. I need it to *stop*. But the flood of sensation only swells, upending my own awareness. My feet stumble under me, a pang shooting through my warped foot. My elbow bumps one of the other spectators, who jerks back with a frown.

I have to get away. Maybe if I go far enough, I can outrun this awfulness?

Please, come back. I know you must be startled too, but—

Spinning around, I stop paying attention to his words, thinking of nothing but propelling myself in the opposite direction. My balance is off; the ground seems to sway. A hand catches my arm, and I flinch, striking out instinctively.

"Whoa there." It's not an enemy—not *him*—but Astrid, the fae warrior woman who's acted as a sort of bodyguard when the lord of my pack and his cadre can't watch over me themselves. Staring down at me, she blocks my reflexive jab easily and gently. My awareness of her is fractured by other scenes from an angle another pair of eyes are seeing from: the semi-circle of gathered Seelie. The line of Unseelie arch-lords beside—beside him, not me—

Astrid's steady voice breaks through the stream of clashing images. "What's wrong? You don't have to worry —the ravens can't attack us. They'll have taken their vows to come through the border here by the Heart."

I'm not worried about that kind of attack. A totally different sort of assault is already underway within my mind and body. I close my eyes, but that only brings the invading impressions into sharper clarity.

I wrench my eyelids open again with a wild shake of my head. A ragged plea spills from my lips. "I have to get out of here."

Astrid may not understand what's going on, but she knows she's meant to protect me. Without arguing, she adjusts her grip on my arm so she's partly supporting my weight and ushers me toward the Bastion. The gleaming, gold-veined walls of the building where the Seelie arch-lords conduct their business no longer reassure me with their warmth. Somehow I don't think they'll provide enough shelter.

You must— Wait. We can talk about this like reasonable—

No! I think at the voice with a more emphatic burst of panicked resistance. *No, go away, stop, get out of me.*

I've never experienced anything like this before, but I've heard it described. This splitting down the middle, this rush of another person's awareness sweeping in—it's how a soul-twined mate bond feels when it sparks. But only true-blooded fae are supposed to make soul-twined connections. And I'm not fae at all, except for the tiniest trace somewhere in my heritage. By every measure that matters to the folk around me, I'm human. This is impossible.

But then, other things about me have been impossible since the moment my path crossed with the fae in violence and bloodshed and the murders of my family nearly ten years ago. Why not this too?

Oh, God, I don't want to think that. I just want this unwanted invasion to be done.

We duck through one of the shadowed doorways. Footsteps thump after us. I flinch again, but when I look up, relief washes over me. August, the lead warrior of our pack and the tenderest of my lovers, is hustling over to us, his boyishly handsome face tensed with concern. Astrid must have managed to signal him while she was leading me here.

"What's going on?" he asks, grasping my shoulder. "What happened to you, Talia? What do you need?"

The impressions rising through me have jumbled into some sort of commotion—urgently spoken words, a glare, a flash of frustration. *Come back*, the voice demands, but then it falls away as if the man out there is distracted by whatever's going on around him.

I gulp for air. "I don't know. I—I think— It doesn't make any sense."

August gathers me in his arms, tucking his chin over my head. His hand strokes up and down my back. An uneasy twinge I've never experienced in his embrace before runs through my gut. A flare of hostility carries through the connection—

And then it's gone. *He's* gone. But I'm not the same as

I was before. The seared-open space inside of me echoes with the sudden emptiness. I can't shake off my awareness of the Unseelie man's absence, as if he's carved a mark inside me that will linger no matter where he goes.

No. I clench my teeth against a sob. August hugs me tighter, murmuring reassuring words, and my stomach knots with an ache so sharp I shudder.

How can I tell him? How can I tell any of them after they just offered me so much devotion, even committed to making me their mate?

I love the three fae men who've become my saviors and protectors, and they care for me so much in return, as impossible as I thought that would be too. I'd never been happier than I was moments ago in this building when they swore they'd find a way to make our shared relationship official in the eyes of all their peers.

And now this—this whatever it is—has betrayed them and me.

"Just tell me when you're ready," August is saying.

I swallow the lump that's filled my throat. My voice comes out thin and scratchy. "I—I don't—"

Two more sets of footsteps ring out across the stone floor. Sylas, lord of our pack and newly proclaimed arch-lord, and Whitt, his spymaster, stride over to us. There's a storm already brewing in Sylas's mismatched gaze—one eye dark as chocolate and the other one ghostly white amid the scar that cuts through his brown skin. It turns even wilder when he takes in my expression.

"Did they injure you in some way? If those blasted ravens—"

"No," I say quickly. The last thing I want is for his first

move as arch-lord to be charging back out there to start a full-out war. He became arch-lord partly to *prevent* all Seelie kind being sucked into an even more massive conflict against the Unseelie, who've been launching raids along the border between the summer and winter realms for a few decades now. "I—"

My voice wavers with another burst of sensation from deep within, this one more like a brief punch than a flood. A harsh female voice rattles through my mind. *—can't seriously be saying that—* It comes with a clenching of loss and dismay, a glimpse of pale walls and fierce eyes, and then it's gone again.

The connection hasn't been broken. The Unseelie man on the other end of it must be shutting me out—or at least trying to.

I lean back against August's brawny frame, inhaling slowly and scrambling to regain my bearings. I can't hide this problem, and I sure as hell have no idea how to deal with it on my own. Bracing myself for my lovers' reaction, I force out the best explanation I can offer.

"I was in the crowd, watching the Unseelie arch-lords for any clue about why they'd come. And then—the one at the end of the line, the younger man—he glanced toward me, and our eyes met, and—" My chest hitches. I gather myself and press onward, quieter than before. "It felt like I was being seared apart inside. And I started seeing what he must have been seeing, feeling— I heard his voice in my head."

I press my hand to my temple. It *is* my head. I can't even explain how wrong it feels to think that someone else could slip into it like that. How many of my thoughts did the Unseelie man catch?

August's arms tighten around me. Sylas and Whitt are gaping at me, Sylas's stance gone rigid, the color draining from Whitt's tan face. The fae lord speaks first. "You can't mean…" He doesn't seem to know how to go on.

"I know how impossible it sounds." I cringe, misery coiling all through my abdomen. "I know it shouldn't have been able to happen. I wish it *hadn't* happened. But that's—"

"Wait." Whitt's tone is taut and urgent, with a thread of the anguish creeping into his ocean-blue eyes. "If that kind of bond has formed between you and one of the Unseelie arch-lords—he'll be able to see and hear all this through you."

I stiffen. The winter fae could be spying on us, on the Seelie's newest arch-lord, through me. We haven't said anything it'd hurt for them to overhear, but if he can read even my thoughts…

"How do I stop it?" I blurt out.

Even as I speak, another flash blazes through my mind: cold, raised voices clashing, a gleaming silver table. It snaps away as quickly as it rose up.

I shiver. "I think *he's* trying to stop it. At first so much was coming at me from him, and now it's mostly cut off. I just feel kind of… empty."

Sylas grazes his fingers over my head, but his expression is too grim for me to take any comfort from the gesture. "That serves us well. No doubt he's as worried about you reporting what goes on in the winter realm back to us as we are about the reverse. The arch-lords left rather abruptly—it did seem that one raised some kind of issue with the others—but they'd already started making demands of other sorts that we weren't interested in entertaining. I can't imagine they were expecting a sudden soul-twined bond to take hold during their foray here."

He's said the words I hesitated to. *Soul-twined bond.* I'd already thought them, but hearing the fae lord voice them out loud brings the full impact of the situation crashing down on me.

I rub my hands over my face. "How could it have happened?"

If it was going to happen, why couldn't it have been with one of the men around me—the men I already love so deeply?

"I don't know," Sylas says, softly if a little raggedly. "But first let's give you whatever measure of control we can over the connection. There are ways to tune out a soul-twined bond, as I know too well. Are you ready for me to talk you through it?"

I can't imagine what a frantic mess I must look. I lift my head as straight as I can and nod.

"All right." He takes my hand, and August releases me so Sylas can guide me to sit cross-legged on the stone floor across from him. The fae lord lifts his gaze from me for only a moment to his cadre-chosen. "Make sure we're not disturbed."

August moves to the hall we entered from, Astrid taking the initiative to do the same at one of the other doorways to the room. Whitt stays poised over Sylas, crossing his arms tightly over his chest.

Sylas grips both of my hands in his. "You want to pick

some element or material you feel closely connected with. I used living wood. Whatever speaks to you the strongest, picture it sealing over the space inside you, blocking anything that would try to travel through either way."

I wet my lips. "Does it have to be something you're magically connected to?" One of the other impossible things about me is that despite being human, I've managed to wield a few true names like the fae do, conjuring and manipulating things with them. But my skills are weak, and I don't have many options to draw on.

Sylas's gaze flicks to Astrid, who doesn't know about my fledgling powers, but he seems to decide that if she follows this part of the conversation, there's no harm in it. "I expect that's more likely to form a strong barrier, yes."

Then I'm choosing between bronze, light, and air.

I close my eyes, thinking back to the times when I've called to them, and the answer comes to me faster than I expected. Bronze has defended me and air has brought information to me, but light is the magic of my heart. The power fueled by the joy I feel when I'm with these men.

If anything can shut out this unwanted intruder, that'll be it.

I imagine the light I've summoned between my hands with its true name and the brilliant sun streaming over the castle in our home in Hearthshire. The way August's face lights up every time I tell him I love him, the playful spark that so often dances in Whitt's eyes, and the heady warmth that passes from Sylas into me with his touch. All those glowing sensations wrap around my chest and spread through my limbs.

Collecting that impression of brightness, I picture it

pouring into the gap that's split open inside me. I will the warm glow to thicken until it's an impenetrable mass of light.

The impression of emptiness fades. No further flickers reach me from that other mind. I feel… almost complete again as I am.

A shaky breath spills out of me. "Okay. I think—I think I did it."

"Good." Sylas squeezes my fingers. "It'll take practice to perfect it. You'll need to stay watchful and notice when any awareness from the other side begins to seep through. But with every breach, you'll get better at telling whether you've gotten the seal solid."

I meet his solemn gaze. "This isn't a real solution, though, is it?"

His jaw tenses. "No. It's a temporary fix. The rest…"

He glances up at his spymaster. Before they can discuss the subject any further, a voice carries down the hall.

"Sylas?"

It's Celia—his new arch-lord colleagues must want to discuss the visit from the Unseelie. They don't know about me yet—about what happened to me. What will they think when they do?

Sylas grips my hands firmly as we stand together. "Over here!" he calls, and turns back to me. "You'll go with Whitt and August while I see to other business—I'll be back as soon as I can. We won't mention this to anyone else until we know our next steps."

That reassurance only soothes my nerves a little. As the fae lord goes to meet his fellow arch-lord, giving a few quick instructions to his cadre on the way, I hug myself.

The glowing patch inside me wavers. With a hiccup of my pulse, I gather more light together, putting all the power I can summon into it.

What next steps can there be? My soul is somehow intertwined with one of the Unseelie—one of the leaders of the raven-shifting winter fae who've been attacking the Seelie since before I was even born. No matter what benefits my blood offers the summer fae, no matter how much affection my lovers have for me, I can't picture any solution that won't come with a whole lot of pain.

2

August

As I stalk from one end of the make-shift office to the other, I can barely rein in my wolf. It stretches within me, fangs gnashing and claws raking, every nerve reverberating with the desire to leap free and launch myself at the mangy raven who somehow twined himself with Talia's soul.

I love her. I meant to make her my mate. The thought of losing her to anyone, let alone the wretched Unseelie, brings a roar to my throat even while she's sleeping just down the hall. If the feathery bastards actually try to take her away from us…

The only things holding me back from unleashing the beast inside are the fact that murdering an Unseelie arch-lord would ruin all of us, not just Talia—and the possibility that severing her from a soul-twined bond that's already formed might hurt her even more than *I'm* hurting right now.

"We can't throw her into the winter realm," I say, unable to restrain the growl that creeps out with the words. "None of this makes sense. She belongs with *us*."

Whitt's voice comes out as strained as it is dry. "The bond would appear to indicate otherwise." His face is drawn where he's propped against the rough desk Sylas has been using for work while our castle here by the Heart is still in the early stages of construction. The tart scent of fresh oak sap laces the air.

I don't think either of my older brothers are any happier than I am with the situation. Sylas stands next to Whitt, his arms crossed and his unscarred eye smoldering with dark emotion. "We aren't sending her anywhere until we have a better idea of how this happened. And not even then, if I have any say in it."

I stop, swiveling toward them. "*She* should have the say—and she doesn't want it. You saw how upset she was."

Sylas steps forward to set his hand on my shoulder. "I did, and that's why I'm going to do everything in my power to get to the bottom of this."

As always, my lord's steady authoritative air helps settle my temper. If anyone can find a solution, it's him.

But what if no one can? What if Talia is doomed to be tied to some vicious winter fae for the rest of her life?

As soon as Sylas lowers his hand, I start pacing again, unable to keep myself in place. Wary of what might spring free of me if I did.

Whitt swipes his hand over his face. Afterward, his expression only looks more uneasy. "We've always known she's more than a regular human. The way her blood counteracts our curse, and her minor capacity for learning true names. But for a soul-twined bond to grip her—that's an immense escalation. Most *fae* don't experience that."

Sylas inclines his head in agreement. "I can't see how Nuldar's statements shed any light on this development either. A trace of fae blood in her ancestry and a coincidence of synchronicitous timing might explain her connection to the curse, and that connection could conceivably have allowed her to tap into a small amount of the Heart's power. But as you say, for a soul-twined bond to form… and with an Unseelie, no less!"

A miserable thought occurs to me. "The sage never said the fae heritage she got through her great-grandmother's line was Seelie. For all we know, the trace she has is winter blood."

"But for her to be connected to *our* curse—" Sylas cuts himself off with a violent shake of his head. "No, there's no debating it. It remains a mystery—far too much of one for us to draw any real conclusions."

He glances at Whitt. Things have been tense between them for the past few weeks because of a horrible admission Whitt made that I don't want to think about right now, but in this moment, with a much more urgent concern in front of us, any hesitation Sylas felt before has fallen away. Say whatever you might about Whitt's behavior, there's no doubting his skill at his work.

Sylas motions to him. "Have you ever heard any report, current or historical, of *any* faded fae having a soul-twined bond come upon them?"

Whitt grimaces. "Not one that I can think of—and while I don't expect my mind has held onto every story that's reached my ears, one like that would have been remarkable enough to stick."

My hands ball at my sides, the claws I can't quite will back pricking my palms. "Should we go back to Nuldar and request another audience? Before we only asked him about her connection to the curse."

"He's never had patience for those who fail to ask the 'right' question the first time, and after that first answer, I have my doubts about whether we'd glean much more from him anyway." Sylas pauses, his gaze going momentarily distant. His mouth curves with a frown. "There is another way we could discover more about her history and how her soul might have become intertwined with fae kind."

Whitt stiffens just slightly. Between that and his frown, I can guess he knows what Sylas means and that I'm not going to like it. Still, I have to ask. "What is it?"

Sylas gives me a pensive look before answering. "We could bring her to the Pool of the Clouded Past and see what it shows her."

"The—" My hackles rise even though *he* hasn't done anything to offend me. "We'd have to go back to Thundervale."

He nods grimly. "And request permission from its lord. I know you have unpleasant memories there. If you'd rather not—"

"No, I'll go. Talia needs all of us." I'm not going to abandon her over my own past ordeals, even if the thought of returning to that place makes my chest constrict.

All three of us are incredibly familiar with both the

domain of Thundervale and its lord… because we all grew up there, and Lord Eldris is our father.

The closer the carriage brings us to Thundervale, the tighter my ribs seem to compress around my lungs. I sit in the bottom of the vehicle next to Talia, my arm around her, sheltering her from the whipping wind. At least I *can* shelter her from that when there's so much else I can't.

We've made the journey to Thundervale at a swift pace so that we're not keeping Sylas from his new duties as arch-lord for very long. He told his colleagues that the trip was to gain insight into a matter involving both the curse and the Unseelie, which is technically true.

Whitt volunteered that he and I could escort Talia on our own, but our lord vetoed that idea immediately. I'm not sure how much it was because he wants to hear Talia's account firsthand and how much because of the brightly brittle note in Whitt's voice that suggested if left to our own devices, the two of us might unleash so much of our honest opinions on our father that we'd never get to the pond in the first place. The man's love of criticism has never extended to any aimed at himself.

I suspect I'm going to spend the better part of the initial meeting biting my tongue. It's been a long time since I thought of Lord Eldris as anyone I'd want to call Father. In my head, he's not so much a father or a lord as the man who ordered my mother's death.

Even a century and a half later, the memories rise up with

brutal vividness: her screams and his guards' claws gouging into her flesh, my muscles straining against my father's magic as I struggled to spring to her defense. A "lesson," he called it. All it taught me was never to trust that anything I cared about would stay safe in the presence of that man.

And now we're taking Talia straight to him.

I must be letting too much of my discomfort show. Talia adjusts her position in my arms so she can peer into my face. "Are you worried about seeing him?"

A flash of regret passes through me that I shared so much of my history with her. Not because I don't want her to know me in every possible way, but because it gives *her* more reason to worry about this trip. But then, maybe it's better that she knows the darkest side of the man she's about to meet.

"I don't enjoy having to see him or speak to him," I say over the warble of the wind. "And I'd rather you never had to come anywhere near him. But he's proud of Sylas, even though Sylas struck out on his own rather than waiting to continue the Thundervale legacy. He respects him. I don't think he'll challenge Sylas's authority or act against us in any way."

And Sylas will be on his guard just in case I'm wrong. Our father may respect *him* as his true-blooded son, but Sylas didn't turn a blind eye to how things were run in the domain while he was coming into his own. I never told him exactly what went on with my mother, but he found me during the anguished rampage I went on through the woods afterward, cooled me down and comforted me as well as he could without demanding anything from me.

I'm sure he gathered enough from other witnesses to put the pieces together well enough.

He told me once that the day when he heard Eldris had ordered my mother's murder was the day he decided for sure that he was leaving Thundervale. And as soon as I was of age to officially join his cadre, we left that place behind. I've only been back a few times in the many decades since then when official business required it, and not at all since our banishment.

Talia shudders and squeezes my arm in sympathy. "I wish we didn't have to come anywhere near him. Do you really think this pool will tell us something that could help with the soul-twined bond—or at least explain how it happened?"

I make a face. "I don't know. Like the sage, the sorts of responses it gives aren't always straightforward. You have to word your requests carefully. But it does at least show a literal representation of whatever past moments you're able to summon to the surface." My lips slant into a half-smile. "I'll admit there were a couple of times I used it just to find out where I'd left some object or another I'd misplaced."

Talia laughs. It's a beautiful sound, over far too quickly as the weight of everything she's struggling with descends on her again with a shadowing of her eyes. She tucks herself closer to me.

"Is your barrier against the soul-twined connection holding?" I ask.

She nods. "For the most part. I have to stay focused and keep bolstering it. Every now and then if I'm distracted, bits and pieces trickle through. He's been trying to talk to me."

I hug her and kiss her forehead. "You don't have to listen to him. The bond doesn't give him the right to demand your attention."

It just means it's much easier for him to make demands of her anyway. The toll her efforts at fending off the Unseelie arch-lord are taking comes through in the thread of weariness in her voice, the way she sinks into my embrace rather than insisting on holding herself straight and strong.

I grit my teeth in frustration. I should be able to protect her better than this. But the best I can do is stay beside her while we carry out this quest. I just hope something useful comes of it.

The carriage slows. We're almost there. I lift my head and catch Whitt's gaze. He offers me a crooked smile that's closer to a grimace. Eldris might have gone easier on him as the child of a fae dalliance rather than a human one, but my oldest brother has never made his disdain for our father's tyrannical habits a secret. For all the ways we're different, there's something reassuring in knowing we're united on that one subject.

It probably is a good thing Sylas insisted on coming along. If Eldris made one cutting remark about Talia in front of just the two of us, he might very well have ended up equally lashed by Whitt's words and my claws.

When the carriage comes to a halt, Sylas hops out alone, as we planned. I ease onto one of the benches, keeping an arm around Talia, and watch my lord stride up to the castle.

True to Eldris's magical affinities for plant life, which Sylas inherited a fair amount of, the massive structure is constructed out of interwoven vines. In the time since I was last here, they've darkened from green to brown and melded together at the edges with age.

They aren't the only things about this place that have altered as they've gotten older. The man who marches out to meet Sylas is grayer and more weathered than I remember, the dark purple-brown hair Sylas also inherited grizzled along his temples and through his short beard, new crow's feet lining the skin at the corners of his eyes. Eldris smiles the same way as ever, though—wide but thin, as if he doesn't quite trust anyone enough to offer a glimpse of his teeth.

The smile he offers Sylas does reach his eyes though, with a gleam of the pride I told Talia about. "My son, now Arch-Lord Sylas. I wish I could have come to the crowning, you know—there were just too many things that needed my supervision here. I'd have arranged to come to you to offer congratulations as soon as I could."

We all know that "as soon as I could" means never. I'm not sure Lord Eldris has left his domain in the entire time I've been alive. He rules with a tyrant's fist—and a tyrant's fear of how his pack might revolt if he gave them any room to breathe out from under his thumb. From what I've gathered based on Whitt's and Sylas's stories, that paranoia has only grown as his cruelty did in the wake of his soul-twined mate's departure.

When I was younger and I heard people refer to how much milder Eldris's temper was when he had Sylas's mother by his side, it made me angry at her for leaving.

Now, with an adult's perspective and the understanding that a milder cruelty still wouldn't offer much happiness, I can't blame her. After all, we left as soon as we easily could too.

"I'm glad to receive those congratulations now," Sylas says evenly. "Unfortunately this matter is too urgent for us to enjoy a full visit. Do we have your permission to journey to the Pool of the Clouded Past?"

Eldris dips into a small bow, remembering a little late the extra respect he owes Sylas's new position. "Of course. I wouldn't deny an arch-lord or my son."

Not that son, anyway. His gaze slides over the carriage, taking in Whitt in his careless pose by the bow, me on the bench, and Talia next to me. A different sort of gleam lights in his eyes, one closer to greed. "Is that the human of the cure?" he asks without any sign that either of us with her deserve his acknowledgment.

Talia's stance goes rigid. I react automatically, even though inside I'm recoiling at the sight of my father. I get up and step in front of her to fully shield her from his view. My fingers curl over the sides of the carriage, gripping it hard. Just shy of digging my claws into the wood.

Let him look at *me* all he likes. I can hold my other urges in check, but I'm not letting him subject her to his malicious stare.

Sylas's voice goes firmer. "It is, and she is part of our business here. We'll take our leave of you. I assume we can count on being undisturbed?"

Eldris scowls at me, and I stand there immovable, glowering right back at him. After a moment, he jerks his gaze back to Sylas. I get the sense he's bitten back a few things he might have wanted to say to me if he weren't faced with the son he actually values with all the authority that son now wields.

"I'm pleased I could be of service," he says, only a hint of annoyance leaking into his formal tone. "You will have the pond to yourself."

He draws back, and Sylas returns to the carriage. I stay where I am, poised in front of Talia by the edge of the canopy, until the vehicle glides forward and Eldris hustles back into his castle.

That's one minor challenge we've dealt with. There's far more than I'd like to measure still ahead for us to tackle.

3

Talia

$\mathcal{A}$s Sylas directs our carriage toward this magical pool, my brief observations of my lovers' father replay in my mind. I've heard enough about him to know I wouldn't want to spend any more time around him than I have to, so I should have been prepared, but my skin is still crawling from the brief encounter. The way he spoke to Sylas with no trace of genuine fatherly warmth—the way he totally ignored his other two sons while they were right there in front of him—and the cool calculation in his expression when his gaze settled on me…

A shiver passes through me. August sits back down beside me and tucks his arm around my back. The tightness of his mouth shows that he didn't enjoy that interaction any more than I did.

Whitt leans back against the wall of the carriage, turning his face to the wind so it ruffles his sunkissedbrown hair. "Looks like the joys of fathering an arch-lord didn't distract the paternal pissant from his obsessions for more than an instant. Here's to another century or so before we require any further dealings with that dung-heap."

Sylas shoots him a chiding glance, but he doesn't dispute Whitt's commentary. He's told me he couldn't call the man I just saw a bad father as far as he was concerned, but I know he hates a lot of things about the ways their father has ruled.

Nevertheless, they all handled the conversation with poised control, none of them sinking to the other man's level to show their contempt in return. Lord Eldris might have fathered them and had a hand in raising them, but they've clearly risen far above anything they could have learned from him. Thinking of their strength, I reach to squeeze August's hand. After what that man did to his mother, this meeting must have been hardest for him out of all of them.

"You could put out a word surreptitiously via your typical methods," Sylas says to Whitt. "See that anyone who'd rather not remain under his tyranny knows they'd be welcome at Hearth-by-the-Heart."

Whitt inclines his head with the faintest of smiles. "I'll make sure the word gets out without him catching wind of it."

I guess our current pack-kin must mostly be fae who left with Sylas and his brothers when they founded Hearthshire. The others must not have disliked Lord Eldris's approach enough to switch their loyalties, but maybe a few of them have changed their minds in the time since. Our pack must be awfully small for an arch-lord. The men have said their numbers dwindled after they were banished, and I've seen how many people arch-lords like Ambrose had at their disposal.

Sylas urges the carriage faster again, and I tip my head against August's shoulder. The wind ripples over my hair—and a fragment of a forceful voice breaks through the mass of light I've pulled together inside me.

—have to listen to me. We can't just—

My pulse hiccups. Closing my eyes, I wrench more of the glowing sensation into the center of me. Let it burn out any impressions trying to slip through and seal over the hole inside me.

I focus on that place until the light feels like a thick, solid thing, a wall as blazing as the sun. It's only when I open my eyes that I feel the sweat that's broken out on my forehead, cooling my skin.

August rubs my arm. "He tried to reach you again?"

I nod, too exhausted in that moment to form words, and snuggle close to my lover. How much longer am I going to have to fight this connection?

How much longer *can* I fight it before I'm completely worn out?

August holds me tight until the carriage slows. We've passed into a stretch of pinkish rocky terrain dotted with tufts of sea-green grass that glitters when the sun's beams hit it. A faint ozone-y scent lingers in the air as if a thunderstorm has just passed, though there hasn't been any rain.

The pool lies directly ahead of us, an oval of water surrounded by a glossy stone bank. The pond's surface is so smooth it looks more like a mirror reflecting the sky above than anything I could dip my hand into.

As I watch it, a breeze trickles across it, rippling the reflection. The water returns to stillness just moments later. It's so eerie, the hairs on the back of my neck rise.

We walk up to it, our boots thumping on the hard ground. Sylas motions for me to sit at the narrowest point on the oval, right at the water's edge.

"Each person can only see their own past, and the pool will only show what you ask it for, however it can best interpret that," he says. "You'll have to look and tell us what you observe."

I inhale slowly, bracing my hands against the marble-like surface beneath me. "And I should ask about anything to do with the fae—any ways I might have been influenced by magic without realizing it?"

"Exactly. But follow your gut. You know your life far better than any of us. There's no limit to how much the pool will show you if you keep making new requests, so take your time and try anything that occurs to you."

"All right." With my legs crossed, I scoot a little closer until my knees jut over the pool. Then I lean over to peer into the motionless water.

My face stares back at me, even paler than usual with dark smudges beneath my eyes. I didn't sleep much last night, jerking awake every hour or two with fears that my barrier of light was failing, building it back up before I could even start to relax again. Not even seeing the dark pink hair August gave me months ago with a combination of magic and fruit-based dye raises my spirits. I tuck a few stray strands behind my ear as I decide where to start.

Why not go back to the beginning? The sage said that my connection to the curse was something passed on through my family. Were there signs of it when I was born, when I was so young that I wouldn't remember?

"Show me when I was first born," I say to the water.

A shimmer skims across the pool's surface, and my reflection falls away into darkness. But no other images emerge. I'm just staring into flat blackness.

I frown. "It isn't showing me anything. It's just gone dark."

Sylas hums, peering into the pool from beside me even though he said he wouldn't be able to see what the water presented to me. "Perhaps it's taking your statement a bit too literally in the sense of when you'd be considered fully 'born'?"

Nuldar's words come back to me. *She started in darkness. Then she came out into the light.* Is the pool being equally obtuse?

"Show my mother holding me when I was a baby," I say, and then quickly add, "less than a month old. When it was light out." Hopefully that narrows it down enough.

The darkness pulls back. And there before my eyes is Mom, swaying from side to side and back and forth in a wavering circular motion. Pale sunlight spills over her from a window beyond my view. A round head with a smattering of brown hair pokes from a tightly wrapped blanket in her arms.

My chest hitches. That's me. That's me with my mother. I can only see her profile, and she's younger than in any of my memories—but I'd almost started to forget what she looked like in all the years since then. This glimpse of her brings so many moments with my family back into startling clarity.

She looks tired, her dark hair rumpled and her eyelids drooping, but she's smiling at my infant self. There's a joyful glow in her face that wrenches at my heart. I find myself blinking hard.

It's been almost a decade since I saw that smile aimed at me, heard Mom's soft laugh or the tsk of her tongue. I have the wild urge to throw myself into the water as if I'd somehow crash into her embrace.

But she's not really there. She's not really anywhere. Aerik and his cadre tore her to pieces along with Dad and Jamie.

My hands clench the rocky lip of the pool.

"Do you see something now?" Sylas asks gently.

Right. I'm here for a reason, not just to reminisce about what I've lost. I clamp down on the rush of emotions and study the image as well as I can. My voice manages to come out steady. "Yes. My mother, holding me. Rocking me to sleep, I think. She had this funny way of doing it—she told me that the first couple of weeks I cried so much she was afraid I had colic, but she tried all kinds of things and finally found this specific motion that calmed me right down."

My lips twitch at the memory. Whenever I started complaining too much when I was older, she joked that she'd have to scoop me up and give me a good rocking. *If it worked when you were two weeks old, I'm sure it'll work now.* In my protesting or laughter, I often forgot whatever I'd been whining about.

August has hunkered down nearby. He strokes his hand up and down my back. Sylas's jaw clenches as if he hesitates to press further, but he goes on anyway. "Is there anything unusual that you notice?"

I peer at the image as intently as I can, keeping a tight hold on my emotions. I can only make out hazy impressions of the room around my mother and me, but it looks like an ordinary children's bedroom. Nothing strikes me as odd about her or me. "No."

I feel more than see Whitt come up behind me. "Ask it to show you one of the times when you were crying, like you mentioned."

Does he think there's something odd about that? I fix my gaze on the water, letting go of the desire to just keep staring at Mom as she is there now forever. "Show me when I was with my mom as a baby crying."

The image wavers and bleeds into another. My mom is hustling me into the house, bundled up in a stroller. The pool doesn't emit any sound, but it's obvious from the ruddiness of my infant face and the shape of my mouth that I'm wailing my heart out. Mom's lips form a shushing sound as she scrambles to undo the straps.

There's still nothing remotely magical or otherwise strange about the scene. I shake my head in anticipation of Sylas's question.

At the edge of my vision, he glances toward Whitt. The spymaster must be satisfied, because Sylas gives the next instruction. "I'd say focus on asking about the fae influence in your life next."

That sounds reasonable. I watch Mom tucking my infant self into her arms for a moment longer, absorbing every detail of her I can make out, and then force out the words to send her away. "Show me the first time I was affected by the fae."

The previous scene is swallowed into the same blackness my first request brought. I wait a few seconds, but the darkness doesn't change. "Nothing again," I say. "I guess the first time I was affected was before I was even born. Um, show me the first time I was affected by the fae *after* I was born."

Only more darkness, stretching across the pool. I knit my brow. "Still nothing. Maybe that means I wasn't ever directly affected, however it's interpreting that word?"

Whitt lets out an irritable sound. "So convenient, these wizened sages and magical places. Try phrasing it as when you first *saw* a fae, so we'll know there should be a visual."

I give the water my best *You'd better start behaving* glare. "Show me when I first saw a fae."

The darkness shatters apart into a dimly lit scene of a preteen girl giggling as she jogs between a couple of trees —just as a massive furred shape leaps out of the shadows.

My heart hurtles into my throat. I choke on it, my breath fading to a rasp with the constricting of my lungs. Icy panic clutches my chest.

I squeeze my eyes shut, but it's too late. I've already watched the beast with the tawny fur sink its jaws into my 12-year-old self's shoulder where scars still mark my skin today, seen the shriek in the contorting of my mouth, and caught the gangly figure of my eight-year-old brother just coming into view with another monstrous wolf charging straight toward him.

"Talia!" August says, alarm ringing through his voice.

I'm rocking against his supporting hand. My breath is still seeping out of me in gasps. I press backward into his touch harder and slam my palms against the smooth stone, training every bit of my attention onto those solid surfaces.

This is what's real. This is what's now. The rest—the rest is done. It's over with.

It's running through my mind so vividly the scars on my shoulder sting.

Other hands rest on my back, my head. Sylas's steady baritone breaks through the haze of panic. "We're here with you, Talia. No one can hurt you. Whatever you saw, it won't happen again."

I manage to drag in a deeper breath. The images retreat but don't fade completely.

And then another voice splits through them from within. *Talia? What happened? Are you all right? Please, if you would just speak to me—*

The Unseelie arch-lord—in my fluster, the light walling off our connection faltered. How much of my distress did he feel? If it was even half of it—

I don't want this total stranger, this enemy of my lovers and my pack, seeing so much of me. My body recoils from the inside out.

No! I shout at him inwardly, and visualize every

particle of light I can summon swelling through my torso, blocking him out.

When that's done, I open my eyes, dragging in another ragged gulp of air. I'm not rocking anymore, only trembling. I can't tell how much that's from the aftermath of the scene the pool showed me and how much from the effort it took rebuilding my inner wall.

Then one new fact catches up with me, hitting me hard enough that I speak without thinking. "He knows my name."

Sylas brushes his fingers over my temple. "Who? What did you see?"

"It's not— There was nothing useful in the pool." I make a rough gesture toward the water. "It was the night when Aerik attacked me, just like I remember it, nothing I'd forgotten. I'm sorry. I should have realized I might see that—I should be able to handle it better—"

Whitt's knuckles graze the back of my neck as he gives my hair an affectionate tug, cutting off my apology. "You don't have to be that mighty, Talia. No one here is going to blame you for carrying scars inside any more than we do the ones on the outside."

Will I never be able to recall that horrible night without a panic coming on, just like the marks on my shoulder will never disappear? The thought makes my stomach twist, but I haven't actually answered Sylas's question yet.

I look up at the fae lord. "When I panicked, the barrier I put up over my soul-twined connection weakened. I think the Unseelie arch-lord felt some of it. And he tried to talk to me again—he used my name."

No sign of concern crosses Sylas's face. He simply drops his hand to caress my cheek. "That's not surprising. If he didn't hear it when we were first determining what had happened back by the Heart, he might have just now. You couldn't expect to keep something that basic from him for very long."

Right. Because fae men destroyed my past life, and now another is attempting to take over my current existence. My throat tightens all over again.

I draw my knees up to my chest, hugging my legs. "If Aerik's attack was the first time I saw any fae, what else can I ask?" What if it all goes back to my great-grandfather and whatever fae heritage he had?

Whitt's hand goes still against my spine. "I think we've put her through enough, don't you two?"

Sylas pauses. "Now that we've come all the way out here, we should try everything we can think of."

"What else is there? We've already forced her to re-experience the worst moment in her life." Whitt leans in to press a kiss to the back of my head. I reach to twine my fingers with his. There was a rawness in his voice that reminds me he had to dredge up what might have been the worst moment in *his* life not that long ago.

I defended him then, and now he's trying to protect me.

"It's all right," I say quietly. "I want to give it my best shot. I'll just be more prepared this time—if it looks like I'm going back to the attack, I'll look away."

The spymaster lets out a soft growl. "Fine. Do what you have to do. But something's occurred to me that might work better."

August perks up. "What's that?"

Whitt is silent for a moment. "It won't be easy or fun. But it doesn't matter *why* this happened if we can make it so it never happened. I may know of someone who can break a soul-twined bond."

4

Whitt

I know we've almost reached the spot when the humidity gets so thick the air might as well have turned to soup. This section of the fringes is a swampland, and the closer we get to the outermost edges of the Mists, the more the slimy water beneath our carriage seeps up from the ground to saturate the space above. It carries a scent like mildew and algae that makes me wrinkle my nose.

I'm going to need not one but several showers the moment I'm back at the castle.

Talia peers into the drifting fog. A shiver she can't hide runs through her delicate frame. "There's a jail around here somewhere?"

"Not a jail." I scan the hunched, half-submerged trees and the bubbling patches of water. "She's a solo prisoner. The lord she offended had a grave enough case that the arch-lords agreed to not only banish her out here alone for the foreseeable future but also to place her under indentured servitude."

"Servitude doing *what?*"

"There are fish that live only in this swampland that are a delicacy among the fae, brought out for special occasions. From what I've heard, they have her hunting them, with a certain quota to be met each month." I grimace. "It won't be pleasant work. There's a reason they're a rare delicacy. As far as I know, no fae has ever been able to 'commune' with them well enough to learn their true name, and their scales repel magic. No one much enjoys going up against their many sharp teeth."

Talia outright shudders. "How long has she been stuck out here?"

"Coming up on four centuries. I wouldn't be sure she's even still here if it weren't for the barbtooth filets that were included in our glorious leader's coronation feast."

Reasonably sure, anyway. And I'm less certain of how exactly we'll find her. I murmur a few words designed to resonate with any magic around us, since presumably the woman has used her skills to build some sort of shelter and other amenities even if they won't help her with her duties. A faint twinge leads me to redirect the carriage.

Talia pulls back from the bow to sit on the bench across from me. We've drawn back the carriage's canopy, since the hazy sunlight that filters through the overcast sky and the fog gives the impression of dusk even though it's mid-day. She closes her eyes for a second, I suspect adding to her internal defenses. My fingers clench around the rim of the hull.

When she opens her eyes again, she looks at me far

more wearily than I'd prefer to see. "And this is the only fae who's ever managed to break a soul-twined bond?"

"To the best of my knowledge. I only have it on third-hand authority that breaking a bond was her crime. The lord and his lady in question stayed on as mates and acted as though they were as bonded as ever until their deaths. The exact matter they brought before the arch-lords was kept quiet. But you know I have many sources always on the lookout for those with loose tongues."

"What did your source say happened?"

"He mentioned that someone or other claimed that the woman we're seeking was in love with the lord. She was supposedly so jealous when he found his soul-twined mate that she went to excruciating lengths to discover a method that would shatter that connection." I cluck my tongue. "I can't imagine the depths she must have stooped to—or whether she still thinks it was worth it."

Watching Talia, I can't hold onto the nonchalance I put into my tone. Her suffering is no laughing matter. I've kept the tension wound through my innards at bay by focusing on the schemes we've come up with to help her, but in moments like this, when there's nothing to do but wait for the current scheme to come to fruition, I can't tune it out completely.

I'd like nothing more than to wrap my hands around the neck of that blasted bird-brain arch-lord and squeeze until there was no soul left for her to be bound to.

Talia holds my gaze with such a pensive cast to her eyes that when she opens her mouth to speak again, I ready myself to tackle some new calamity.

"Are you doing okay?" she asks.

I blink at her, momentarily struck speechless with surprise. "I'm pretty sure I'm the one who's supposed to be asking *you* that question."

Her mouth twists. "I just mean—I know you were still dealing with having all that stuff about Isleen brought up after so long, and things have been tense between you and Sylas. Just because we have other problems doesn't mean yours don't matter anymore."

The mention of my relations with my lord's late soul-twined mate and his feelings about that encounter stirs up a clash of emotion that's becoming unpleasantly familiar. But it only lingers for an instant before the deluge of awed affection that sweeps through me at the same time washes most of the rest away.

I appear to have lost my capacity for words completely now. I reach out to Talia, and she comes to me without hesitation, slipping into my embrace with her head against my shoulder and her legs tucked over my lap as if she were made to fit against me. Hugging her, I dip my head to inhale the tartly sweet scent of her.

This incredible woman. Worried about *me* while she's grappling with a disaster none of us can protect her from. The jolt of shock that hit me when she first told me she loved me seems absurd now. That love radiates from her with every gesture from the squeeze of her arm around my chest to the kiss she brushes to my jaw.

She's seen every part of who I am, including the bits I never wanted to show her, and she's stood by me when even I wouldn't stand for myself.

A large part of me is still far from convinced that I deserve anywhere near the compassion she's shown me, or that the drugged tryst I tumbled into with Sylas's mate isn't my crime but only Isleen's—that I haven't fucked up in *some* way beyond what any rational being would respond to with mercy. I've been carrying the guilt for so long that it's grown roots all through me, and tearing them up has unearthed all sorts of other uncomfortable pangs.

But I'm still here. Sylas hasn't seen fit to cast me out or rend me apart after hearing the full account, and he's possibly the most rational fae in my acquaintance. If I didn't know better, I'd be inclined to say our mighty human has cast a spell over us all that included saving me. There's no denying there's some kind of magic to the feel of holding her against me.

I've never given much thought to love. After the first few rounds of temptresses hoping to score a prized position in Sylas's court through their association with me, I dismissed the possibility as something that wouldn't factor into my life, and I can't say I've anguished over that decision. But now…

What else could I call this unceasing welling of affection and desire from some spring deep inside me? The thought of a wretched raven having any sort of claim on her brings my wolf lunging to the surface.

Talia was meant to be our mate, *my* mate—to stand by me and my brothers for decades more to come. Longer, if I have any say in it with the magic this world can offer.

And even if not that, she deserves so much better than to be torn in two from the inside out by a murderous villain who probably has ice in his veins.

But Talia isn't thinking about any of that right now. She's still worrying about me. She strokes her fingers down the side of my neck, waking up a heat much more pleasant than the sticky humidity wrapped around us. "You haven't answered me. Are you okay?"

She's incredible and also incredibly stubborn. I let out a rough sound and lower my lips to kiss her temple. "I expect it'll take some time getting to 'okay,' but at least I *can* get there properly now that those secrets are out in the open. I still—" Just talking about it revives the clashing emotions. "I have many regrets that I haven't fully come to terms with, and I can't blame Sylas for feeling betrayed that I kept so much from him even if he absolves me of my greatest theoretical crime."

Talia nuzzles me. "I don't think he'll hold that against you for very long. It was understandable that you didn't know how to bring up the subject."

"I suppose. But also… somewhat bizarrely, I find I'm a little angry with *him*. Which isn't exactly fair, because I should be glad the idea that I'd have been involved in Isleen's unfaithfulness was so unbelievable to him that he never considered it, but if he'd simply dealt with *her* betrayal to begin with, it could have all come into the open so much sooner."

"I think he's pretty angry with himself about that too."

"Yes. Well. And as I said, it's hardly fair. But that feeling is there along with everything else. I suppose it's just a matter of continuing to go forward and work together until the broken edges of this division between us smooth out and fit back together more easily again." I pause, considering. "I don't know exactly how long that'll take, but we do have a long time. I trust that we'll get there."

"Good." Talia brushes one more kiss to my cheek and then turns her head to glance out over the swamp.

We both spot the light at the same time—I can tell from the tensing of her body. It's only a reddish glimmer through the fog, but it's no natural part of the landscape around us. We've found our fae convict.

Talia eases away from me so I can stand. I walk to the bow, adjusting the carriage's path with a gesture of my hand. I assume a casual stance, but my spine has gone rigid.

I don't expect what we find here to be pretty. I'd have embarked on this journey alone if Talia hadn't insisted with that stubborn spirit of hers on keeping me company. *You're doing this for my benefit*, she said. *I should be there.*

The fog thins to reveal a patch of solid, muddy ground holding a shack formed out of woven reeds, which sag here and there with patches of rot. The reddish light is a magically-charged fire flickering in a ring of stones near the door. As I motion the carriage to a halt, a figure emerges from the shack with a combative stride and a spear clutched in her hand.

It's worse than I anticipated. Four centuries in this fringe swamp wouldn't do anyone good, and it's clearly punished the woman before me in all sorts of ways. The deep, angry scars of piercing teeth mark her limbs, even her chin and cheeks. One of her ears is outright missing amid the ragged strands of her hair, and she's lost three fingers and more than half of her nose as well.

But perhaps the worst is that the same rot that appears to be spreading through her home has infected her as well. Dark brownish-green hollows seep into her bare arms, calves, neck, and face alongside the scars, as if the swamp has made her its home as much as the reverse. My gut recoils.

The woman raises her spear and snarls. "You're not the usual one—and it's not the right time. What do you want here?"

I hold up my hands in a gesture of peace. "I'm not here to make any demands or cause you any trouble. I simply have a few questions to ask. And I've brought gifts to compensate you for your time."

I bend down—carefully, so as not to appear threatening—and raise the large basket some of our pack-kin put together without knowing its destination. The woman's bloodshot eyes rove over the block of cheese, the fresh-baked pastries, the gleaming mirrornuts, and the bottle of dusk-apple wine.

As much as the fish she catches are a delicacy to the fae who can afford them, the common foods I've brought will be a treasure to her. Her diet won't have been comprised of much more than aquatic creatures and swamp plants in close to four hundred years.

She licks her mottled lips, revealing a flash of fangs. Then she turns the spear so she's holding it like a staff rather than a weapon, her fingers clenched around it. "What do you want to know?" Her gaze flicks past me to Talia still crouched on the bench.

I snap my fingers to bring her attention back to me. Better we get this over with quickly. "I've had it that the crime you're being punished for involved the severing of a soul-twined bond. Is that true?"

The stiffening of her posture suggests it is, but her lips

press flat too. She glowers at me. "I'm not to speak of my crime."

I wave her objection off. "What can they possibly do to you that's worse than this? Besides, I come on the request of one of the arch-lords as his cadre-chosen." I produce a token from my pocket that gleams with a power only those with the closest bond to the Heart can access.

The woman studies it for several seconds. Her shoulders come down. She eyes the basket and then my face. Her voice comes out much less strident than before. "All right. Yes. What about it?"

"I want to know, if an arch-lord requested it, if you could do it again."

Her jaw slackens. She composes herself again with a shake of her thin frame. "Your lord wants me to—to break another soul-twined bond?"

"Perhaps. It depends somewhat on the process involved." We're assuming it would be much more expedient to have someone who's learned the magic already carry it out rather than asking her to try to teach something so obscure and presumably difficult to one of us.

"Well, I—I suppose I could. I believe I remember all that's required, or at least how to remind myself. There hasn't been much to think about out here other than my life before." She rubs her mouth. "You can tell your lord it could be done, but he may not like the results."

I raise my eyebrows. "What do you mean by that?"

"The only method I found—and I did try—I didn't *want* to hurt him…" She pauses, her gaze drifting away, and then appears to gather herself. "It's very painful for both parties. Neither… Neither may come out as whole as they were when the bond formed. I think something in each goes into the connection and then is burned away with it."

A chill prickles down my back. I don't like the sound of *that* at all. Although— "What if the bond hasn't been confirmed and consummated yet?"

She lets out a hoarse bark of a laugh. "The magic I know won't work at all then. It draws on the power of the bond to turn it around on itself… If the connection isn't fully formed, I won't have anywhere near enough energy to apply. It's a close thing as it is."

"Ah." My heart sinks. I grope for another question or suggestion, but her last statement cuts off most other avenues. The only thing left to ask is, "Would you need anything other than the presence of the bonded pair?"

"There are a few supplies, things I'm sure an arch-lord could arrange." Her expression turns more calculating. "Better I don't spell too much of it out for you or I'll have nothing left to bargain with, will I?"

A fair point. I direct the carriage a little closer so I can hand the basket to her. "Thank you. I'll return should we decide we're in need of your services, and I'm sure if we are you can expect a far more extensive reward."

She snatches the basket and hurtles into her shack. As I back the carriage away and turn it to leave, the sounds of teeth gnashing into the gifted food carry through the frail walls.

I wait until the shack and its occupant are well behind us and the carriage steady on its way before I return to Talia's side. She's staring straight ahead, her eyes unnervingly glazed, her hands twisted together in her lap. For an instant, I think she may be caught up in some sort of vision through her soul-twined bond, but her gaze slides to me when I join her.

Her voice sounds as brittle as charred paper. "What does it mean to confirm and consummate a bond?"

Of course she has to ask that. I swipe my hand back through my hair, my stomach knotting. "There's a brief ceremony in which you acknowledge and accept the bond with words and magic. And then you accept your mate with your body as well. Only after both happen is the connection complete."

A tremor runs through her. "It gets even *stronger* than this?"

I have no idea what she's already experienced. I ease my arm around her shoulders, hating how poor a comfort the gesture must be. "Sylas was still able to dull his. From what I understand, it gives you a greater ability to convey thoughts and impressions you *want* to pass on, and brings those of your mate into greater clarity when you focus on them."

Talia nods, a defeated motion. Her arms come up to fold over her chest. Her whole body closes in on itself: her head drooping, her jaw clenching, her shoulders drawing tight, her knees pressing together. Trying to hold in what a moment later comes spilling out anyway.

A sob wrenches from her throat. She claps her hands to her face, but the sudden flood of tears streams past them, down her cheeks and her wrists. Her gasps for air shake her entire frame.

Her misery tears right through my chest. I scoop her

up and hug her tightly against me, caressing her hair, absorbing her weeping as well as I can, which isn't very well at all. I can't remember the last time *I* cried, but tears prick at my own eyes on her behalf.

I've never seen her break down like this. Even when she was huddled in Aerik's horrid cage, even when she had to come face to face with that prick and his minions afterward, even when the arch-lord whose place Sylas took threatened to use her as breeding stock—throughout all the torments and indignities she's faced in my presence, she's never bawled her heart out as she's doing now.

Seeing just how much anguish she's been holding in, I realize I didn't appreciate how much strength she's been expending over the past few days. My fangs emerge, gritting against each other with dark thoughts of all the many ways I'd like to apply them to the feathered bastard who's brought her this low.

The only words I can think of to say, nowhere near adequate, tumble out of me in a murmured string. "I've got you. *We've* got you. Whatever we have to do, we'll figure it out. None of us is going to leave you while you're facing this."

Talia's breath hitches. She paws at her eyes, but the tears keep gushing out. All I can do is hold her and murmur those pale reassurances to her over and over until the torrent finally ebbs.

When her sobs have dwindled to sniffles, she cringes against me. "I'm sorry," she whispers hoarsely.

Somehow the apology makes me twice as furious as before. I kiss the top of her head, hugging her with all the adoration I have in me. "*You* have nothing to be sorry for.

By all that is dust, mite, it's a wonder you've held yourself together as well as you have up until now. Not one bit of this changes how mighty I think you are."

She manages a short, watery-sounding laugh. "I just— after all that time with Aerik, everything I've been through since then was at least *better*. It was hard to get too upset when I knew how much worse I'd endured. But this…"

Her voice breaks, and she pauses, swallowing audibly. "It's like I've been caged all over again. Except even more than before, because it's not just my body that's trapped but my mind, my soul—there isn't any part of me that can get away. Not when the person I'm trying to get away from can reach me from right inside me. And to have any chance of getting out of it, I'd have to let him in even *more*. We don't even know for sure that I'd survive the magic she was talking about if it'd hurt even a true-blooded fae."

All of that is true. None of the anguish spreading through my own body can change it.

I love this woman, and I might lose her.

I hold her and press my lips to her forehead, hoping she's taking at least a small measure of comfort from my embrace. "Whatever it takes, whatever I have to give, I won't stop until I've done everything I can to figure out how to get us out of this catastrophe."

Heart help me find the way to protect her as much as she's been here for me.

5

Talia

The grass ripples around me in a sunlit field, the scattered daisies swaying with the breeze. Pale glimmers drift on the currents. It takes me a moment to recognize them as snowflakes, impossibly tumbling down from the clear sky.

This is a dream. The awareness of that fact creeps up over me as I turn on my feet, taking in the hazy sensations, the lack of pain in my foot even though I'm not wearing my brace. It's a *good* dream for once, without vicious teeth or splattered blood, just me and—

My legs stiffen in mid-swivel. I back up a step, staring at the figure who was standing behind me: the Unseelie arch-lord who's been invading my mind for the past few days.

Maybe this is a nightmare after all.

But the fae man doesn't make any move toward me, just gazes at me from where he's poised several feet away.

His posture is straight and formal, but his expression looks more concerned than hostile. If he's angry at me for how much I've been blocking him, he isn't showing it.

My heart thumps against my ribs, but it is only a dream. He can't hurt me. So I hold myself in place and study him like he's studying me.

His bronze-brown skin is as smooth as I remember, broken only by the darker lines of the true-name tattoos that unfurl up from the corner of his jaw, down his neck, and across the backs of his hands. No hint of gray shows in the blue-black hair that curls around the peaks of his sharply pointed ears, but I get the impression he's a little older than I assumed when I saw him next to his stately colleagues. Older than August or Arch-Lord Donovan at least, maybe closer to Sylas's age. There's a solemnity in his dark eyes and the set of his jaw that suggests a certain amount of experience—and not all of that experience good.

He's dressed less formally than he was when I saw him before. Ivory trousers and a trim, dove-gray tunic with just a smattering of silver embroidery clothe his tall, lean frame, which is less brawny than my wolfish men but emanates understated strength.

He doesn't have his expansive raven-like wings out now. I guess the Unseelie probably keep those restrained most of the time like the Seelie do their fangs and claws, only revealing them to threaten or intimidate.

In that way of dreams, I simply know that he's dreaming this too—that we're still far apart in actuality. He's slipped his way through my barrier of light into my mind yet again.

My shoulders tense. I close my eyes, willing myself to wake up so I can rebuild that wall, but nothing happens. The falling snow tickles my arms with specks of cold. The summery breeze licks over my skin, warming me again.

"Talia," the Unseelie man says quietly, his voice cool and as smooth as his burnished skin. "I know you must be startled by this connection. I am too. But the bond is there. We can't simply dismiss it. I believe it would do us some good to talk it over—to see what we can make of it."

I raise my eyebrows at him defiantly. "Did you make this dream happen because I wouldn't let you in while I'm awake?"

He shakes his head in a subtle movement. "I wasn't expecting to meet you like this either. But with the bond tying us together, it isn't surprising that we'd find even some of our dreams merging."

Frustration grips me. I cross my arms tightly in front of me. "I don't want this. I don't want *any* of it. You hate the Seelie. You've been attacking us—your people have *killed* my pack-kin."

The fae man's mouth tightens. "I—" He pauses, looking as if he's holding back a frown. "You were with the new Seelie arch-lord—Sylas. You're of his pack."

"I am." It's true enough. He doesn't need to know exactly what role I play in that pack or among the rest of the Seelie. If the Unseelie knew just how valuable I am to their enemies—

I clamp down on that thought with a shiver. What if this man can pick up on my thoughts as well as what I say out loud?

He doesn't give any sign that he's noticed my concern,

though. "If the arch-lords brought on your lord to replace the one they lost, then they must have trusted him. Has he said anything about a note of warning?"

My pulse hiccups. Sylas told us that the arch-lords had gotten a note that appeared to have been left by someone from the Unseelie side, warning them about the raven shifters' plans for an attack during the full moon. Whoever did that went against their own rulers to help us, whether they regret that now after the summer fae were able to beat the Unseelie warriors back or not. Is the arch-lord attempting to figure out who betrayed him?

"I don't know everything the other arch-lords have shared with him," I hedge.

"Well—perhaps you could speak to him about it, and he can confirm. I don't agree with many of the tactics my colleagues have been taking, but my vote is only one out of five. To strike out when you couldn't even defend yourselves…" He gives that little shake of his head again. "I couldn't let your people face it unaware."

My jaw drops. "*You* left the note?" I realize after the words have already spilled out that I've just admitted to knowing about it, but I'm too overwhelmed by shock. This man, this *arch-lord*, warned us against his own people?

He inclines his head. A glimmer of what might be pain shines in his eyes. "I did. I didn't anticipate the results being quite so catastrophic for our own, but—they wouldn't listen when I made my case against the assault. There was going to be too much blood shed either way. As much as I hated to see the results, we brought it on ourselves by sinking so low."

As I take that in, a sudden prickling of guilt fills my stomach. All the horrible things I've thought about him, all the assumptions I've made... but how could I have known?

My arms loosen where I was hugging myself. "Thank you," I have to say.

A muscle at his jaw ticks, and it occurs to me that he's just revealed a secret to me that could end his entire career, if not his life, if his fellow arch-lords found out. Not that I have any means of telling them or any desire to. But he doesn't know me that well yet.

And still he trusted me enough to say it. Because earning *my* trust meant that much to him.

"Obviously you should ensure that information doesn't get back to any of my brethren," he says, a little stiffly. I think he's trying to avoid showing how precarious a position he feels he's put himself in. "It would be to your people's benefit as well as mine if I could continue to speak up for a more peaceful resolution to the present conflict."

"Of course." I open my mouth and close it again, unsure of what else to say. Even if he isn't a monster, I don't want to be tied to him like this. Can't he understand that?

No, he probably can't. He'll have lived his whole life as a true-blooded fae knowing that he'd meet his soul-twined mate eventually. He was ready for this, maybe even looking forward to it.

Whatever he imagined, I know I can't possibly be it.

He takes a step closer, and I manage not to shrink back. "Talia," he starts, and I'm struck by the discomfort of how familiarly he says my name, as if I offered it to him rather than having it stolen out of my awareness.

"I don't even know *your* name," I blurt out.

He blinks, looking briefly taken aback, but his cool composure returns a moment later. "Corwin," he says. "Corwin of Heart's Cadence. I apologize—it is… strange, feeling so close and yet knowing each other so little."

No kidding. But the fact that he's acknowledged the strangeness lets me relax a smidgeon more. I try out the sound of his name. "Corwin. Yes, it is strange."

A different sort of light flickers through his face, something hopeful if fleeting. "I don't want to tear you from your home. I don't want… I don't want this unexpected bond to harm either of us. But can you see that it could be a good thing for both our peoples? A chance to find more of a common ground, to ease the tensions—build a bridge between summer and winter, a demonstration of unity. I think that's worth giving a try."

A lump rises in my throat. He makes it sound so easy. He has no idea—there's *so much* about my life he doesn't know.

Corwin steps even nearer. "All I'm suggesting is that we give it a fair chance. See what comes of it. I understand there would need to be compromises made, but that isn't impossible."

He raises his hand, his fingers grazing my forearm, and a jolt of sensation shoots through my nerves like a burst of sparks. I gasp for air, half of me compelled to lean into his touch, the other half gripped by the urge to wrench myself away.

From the widening of Corwin's eyes, I don't think he

was prepared for this either. Emotions that aren't mine trickle through the turmoil rising inside me: uncertainty and alarm but also a glimmer of joy.

That last impression brings me back to myself, to the echo of joys past it stirs in me. I jerk my arm away, stumbling backward, my heart outright hammering now.

"I can't— It isn't—" I heave in a breath, fighting to get my protest out with some kind of coherence. "It isn't just about giving this a try. I already—there are people here I love. I don't want to leave them. We were going to be mated…"

I trail off at the flinch Corwin doesn't manage to restrain. He masters his expression an instant later, but it's too much—the pain my admission caused him echoing into me, the fact that we're twined enough to be having this conversation at all. Driven by instinct and panic, I whirl around and fling myself away from him—

—and wake up with a hitch of breath in my bedroom in Hearthshire.

I'm not alone here either, but at least my present company is much more wanted. As I sit up, clutching the covers around my legs and swiping my hand across my eyes, Sylas rises from the armchair across from the bed, his massive form unmistakeable even in the thin moonlight that's the room's only illumination.

"Are you all right?" he asks. "You didn't sound distressed, but you were murmuring in your sleep—I was keeping watch in case one of your nightmares took hold."

"I—" I cut myself off, at a loss for how to explain what just happened while my mind is still whirling. Reaching inside me, I summon up another shield of light to block off my connection to Corwin. I'm not sensing anything from him right now—maybe he's still sleeping— but even if I find him less horrifying than before, I don't want him sneaking peeks into my thoughts or my conversations.

"When did you get back from the Heart?" I say instead. Whitt brought me to Hearthshire on the fae lord's orders—we agreed that I'd feel more secure on familiar ground rather than in the unfinished rooms of the castle still under construction. Sylas, of course, needs to uphold his new duties as arch-lord. My situation has already disrupted that transition plenty.

"About an hour ago," he says, which judging by the dark sky beyond my window means he traveled through the night. "As soon as I could reasonably get away. Whitt said that your venture did not prove as helpful as we'd hoped."

A broken laugh falls from my lips. No, it didn't. Not at all. But thinking about it brings a fresh burn into the backs of my eyes. I'm afraid if I try to say much about it, I'll burst into tears all over again. It's bad enough that I melted down in front of Whitt. I have to hold it together better than that.

I'm *stronger* than that. I know I am, as helpless as I felt after hearing what that unsettling fae woman had to say about breaking the bond. And really, talking to Corwin in the shared dream has left me calmer as everything he told me sinks in.

I hold my hand out to Sylas, and he sinks onto the bed next to me, opening his arms so I can tuck myself into his embrace. I lean my head against his solid chest, absorbing his warmth and his smoky, earthy scent. The words work their way up my throat.

"I had a dream with the Unseelie arch-lord. He was dreaming it too. We talked a little."

Sylas hugs me closer. "If he threatened you in any way—"

"No. He was actually very… kind about it. It was important to him that we talk, but he didn't try to push for anything else." I pause. "He knew about the note that warned the arch-lords about the full-moon attack. He said he's the one who left it for them, that he's been trying to convince the other Unseelie arch-lords to stop the fighting. It sounded like he was telling the truth. I mean, he couldn't have known about the note otherwise, right?"

Sylas hums, a rumble reverberating through his chest into me. "If they caught the one who betrayed them, they might have found out. He could be using that knowledge to convince you to trust him. Did he phrase it in a way that only *implied* he sent it, or did he say it outright?"

His voice stays mild, just stating a possibility rather than insisting on it. I think back to the dream. The details of it are already turning foggy, but nothing about Corwin's demeanor gives the impression of deception. He was nervous and trying to hide how nervous he was making that admission.

And fae avoid lying, especially when close to the Heart. Apparently saying something false can damage their connection to the Heart's magic. Corwin didn't say he left the note in so many words—I was reading between the lines—but he confirmed it openly, and he said lots of other things directly stating that he disagreed with how the other arch-lords are handling the conflict.

"I believe him," I say. "I could be wrong, but—everything about it felt true."

"I suppose there's some comfort in knowing the one you've ended up tied to has less hostile intentions toward us than many of his brethren. Did he say anything else?"

"He told me his name—Corwin. And that he wanted us to try to see where the bond could take us. He thinks it could be a way of ending the fighting, like a bridge between the summer fae and the winter fae."

Sylas rests his chin against my temple. "And how do you feel about that?"

I grimace. "I don't know. It's a nice idea. But… I'm happy here. I don't want to give this up. I don't want to give *you* up." I hesitate with a wince. "I kind of told him so. That I had someone—or someones—I'd already meant to take as mates. He definitely didn't like hearing that. Then I woke up."

"Did you say anything about what you mean to the rest of the summer fae?"

I shake my head. "I didn't mention anything about the curse. I tried not to even think about it. He didn't seem to have any idea." But that is yet another complication.

Sylas is silent for a stretch, just holding me, his thumb tracing a curved line up and down my arm from shoulder to elbow. "I don't like any of this," he says finally. "I hate that you've found yourself in this position, and I hate that I haven't found any way to get you out of it. Whatever you decide will be your free choice. I'm still committed to that, even if it takes you away from me."

The rawness in his voice makes me lift my head. He sounds as if he expects me to leave even though I just told him I don't want to. "Did something happen in your meetings with the arch-lords? Do you think I'm in more danger here?" That's the only reason I can think of that he'd suggest even vaguely that I should leave.

"No. I—" He lets out a strained huff. "I don't know if I should tell you this. I've always kept the knowledge to myself, so as not to influence—but I don't want to keep anything from you either." He eases back far enough that I can see his face. "You've never asked how I got my scar."

I'm sure he has others, but it's clear he's talking about the most visible one that cuts through his ghostly eye. I've wondered enough times, but— "It seemed like a pretty personal question."

He chuckles with a hint of genuine emotion despite his still-somber expression. "I'm not sure we can get much more personal than we already have, my love."

Those last two words provoke a flutter in my chest, even though he already declared the depths of his affections the night of his coronation. It's still a little hard for me to believe that this powerful, magical man loves *me*.

I squeeze his arm where it's wrapped around me. "How did you get it, then?"

Sylas's mismatched gaze drifts away from me, going distant. "When I was what a human would consider an adolescent, still finding my footing within my father's domain, a small group of Murk got it into their heads to stir up trouble for the sentries watching over our borders. I volunteered to deal with them. I was... somewhat overconfident in my abilities and how easily a pack of rats might be subdued. I located the den they'd made and came at them alone."

I trace my finger along the pale, jagged line that marks his cheek. "And they did this?" I haven't encountered any of the rat-shifting fae called the Murk yet, but from the way I've heard the Seelie talk about them, they distrust them even more than the Unseelie. The winter fae they at least see as equals, if enemies. The realm-less fae that lurk around the edges of this world and the human one, they talk about with disdain as well as animosity.

"They nearly ended me. Three of their number I dispatched quickly enough, but the fourth had more magic than I'd bargained for. She threw a curse at me that would have killed me if I hadn't managed to deflect it at the last second. As it was, it still caught the side of my face rather than burrowing right into my brain."

I shudder. "That's awful."

"My own fault for going in too cocky." He dips his head to nuzzle my temple. "But whatever the spell would have done to my mind, it had something of an odd effect on my eye. I can't see in the regular way through it—in that sense, it's essentially dead. But here and there it shows me brief images from the past or the future or hints at a reaction someone is holding in. Sometimes literal, sometimes more the gist of a situation. It can occasionally be useful, but often I'm not sure enough of the when or how to make use of those impressions."

My thoughts slip back to the comments that got us started on this tangent. "Did it show you something today?"

"Yes." He inhales slowly. "When I left the Bastion after

my last meeting with the arch-lords, I got a glimpse of you, walking toward the border right by the Heart as if you were going to pass through."

My stomach twists. "And that couldn't be from the past, because I've never gone through before."

"Exactly." He turns me to look at him straight on. "I don't know how far in the future that glimpse might have come from, what might have led to it, or whether it's unavoidable. Don't make any decisions based on that." His tone turns vehement with a trace of a growl. "As long as you want to stay here, I'll fight for you with every shred of my being."

An answering emotion floods my chest. I grasp his shirt and burrow my face against his neck. "I love you."

I wish that was *enough* of an answer. Not that long ago, I thought the only thing standing in the way of my staying with the men of Hearthshire was that they'd never return my feelings as strongly. Now…

Now I'm no longer sure that even a fae lord's love will be enough to save me from whatever awaits us.

6

Sylas

Stepping into the Bastion of the Heart used to fill me with a sense of wonder. To some extent, the sandstone walls with their glowing veins of gold that pulse in time with the energy flowing from the Heart still do. But as I stride through the halls to the central meeting chamber on an urgent summons from the two arch-lords who are now my colleagues, that awe is dampened by a sinking sense of dread.

These days, the weight of my multiplying challenges and responsibilities doesn't leave much room for wonder.

Celia and Donovan are huddled in quiet conversation by Celia's throne. A few of their cadre-chosen stand at a respectful distance. With August stationed in Hearthshire to watch over Talia for the day and Whitt off making more inquiries, I've brought only Astrid with me—a loyal warrior but not official enough to be allowed into the room for whatever discussion we're about to have.

I make a brief gesture to her, and she stops without hint of protest to wait in the doorway in case I have need of her. As my fellow arch-lords glance up to mark my strides to meet them, I feel my lack of support with a prickle down the back of my neck.

It's the risk you take, setting off to found your own domain rather than lingering to take over from your parents. Split the pack, and you end up with one much smaller than you'd have been able to call on otherwise. Hearthshire was growing well in those early decades, but the banishment set us back to even worse numbers than we'd had when I first struck out on my own. And I couldn't justify asking any of my pack to make such a heavy commitment as adding to my cadre when I hadn't even been able to hold onto our home for them.

Something I'll have to put a mind to changing… once I no longer have quite so many other pressing concerns on my mind.

Celia and Donovan turn toward me as I reach them. It's easy to discern that there's been bad news. Despite her advanced age, Celia has never lacked for energy, but today her ebony face looks tired. Donovan's mouth slants downward. He rakes his hand through his flame-like hair with a jerk of his arm.

"Has some new trouble arisen?" I ask, tamping down on the urge to add a frustrated *What now?*

Celia draws her willowy frame up even straighter. "We've had word from the Unseelie arch-lords. They're threatening an assault on our own domains."

I blink at her, the statement so bewildering it takes me a moment to regain my composure. "On *our* domains—

around the Heart? They'd have a hard time reaching us from any place they could cross the border without taking the Heart's vow."

"They say that circumstances will allow them passage without the vow," the younger arch-lord says, his voice strained. "That keeping one of their soul-twined mates from her bonded partner is in defiance of the Heart, and the Heart will allow them passage to rectify that offense."

Every muscle in my body tenses. It is true—there is a minor loophole in the spell the summer and winter fae created together all those centuries ago. If we committed a severe enough crime against the Heart's will, it would let their warriors pass through without their oath to do no harm. We could still defend ourselves—we have no shortage of our own warriors, after all—but imagining how they might ransack the sacred lands here brings my fangs springing forth.

"We haven't been *keeping* Talia from him," I retort. "She has her own mind—she doesn't want to go to him."

Celia sighs. "And we don't particularly want her to go either, considering her role in defying our curse. The entire situation is incomprehensible. Are you absolutely certain that it's a soul-twined bond and not some awful magic they cast on the girl?"

Of course she'd only think of what Talia can offer through her blood, not anything else. But then, that's exactly why I haven't told my colleagues about my intention to take the woman I love as my mate. Until I *can* do that, starting what will likely be an argument over it will only be another complication.

I'd rather not even have told them about her soul-twined bond, but after our initial attempts to overcome that problem failed, I couldn't keep the information from them any longer.

I gesture toward the Heart. "The Unseelie wouldn't be able to say we're keeping his soul-twined mate from him if that's not the case. *That* would be an immense offense against the Heart—can you imagine the consequences of a lie so immense?"

Donovan rubs his narrow chin. "And you haven't found any explanation for how this could happen to a human or whether it could be undone?"

I grimace. "Our efforts have brought little result. The only possible solution we've come across requires that the bond first be consummated, and it might very well kill Talia in the breaking of it. Do you really think the Heart will allow them to attack us when the choice is hers?"

Celia gives me a measured look. "Soul-twined bonds are one of the Heart's greatest gifts to us. To deny one… I don't know how this would play out. She isn't making the choice entirely for herself, is she? I find it hard to believe that your cadre-chosen who's so enamored with her hasn't swayed her on the matter at all."

It *is* impossible to know exactly how the Heart will react to these circumstances. None of us would have believed it would ever create a bond between fae of opposing seasons, let alone bestow one on a human. The Unseelie might attempt an assault and be pushed back— or they might descend on us like they did on that full moon night several weeks ago.

There would be no withdrawing to a defensive position and regrouping. We'd be locked in an unceasing battle to the death until one side or the other came out on top. If we lose these lands, our connection to the Heart will falter, and our magic alongside it. Once the Unseelie gain that foothold, we may never regain it.

But to lose *Talia*… I have to hold in a snarl of defiance. Fury reverberates through every nerve in my body at the thought.

I rein in my temper, though I can't quite keep the edge out of my voice. "What do you suggest, then? You can't mean to give up our only current means of controlling the curse. Especially when she *wants* to remain with us."

"You're a skilled negotiator, Sylas," Celia says evenly. "We saw that when you made your appeal to us to protect her position with you. If she spends a short amount of time with her mate and rejects the bond with no influence from us, then her will in the matter is undeniable. I say we have her make whatever arrangements you need to through their connection to ensure her safety and her return to us should she wish it—and to keep our secrets uncompromised."

I probably could ensure that with an oath or two solidifying the promise. My heart balks at the idea, though. I keep my mouth shut for a moment, lest the anger burning through me sear from my tongue into my colleagues instead.

Celia is right. I know she is, as much as I detest the fact. And when I accepted the role as arch-lord, I made a graver commitment to my people—to all the Seelie—than ever before.

Either I fail as a mate-to-be or I fail as leader of my

people. One injures at worst four of us, the other thousands. May maggots eat those raven bastards.

"I'll put it to her," I say. "I won't force her." But I already know how she'll answer if she knows the potential disaster we face, don't I?

Talia should know just what sort of man she'll be dealing with on the other side. My gaze flicks between my fellow arch-lords. "Did the threat come from her mate— the one named Corwin?" If he thinks he can go from making a plea for peace in her dreams last night to calling for war less than twelve hours later—

But Donovan is shaking his head. "It was from the woman who spoke for them on your coronation night— the one who seemed to carry the most authority if not the most seniority—Laoni?"

Then there's no telling how much Corwin was or wasn't directly involved. "And you agree with Celia's proposal?"

The younger arch-lord has been my greatest ally outside of my pack. He supported my return to Hearthshire whole-heartedly, let me into his confidence when he came under attack from the arch-lord before me, and put me forward as Ambrose's replacement. His pained expression tells me he knows more than Celia does how much this means to me. But he tips his head in acknowledgment anyway.

I can't even blame him.

I force my hands to unclench so I look reasonably in control of myself. "All right. I'll think on it and speak to Talia. Inform the Unseelie that the mate in question is coming to *her own* decision on the matter, and that it'd be an offense against the Heart to rush the acceptance of the bond."

As I march back to the hall, I hold my rage in check, but only by a thread. Astrid falls into step beside me, alert enough to my mood to stay silent.

The beaming of the sun feels like an insult to the turmoil inside me. I turn to Astrid. "Whitt was making use of the library at Blossom-by-the-Heart. Find him and inform him that I want him to look into every obscure detail he can find on oaths, especially as it regards the Unseelie."

She bobs her head. "Is there any way I can assist after that, my lord?"

Turn back time so I never became arch-lord after all? I grit my teeth, knowing that even if such a thing were possible, even if I'd actually ask for it, it wouldn't solve anything. I'd know what I owe my people regardless of my title.

Blast it all to dust.

I nod toward the border. "Keep a watch by the Heart for even the slightest sign of Unseelie intrusion, however innocuous. Report back to me if you see anything at all."

She grins tightly but fiercely, showing her fangs. "If they show more than a beak, I'll happily tear their feathered heads off as well."

I watch her set off and then stalk toward the half-finished castle in my newly-granted domain. She's done well, this loyal warrior who's followed me so far—protected Talia when I couldn't be there.

As much as any of us have been able to protect Talia in the end.

The several pack-kin with the true names needed to construct the castle and its furnishings are gathered around one of the outer corners, coaxing the massive fused tree trunk there into the shape of a ballroom. As if we'll have anything to celebrate anytime soon.

I swallow my growl and wave them off. "Take an hour or two. Have a run if you feel you need it."

They disperse without argument. I snatch up a fallen leaf and murmur a few syllables to it that'll send it on a course back to Hearthshire. When it reaches August, he'll know it's his summons to bring Talia.

He just won't know what he's bringing her to.

The fury I've been shoving down on so forcefully flares despite my best intentions. Claws prick from my fingertips. My jaw aches to stretch.

Hanging onto the last shred of my self-control, I stride into the castle and down the stairs to the roughed-out basement exercise room where sounds are least likely to carry outside. As my heel kicks the door shut with a bang, my wolf explodes out of me.

The animal I've become lashes out in every direction. I lunge at the walls, fully extended claws gouging the wood with a friction that's not remotely satisfying. A strangled howl rips from my throat. My muscles coil and hurl me one way and another, my fangs gnash at the air, and my lungs ache with a chorus of snarls. My awareness narrows down to a rage-hazed blur.

The rage stretches on and on, my body battling to find a release I can't quite reach, until a smooth, quiet voice breaks through my furor.

"Sylas."

My shoulder slams into one of the walls. I spin, panting and paws throbbing, to see Whitt standing by the now-open door. He gazes back at me, his expression mild but his stance uncertain in the way it's been almost always since our confrontation over Isleen's crime against him.

My senses refocus on the room around me. Claw marks scour the walls. The moss padding on the floor lies torn in jagged chunks. The bar mounted at the far end of the room is snapped right through, the broken ends punctured with teeth marks.

Shame trickles through me. I haven't let my most feral emotions take over like this in—possibly ever. Even when Isleen betrayed me, even when we were banished, I stewed and I snapped here or there, but I held onto the steadiness my pack needs from their lord.

I can't help thinking of ages ago when I found August rampaging around a glade in the woods near the castle at Thundervale, taking out his anger toward our father and his grief over his mother's death on every tree and shrub in the vicinity.

He was barely more than a child then. I'm a grown man of over three centuries. I'm a blasted *arch-lord*.

Whitt's posture still looks tense, but his voice comes out typically wry. "As much as I'm sure your honor is compelling you to do so, may I suggest not beating yourself up to anywhere near the same extent that you've demolished this room? The wood can be mended. I'd say we're allotted at least one good blow-up per century, and I suspect you've been stockpiling."

I don't pick up on the slightest hint of judgment in his tone, which is light and calm in its breeziness. Puncturing the tension of the situation by making a joke out of it, like he has in our favor so many times in the past. As I pull in my wolf and straighten up, I'm struck with an odd pang that's almost like homesickness, as if I've missed something about this, something about him, even though he hasn't been elsewhere for more than a day.

I miss the ease with which I used to trust him—and my belief that he trusted me the same way. When I look at him now, I find I don't have any anger left about the past. All that remains is the hollow of mourning within my gut.

But maybe I have some control over whether that hollow is filled back in.

"Thank you," I say to him. "I—" I glance at the room again and flinch inwardly.

"Think nothing of it," Whitt replies as glibly as before, but then his expression darkens. "As much as I'm dreading hearing it, you'd better tell me what put you in this state—and what it has to do with Unseelie oaths."

Not wanting to wallow in the results of my rampage while we discuss the cause of it, I motion him down the hall. My collection of frivolous human movies and August's video games haven't been moved here from Hearthshire yet, but the soon-to-be entertainment room does have a sofa. I sink down at one end of it. Whitt hesitates by the other end before flopping down next to me.

There's no point in beating around the bush, especially with my older brother. "The Unseelie arch-lords have threatened to attack our domains by the Heart if we don't deliver Talia to her soul-twined mate. My colleagues are concerned that the Heart might sway in their favor and allow them free passage. They want us to send her to him for long enough that it's clear she's making her own decision when she leaves."

If she leaves. That possible phrasing sticks in the bottom of my throat. I know firsthand how intense and compelling the intimacy of a soul-twined bond can be. As much as I hate to admit it, that wretched raven has a more valid claim over Talia than any of us do.

She may not want to return after all.

If he truly has been working against his own people to protect us, he might not even be the villain I'd like to see him as. Letting her go to him may be in the best interests of not only my Seelie brethren but Talia as well. If the Heart has blessed her with such a connection to a lord who turns out to be deserving, how can I deny her that?

Whitt paints the air with a colorful string of curse words and then slumps back in the sofa. For a second, I'm half-afraid that he'll shame me for even considering their proposal even though he didn't for my rage.

But he's my spymaster and strategist for a reason. His swift mind probably worked through the factors faster than mine did.

"We'll bind that mangy bird brain in so many oaths he can barely breathe without double-checking," he says. "We'll make sure she comes back. She *will* come back—you know that."

I do. "She'll come back because she feels she owes it to us. Because she wouldn't abandon us to the curse." I know how much honor Talia contains in that slip of a body. The real question is whether she stays or returns to the winter realm once her sense of obligation has been fulfilled.

Whitt looks steadily back at me, the pained set of his mouth revealing that he's making the same considerations. That they wrench at him just as deeply as they do me.

In that moment, the transgressions of a century past feel as substanceless as the visions of my deadened eye. Right here, right now, we are two men united in our love for one startlingly magnificent woman, and I trust that my brother will work as tirelessly toward ensuring her safety and happiness as I will—regardless of where she finds that happiness once every part of this unexpected situation has all played out.

Whitt pushes himself straighter again, clapping his hands together on his lap. "Well, then. Let me tell you the few new tidbits I've gleaned about oaths relative to the winter fae, and we'll see if we can't come up with a plan so air tight it could suffocate a raven."

Talia

Harper stares up at the towering obsidian castle that once belonged to Arch-Lord Ambrose. Her expression tenses as if she's half-afraid he'll come storming out to berate her, even though we both know the vicious schemer who attempted to steal me away from my pack is dead. Then a fiercer spark lights in her eyes, and she makes an obscene gesture at the walls before turning her back on them to look instead at the castle that will be our new home.

"I hope they smash it to dust when our castle is ready," she says, hugging herself.

I have no doubt that she means that whole-heartedly. Weeks ago, Ambrose's pack-kin managed to coerce the young fae woman into helping them with their plot. She made a dress for me with enchanted embellishments that would have recorded my private conversations with my lovers, which Ambrose would have exploited any way he could. Sylas was furious when he found out, but I asked that we give her a second chance rather than banishing her. She used to be my closest friend in the pack.

Since that incident, she hasn't wavered from her efforts to prove how much my friendship and her place in the pack mean to her. Pink lines mark her slim forearm from the slashing claws of one of Ambrose's guards. Harper and I and two of our other pack-kin managed to delay those guards while Sylas was protecting Donovan from Ambrose's murder attempt. She's hardly a warrior, but she threw herself into the skirmish—and between me and those claws that I'm even less equipped to fend off than she is—without a second's hesitation.

Talking with her doesn't feel as comfortable as it did before, back when we bonded over a mutual desire to see more of the world, but the sting of her betrayal is fading. I know she didn't *want* to hurt me. She fell for a horrible trick and didn't know how to get herself out of the mess. I don't know if I'd have made better decisions if our positions were reversed.

I gaze up at the ominous castle too. "I wonder what-all Ambrose had in there. Sylas let his pack-kin take all their belongings from their homes, but he didn't let anyone in the castle."

Since our lord was the one who ended Ambrose's life in fair combat, by fae law the arch-lord's possessions immediately became his own. I suspect he was concerned that if any of Ambrose's pack-kin had vengeful thoughts, they might find ammunition against those Ambrose hated somewhere within those walls.

Harper shudders. "I don't ever want to go back in there to find out."

"Me neither," I have to admit. The black stone is intimidating enough looking at it from the outside; standing in the inner halls, it's suffocating. "Well, I guess there'll be lots of other interesting parts of this domain to explore. There's more magic here near the Heart than anywhere else in the Mists, isn't there?"

"There is." My former friend offers me a shy smile, tucking her sleek flaxen hair behind her lightly pointed ears. "Maybe—if you want to, and you'd want *me* for company—we could still do some of that exploring together."

The tangled sensation that rises in my chest has little to do with her past betrayal and much more with the fact that I don't know when I'll have that kind of freedom again. Instinctively, I summon more light into the glowing barrier inside me. "I hope we'll have a chance. For now we should probably get on with the gardening we told August we'd help with."

Gardening isn't Harper's specialty. Her greatest talent is in designing and sewing gorgeous clothes, a talent with which she'd intended to win her invitations to domains all across the summer realm. But when she heard August was bringing me back to our pack's new domain, she immediately volunteered to come along and help however she could.

As soon as we arrived, August hustled into the partly sculpted castle of trees to speak with Sylas and Whitt, leaving Astrid watching over me from a short distance. She follows the two of us over to the growing cluster of smaller houses that'll become the new pack village.

A man already there points us to some roots that need planting, and we spend the next several minutes digging them into the earth and covering them over. The warm late-afternoon sun, the rich scent of the soil, and the rhythmic movements soothe my spirit a little. It all feels so normal, as if nothing all that major has really changed.

"I guess you'll have no shortage of balls to attend and higher fae to show off your dresses to now," I say to Harper. "Everyone wants to mingle with the arch-lords' packs."

I meant it as a casual remark to make conversation, but she looks up at me, her over-large eyes growing even wider with a vehemence that's echoed in her voice. "I don't care what any of the other packs think about me or what I've made. I'm just glad I didn't ruin my chances of staying with *this* pack." She bites her lip. "I haven't done much sewing since... since everything. Every time I do I remember adding those beads to that dress... The fact that *you're* still okay is so much more important to me than any reward those traitors would have given me."

Her declaration and the guilt etched all over her face bring a pang into my chest. I don't know what to say. The best I can manage is, "I still think your creations are beautiful. I wouldn't want you to stop." I pause, and allow a careful smile to curve my mouth. "Who else is going to make me look like I belong next to an arch-lord and his cadre?"

Harper stares at me for a second as if she can't believe I'd trust her to make anything else for me, and then a grin splits her face. "For you, I'll always do my best work. Even if I'm not making anything for anyone else." Her grin turns a bit sly. "First I obviously need to design you some adventuring clothes, since we won't be able to have nearly enough fun roaming around this domain wrapped up in regular dresses."

An unexpected laugh tumbles out of me. It feels good —until I glance up and see August coming over, obviously to get me. His face, once so often cheerful, is as serious as I've ever seen it. Any good humor in me condenses into a stone that sinks to the bottom of my stomach.

I've already wiped my hands on the grass next to the garden plot and gotten to my feet when he reaches us. He tilts his head toward the castle. "We need to speak with you."

"Of course."

Harper watches us curiously but doesn't pry. No one in the pack other than my men and Astrid know about the soul-twined bond. As far as I know, Sylas has kept it secret from everyone other than his fellow arch-lords.

As we walk to the rough castle, August rests his hand on my back. "It'll be okay. We'll make sure of it."

The statement doesn't exactly reassure me. He'd only say it if he knows what I'm about to hear won't sound okay at all.

Sylas and Whitt are waiting in Sylas's new office with its still-sparse furnishings. If I thought August looked serious, it's nothing compared to the dour atmosphere that closes around me as soon as I step into the room.

August shuts the door behind us. I reach inside myself to pour even more light into the inner barrier, shoring it up with everything I have in me, and then I plant myself in front of the fae lord, my chin high. I'm so tired of having this sense of doom hanging over me. Whatever's going on, I need to know before the awful anticipation kills me all on its own.

"Just tell me what's happened. It's obviously bad. I'm going to have to hear it one way or another."

Whitt lets out a choked guffaw, a glint of admiration shining in his eyes.

Sylas exhales sharply. "You have a choice. You can say no. I'm not going to force you into doing anything."

I can tell from his expression that he's already sure of my response anyway. "A choice about *what?*"

To his credit, he doesn't delay any longer. "The Unseelie arch-lords are threatening to storm our domains here by the Heart if we don't hand you over to your soul-twined mate. It's possible the Heart will let them through without the vow to do no harm because we're defying its intentions by keeping you here. My colleagues have suggested—and I can see the merits of the suggestion—that we allow you to spend a short amount of time with Arch-Lord Corwin so that you can decline him completely of your own free will, without any hint of persuasion from us."

My stomach plummets right to my toes. "You want me to go to the winter realm?"

Sylas's lips draw back with a flash of bared teeth. "I don't *want* you to go anywhere, Talia. If I had my way—" He cuts himself off and shakes his head. "You don't *have* to go. If you say no, even though we're giving you the clearest avenue there that we can, the Heart has to recognize that."

The strain in his voice implies he's not really sure of that statement. I could refuse and spark a battle far more catastrophic than anything the summer fae have faced so far.

I swallow hard, resisting the urge to hug myself. "The Unseelie arch-lords threatened us? *Corwin* threatened us?" After all his talk about peace and building bridges last night…

Anger flares in my chest. Before Sylas can answer, I spin around, putting my back to him and closing my eyes. Whitt inhales as if to speak, but I hold up my hand for silence.

Carefully but quickly, I peel back the mass of glowing energy that's sealed over the open space inside me. Not completely, only paring it back enough so that I can send my thoughts through that ephemeral channel.

Corwin!

I don't know if he had his end of the connection totally unguarded or if my irritation propels the name with enough force to break through. His voice carries back to me an instant later, hasty but with a sense of distraction. *Talia. I'm here.*

It's the first time I've ever reached out to him. The first time we'll have a conversation I initiated consciously. The realization sends a wobble through my gut, but I press on so that our talk can also be *over* as quickly as possible. *Did you tell the Seelie arch-lords your people would go to war over me?*

I get the impression that he's attempting to muffle his emotions, but some slip through anyway: a jab of frustration, a ripple of horror. Enough that I believe him when he says,

No. I'm trying to talk my colleagues out *of that course of action right now. I meant what I said last night. Unfortunately, what I said about only being one vote is also true.*

Fragments of other sensations slip through: a glimpse of a cavernous, pale room and a long marble table in the middle of it, four figures sitting around that table, a woman talking in brittle tones. *—can't let these tender feelings prevent us from—*

"I'm talking to her right now," Corwin breaks in— aloud, to the other arch-lords. The woman's mouth snaps shut. He turns away from them, closing his eyes so I'm left with darkness and silence until his voice returns. *I promise you, I had no hand in this decision. I should be able to at least delay them taking further action.*

Resignation and resolve have already coiled together around my heart. *All right. I'll reach out again when I have more to say.* Dragging in a breath, I summon another swell of light until no hint of his presence reaches me.

When I turn back to my lovers, they're watching me with varying expressions of anguish. They know what I was just doing—that I was communicating with another man on a level of intimacy I'll never be able to with any of them.

"He didn't have anything to do with the threat to go to war," I say. "He's trying to get the other arch-lords to back down right now, but it doesn't sound like he'll be able to."

August stirs on his feet. "But maybe if we give him time—"

I interrupt him before he can fully express that

thought, that hope. "I don't think we should count on that, and it doesn't seem worth the risk." Swallowing hard, I meet Sylas's mismatched eyes. "You'd be able to make sure I could come home?"

The fae lord inclines his head. "We've already been working out the exact wording of the oaths we'd ask him to take to ensure your safe return and the security of our realm. You'd be back before the next full moon. He wouldn't be able to harm you while you're there or compel you to return afterward if you refused to."

"But I'd have to go alone."

Whitt answers for him, smooth as ever but gentle. "None of us would be able to join you. I don't imagine they'd allow any Seelie warriors as part of the bargain either. If you had someone else in mind you wanted for company, I can see ways we could make a case for a single unmenacing companion."

"And I wouldn't be committing to anything just by agreeing to stay with him for a while, would I? He couldn't... force the issue?" The man I've spoken to didn't sound like he would, but he is Unseelie and therefore one of our enemies, no matter what else he's done. I barely know him at all.

Sylas growls. "You can be sure *that* would be an essential part of the oaths we'd require."

For a few minutes, I stand in silence, sorting through my thoughts. To spend a week or two in Corwin's domain, to share his home with him—but without any obligations... I've survived nine years in a cage, starved and beaten down, without knowing there was anyone left in the world who'd care what was happening to me. Compared to that, this plan is nothing.

Except I'd be treading into a totally unfamiliar realm, surrounded by unfamiliar fae who've been slaughtering my own every chance they get.

My mind travels back to weeks ago when Sylas took me to the domain of his former mate's family to pay our respects over the death of Isleen's half-brother. He was a man who despised me and attempted to mutilate me. His family is one that sneers at humans and considers us to be worth no more than dung.

But witnessing their mourning, speaking with them afterward, I couldn't see them as just villains any longer. They were simply people—people with some awful attitudes, but also devotion to their family and grief over those they'd lost, who were willing to offer me respect when I showed I respected them.

I don't know if I'll see the same in the Unseelie, but I can believe Corwin has good in him. I can stand up for my people and maybe even discover something that could put an end to the fighting forever. How can I say no to that just to protect myself from the unknown?

My men have kept their own councils while I've debated with myself. The emotions roiling behind their gazes are obvious, but they give me the space to think. They don't try to argue or persuade me.

Because they know me well enough to have guessed what I would decide before I even set foot in this room, and they're not going to take that choice away from me.

That realization is what solidifies my resolve. I square my shoulders and look around at the three men, reveling in the depth of faith and understanding that's formed between us. We're bound together too, in ways I won't let any twist of fate shake. We'll get through this—we just have to.

"I'm going," I say. "Tell me what I need to tell Corwin so we can get all the details settled."

8

Talia

By the time we're done hashing out an agreement, with me passing on Sylas and Whitt's instructions through the soul-twined bond and relaying Corwin's replies, the conviction that carried me through the decision and the conversation that followed is dwindling. As I wearily reconstruct the wall of light inside me, all I can feel is the ache around my heart.

No matter what effort I put into this shield, tomorrow it won't matter. Tomorrow I'll be stepping into Corwin's domain—I won't be able to avoid him.

I'll be leaving behind the three men I've come to love so much.

Beyond the study's window, the sky has darkened. August tucks his arm around me, and we all head down to the unfinished kitchen. Rather than bothering with the equally unfinished dining room, we find places around one of the islands and put together a makeshift dinner out of the sparse assortment of ingredients August has on hand. He shoots more than one offended look at the spot where the not-yet-molded oven will be.

I force down as much of the smoked pheasant sandwich as I can. None of us says much. Maybe we're all talked out after the extended negotiation. But when we've done a quick clean-up and we all move toward the stairs, something in me balks so hard I stop in my tracks.

August sets his hand on my shoulder. I reach out to grasp Whitt's hand and Sylas's wrist.

The fae lord turns with a frown of concern. "What's wrong, Talia?"

I feel weak saying it. I made this choice. I want to go forward full of boldness and resolution. But the ache in my chest is spreading all through my limbs and up my throat. My voice comes out hoarse.

"I don't want to lose you. Any of you."

"Oh, mite." Whitt leans in to press a kiss to my hair. "We're not going anywhere."

August rumbles low in his chest. "If those stinking ravens try to keep you from coming back to us, we'll slaughter every one of their pompous arch-lords."

Sylas twines his fingers with mine and raises his other hand to caress my cheek. "We're yours, no matter how much distance lies between us. But right now, we're here. What do you need?"

I need this soul-twined bond to disappear as if it'd never formed. I need the certainty that no one will threaten my place among the Seelie and this pack ever again. But since there's no way I'm getting either of those things, I let the longing growing inside me take the lead and ask for one thing I'm pretty sure I can have.

"I want to be as close as I can get to all of you tonight. Together. If—if that's okay. If it isn't some kind of horrible offense against the Heart and the bond."

The heat that kindles in all three of the gazes fixed on me sears across my skin and brings a flush to my cheeks. I can feel it even from August behind me, in the slide of his hand to my waist where it burns like the most delicious of brands.

"You've made no commitment to Arch-Lord Corwin," Whitt says. "Even if you did, the decision about how much mates might seek companionship elsewhere is a matter of negotiation and personal preference, not dictated by the Heart. Enough lords seek other lovers to add to their chances of heirs. If you want this—"

"I do," I say determinedly before he has to go on.

Sylas strokes my cheek again, letting his knuckles trail down the side of my neck this time, and my body sways toward him of its own accord. "Then you'll have it. The tryst room here isn't furnished yet. My pack-kin did insist on ensuring *I* had a well-constructed bed while I work from this castle. If that's acceptable."

My tongue darts across my lips, the longing expanding into a more urgent swell of desire. My body already feels as if it's melting. I find I don't care all that much about where we do this as long as we do it soon, before I burn up from this mix of embarrassment and wanting. "I'm fine with making an exception."

This time it's Sylas who lets out a rumble. As Whitt chuckles, the fae lord scoops me into his arms. He claims a kiss right there in the hallway, tender but scorching. "Let's see how satisfied the three of us can make our mate-to-be, then."

Hearing him call me that, knowing taking me as his mate is still his intention, brings back the ache in my heart. But as we head up the stairs with his arms around me, Whitt's fingers teasing through my hair, and August's thumb tracing the arch of my foot, they conjure enough giddy anticipation for me to ignore the pang.

I'm theirs and they're mine, and not even the bond that tore me open from within can change that. Tonight, we'll prove that not just with words but with our bodies, merging as deeply as any beings can.

Sylas's new bedroom is unfurnished other than the bed, but along with being "well-constructed" it's also even more massive than the one he has back in Hearthshire. I wonder if he requested a larger frame when his pack-kin went to work on it, anticipating that it'd be shared on a regular basis in one way or another.

Then he drapes me across the covers, looming over me with all that passionate devotion in his gaze, and my capacity for any kind of thought goes out the window.

The fae lord holds his body above me, only touching me where he's bent his head to capture my mouth. But I'm hardly neglected in physical contact. As Sylas's tongue coaxes my lips apart and I welcome it with mine, Whitt and August sprawl out on either side of us. August nuzzles my ear and claims the side of my neck. Whitt lifts my hand and begins kissing a path from my wrist toward my shoulder.

I've been with Sylas and August at the same time, and

just having two men utterly focused on me was a dizzying experience. To be enveloped by all three sets my skin alight in all sorts of places they haven't even touched yet. I trace my fingers along Sylas's jaw, tangle them in August's hair, reach to embrace Whitt when he comes to my shoulder and brushes his lips ever so gently to my cheek.

I kiss Sylas once more, so hard a thrum of approval resonates from his chest, and then turn my head to seek out Whitt's mouth. As Whitt cups my jaw to draw me even closer, Sylas takes the opportunity to ease down my body and remove my boots. He kisses each foot and then my calf and my knee just below the hem of my dress, sending a flare of heat straight between my legs.

August strokes his hand down my torso and back up to fondle my breast. The swivel of his thumb brings my nipple to a hardened peak with a jolt of pleasure that leaves me gasping into Whitt's mouth. The spymaster chuckles and devours me with a searing press of his lips, his hand skimming across my waist and up to caress the other side of my chest.

When Sylas slides my dress up to kiss the inside of my thigh, I can't help squirming with the sharpening hunger building in my core. The fae lord brushes his mouth to a spot just a little higher and gazes up at me as Whitt releases my mouth to nibble my jaw.

"Shall we get this off of you?" Sylas asks in a low voice, letting the fabric tease across my thighs.

Eager anticipation shivers through me. "Yes, please. But I'd better not be the only one getting undressed."

Whitt smirks and sits up to strip off his shirt without any further prompting. I only get a few seconds to ogle the planes of tattooed muscle before Sylas is tugging up the skirt of my dress. I lift my hips to give him access, my sex tingling when he leans so close between my legs. As I sit up so he can lift it over my head, the warm air settles against my skin.

August has already shucked his shirt off too. I reach for Sylas's, my grip on the ties by the collar wobbling when the other two men return their attentions to my now-bared breasts. August tucks himself close to me, his broad chest against my back, and it's a wonder I remember what I meant to do well enough to yank Sylas's tunic upward.

He tosses it aside and lowers his head to reclaim my mouth. Searing hot skin surrounds me on all sides. Everywhere I reach, my hand slides over hardened muscle taut with desire.

How lucky I am to be in bed with even one of these extraordinary men, let alone three. I don't know what lies ahead of us, but I'm going to make every moment of this night count. I'm going to hold onto these memories when I'm far away from them, knowing that if I'm careful, if I stand firm, I'll have more of this to come back to.

I tip my head to kiss August next. Whitt eases lower to suck the tip of my breast into his mouth. Then Sylas trails his fingers down my belly to the hottest part of me, and my whimper turns into a moan.

The fae lord growls at the dampness of my panties. With a jerk, he snaps those off me and strokes me skin to slickening skin. My hips arch toward him again, another moan slipping from my lips as he delves a skillful finger right inside me. Bliss burns through me from the rocking of his hand, from Whitt's tongue flicking over my nipple, from August kissing me deeper than ever as if we could meld into one.

Sylas rests the heel of his hand against my most sensitive spot while he slips a second finger inside me. I clutch Whitt's hair, August's neck, riding the wave of pleasure they're summoning together.

It breaks over me far too soon, shocking a gasp from my throat. Electric tingles race through every muscle. My men let me sag back into the pillows, but I'm still burning for more. My fingers snag on August's trousers, my other hand gesturing roughly toward the others, and that's all the cue they need to kick off the rest of their clothes.

Suddenly I'm surrounded by three powerful, predatory, and utterly naked men. Maybe I should be nervous, but the emotions radiating through my chest are nothing but a heady mixture of love and carnal longing. The only question is how exactly we're going to make this work from here.

Whitt moves first—to kiss me on the mouth so tenderly it wakes up the ache in my heart and then withdrawing as if it'd never occur to him that he'd play more than a supporting role in what happens next. Sylas watches his spymaster with an expression I can't read.

As August captures my mouth next, the fae lord teases his fingers through the dampness of my release, stoking my hunger. He nudges my legs farther apart and leans in to swipe his tongue over my slit and across the sensitive nub above, just once.

A keening sound that's more demand than plea breaks from my lips, and Sylas grins. Then he moves from between my legs, dappling kisses across my belly as he goes, and meets my eyes with a smolder in both of his.

"I believe my strategist could conspire to bring even more of those lovely sounds from your beautiful throat, if you'll have him."

My gaze darts to Whitt. The spymaster stares at his lord, so startled it takes him a moment to rein in his shock. At the small but warm smile that crosses his lips, something blooms inside me that's deeper than lust, deeper maybe even than the love I've felt before.

They'd agreed to share me—they already were sharing. But Sylas's statement is an olive branch, an expression of trust and affection, and a dismissal of all the pains of the past to focus on what we have between us right now.

I want nothing more than to be a part of the mending of the ties between them—and it's hardly a sacrifice. I know from experience just how good Whitt *can* make me feel.

I extend my hand to him beckoningly. When Sylas smiles back at him, Whitt bends over me, his eyes alight with passion. He steals a kiss, tucking his hand beneath my back and sliding it down my spine until he reaches my rear.

The head of his erection glides over my arousal-drenched opening so slickly he groans. I wriggle to meet him, and he lets out another low chuckle. "We'll get you there, mighty one. Over and over again."

I just about combust at that promise, and then he's pushing into me, filling me with the hard, hot length of him. I let out a growl of my own.

Sylas has moved to my other side, caressing my breast

and giving my earlobe a gentle tug between his teeth. August hums happily and kisses my cheek, then my mouth when I tilt my face toward him.

I grasp the back of Whitt's neck with one hand, rising to meet his rhythm, wanting every movement he makes to flow through my body. The other hand I trail down August's chest until my fingers graze the straining, solid heat of his own erection. I grip him, reveling in his stutter of breath, in the pleasure expanding through my core with every thrust, in this sense of total unity as the four of us join together in the most intimate way we can.

Whitt shifts his angle, plunging deeper. His body presses against my outer nub, and I start to spiral away all over again. As Sylas tweaks my nipple, August runs his tongue along my jaw. I rock my hips faster, urging Whitt on, and he matches my urgency with a blissful groan.

His head bows, the fringe of his hair tickling my cheek. "You're so perfect, Talia. Come all the way with me. Let's see you soar."

A very undignified whine creeps up my throat. "Only —if you come—too."

He mutters a curse, my ragged request sending him over the edge. He clutches my thigh and thrusts into me so hard I do soar, up and away on a tsunami of sensation that sets every nerve blazing. As Whitt slows, both of us drifting down from the high of release, I sink boneless and giddy into the covers.

"Mmm," he says, a sly glint dancing in his eyes. "Don't think we're done with you yet."

A sound slips out of me that's equal parts disbelief and encouragement. With a low laugh, he eases out of me, his hands still on my hips. He tugs them. "There are so many more angles we can explore. I'm sure my lord can take you even higher."

As I flip onto my hands and knees at his urging, I glance at Sylas. If his invitation to Whitt was an olive branch, I guess this is Whitt returning the gesture. Saying in his own way how much it means to him to be part of this union.

The twitch of the fae lord's mouth hints at amusement, but the rest of his expression is all hunger. "It would be my pleasure in every possible way to take up that challenge, if our lady so desires."

Is he kidding me? I wet my lips, holding his gaze. "I want to feel all of you."

Somehow the smolder in his mismatched gaze burns even hotter at that statement. He kisses my shoulder blade, the curve of my waist, and the side of my hip before positioning himself behind me.

I've only had one of the men enter me from behind once before, in the pool at Hearthshire when August and I were both upright. Bent over like this, the stretch of Sylas's shaft penetrating me sends an even stronger jolt through my nerves. I gasp, unable to stop myself from pressing back into him.

But I didn't just mean that I wanted all of him. As my head tips back with the bliss of Sylas's first stroke, I direct the rest of my attention to August, who's lying patiently next to me, skimming his fingertips over my arm and my chest. I'm not done with *him* yet.

I can't get him off with my hands when I'm braced in this position, though. As I waver, caught up in the pleasure Sylas's measured thrusts are propelling through my body and a momentary uncertainty, Whitt provides a spark of inspiration—by sliding his head beneath me so he can lap his tongue over one of my breasts and then down to the sensitive point just above where I'm joined with Sylas.

A cry escapes me. Whitt works over that bundle of nerves with his skillful tongue with enthusiasm, following the swaying of my hips with Sylas's thrusts, and I'm struck with the impulse to do a little tasting of my own.

Not letting myself second-guess my instincts, I jerk my head toward August. "Come closer? I want to—" My cheeks flare, and the words catch in my throat for a second before I gasp them out. "I want to use my mouth on you. If you'd like it…"

My shaky voice falters completely at the surprise that flashes across his face—followed by a look so heated that his golden eyes may as well be liquid metal. "I'd never say no to you when you ask that way, Sweetness," he says roughly, moving to the top of the bed. "And definitely not when you're offering something like *that.*"

He stretches out so his erection is just inches from my face. I stare at it, never having looked at this part of my lovers quite this close up before. It juts so rigidly, but I know the veined thickness is covered in velvety soft skin. August's natural scent reaches my nose, manly musk with trace of his own sweetness, as if he brings the essence of his baking with him wherever he goes.

Cautiously, I flick my tongue over the head as the sway of my body brings me right up to him. August groans, and a bead of liquid forms at the tip. I lick that up, and his shaft outright twitches. The effect I'm having with just these small gestures is tantalizingly irresistible.

August reaches to trace his fingers over my cheek, into my hair, and back again. Building my confidence, I open my mouth enough to close it around his length. He makes a strangled sound that's all bliss. Whitt swirls his tongue over me, adding an extra jolt to the flood of tingling heat racing through my body, and I decide I'm going to offer August every bit of the same delight that I can.

Bobbing slightly with the motion of Sylas's thrusts, I take as much of August's shaft into my mouth as I can. When I tighten my lips around him, he lets out another groan. "That's it. Just like that. Heart help me, Talia, you're amazing."

I begin to work my mouth up and down, exploring him with my tongue at the same time. August's voice fractures into wordless murmurs of encouragement and appreciation, his fingers tangling in the waves spilling down my face.

As I find my pace, Sylas picks up his own, faster and deeper, as if urging me on while spurring me toward my third peak of the night. Even more pleasure shudders through my body. My arms start to wobble.

I suck hard on August's shaft, Whitt grazes his teeth against my nub, and Sylas plunges into me at just the right angle that I break into a million shimmering particles of joy. I gasp and then tighten my mouth around August again, echoing the clenching of my sex as I ride out the glittering wave.

Sylas bows over me, kissing my back. His hips hitch, and his heat gushes into me.

With a curse, August gently lifts my head. He grips himself. With a few swift strokes, a jet of pale liquid spurts across his abdomen. Then he sits up and kisses me so passionately he must taste himself all through my mouth, but he doesn't show any sign of caring.

Whitt scoots out from under me and props himself up on one elbow with a grin more pleased and relaxed than I've seen him in weeks. As I let myself ease down on the bed, rolling onto my back, my men form a ring of bodily heat around me. Sylas kisses my thigh. August strokes my hair. Whitt tucks his arm around mine.

It reminds me of the first time I brought them out of their curse, when Sylas called me their lady and I watched their wolves shepherding the rest of the pack—when they curled up around me in Oakmeet's entrance room afterward and I fell asleep nestled between them. It was the first time I felt like I truly belonged in this world, with these men.

I lean into all their caresses, absorbing every bit of warmth and affection I can, and try to forget for just a little longer that tomorrow I'll be walking away from all of this.

9

Corwin

As distracted by the day's events as I am, a quiver of awe still passes through me when I soar into view of the glinting landscape of Heart's Cadence.

The spires of my palace appear ready to pierce the sky itself. The vibrant reds and purples of the sunset seep down them, reflecting all across the crystalline walls. The same hues paint over the frozen waterfall that tumbles from the foot of the palace over the curved cliff edge to the mirrored pool far below. Little eddies of twirling snow tease around the regal trees, the pale icicles that dangle from their branches contrasting with the dark gray bark.

But what speaks of *home* the most is the softly sibilant melody that carries on the wind as it ripples across the palace walls and through those branches—the sound that makes my domain's name all the more fitting. A cool gust catches beneath my wings, and I let myself soar higher for a moment.

This splendor is mine.

It isn't long, though, before my thoughts return to all that isn't mine yet. To the uncomfortable hollow running from my chest to my gut, where my soul-twined mate has shut me off yet again.

Tomorrow, I remind myself as I swoop toward the broad terrace that stretches along the eastern side of the palace. Tomorrow I'll see her again face to face, in reality rather than a dream. And for more than a startled second before she's slipping away from me. She's going to stay with me, live with me, for ten days before I have to let her return to the summer realm if she wishes it.

My stomach knots at that thought in a way I don't care for at all. I drop toward the terrace, shifting out of my raven form just in time for my boot-clad feet to hit the polished crystal tiles. Before heading inside, I take in the gleaming splendor of the outer walls for a few moments until my emotions are just as still and cool.

We are soul-twined mates. Even if she's Seelie, even if neither of us could have expected this, the Heart has chosen us for each other. Once we've spent some time together, she'll have to see that accepting the bond is the only reasonable course of action—not just for us but for both our peoples too.

She seems quite loyal to them. There was so much fierceness in her when she challenged me about the harms done or threatened to the summer realm. I allow myself a flicker of admiration at the memory, which seems a fair reaction.

She'll want to do what's best for them. The typical Seelie temper and attitudes might make it difficult for her to understand how important it is for me to do the same for mine... but despite that fierceness, she didn't come across as especially hotheaded or savage when I spoke with her.

We might not get along so badly. Understanding will grow between us as we ease into the bond. If I'm not sure I can expect the depths of love I've seen play out in other couples, well, I've also seen the consequences of such matches. I wouldn't ask for more than a caring ally.

I won't *want* more. It'll be a pleasant enough change simply to have some company in the vast, sparkling halls of my family's long-time home.

As I step into one of those hallways, my footsteps ring out, the sound bouncing off the high ceiling where enchanted domes of topaz glow at intervals along the diamond surface. Of course, I'm hardly *alone* here. The signal of my return brings one of the servants hustling out of a side room with a practiced bow. "We were just finishing making dinner. Did you want to eat right away?"

The girl is human—a young child by fae accounting but somewhere in her adolescence by the mortal lifespan. I like that she waits for my answer without shying from my gaze, looking totally at ease in her role. I suppose she should, given that she was born here.

Some of my colleagues would have muttered about the fact that I let my equally human chef take a partner among the cleaning staff and make a family with her. But then, they'd probably also mutter about having a human prepare my meal over one of fae skill, yet I've never heard any of them complain about the offerings when they've dined here. If you're going to have human servants, I can't see how one born into our ways wouldn't be preferable to those who often have to be drugged or enchanted out of their fears.

"Set it out, covered, on the table," I say. "I'll come when I'm ready."

She bobs her head and scurries back to her father. Charles may not approach his cooking with the same finesse a fae from my flock might, but I can have fae-styled cooking in any other domain on any day I happen to drop in. My father, Heart keep his soul, cajoled the man into returning here with him after a jaunt into the human world where he ate at the man's restaurant, and continued enjoying his work enough to stem his aging. Charles has been with us for over a century now, a fixture in my life since shortly after I reached my adulthood.

In some ways, as absurd as it sounds, he's the closest thing to family I have left.

I stalk through the halls to my private sitting room before any further gloom can descend over me. Though it's getting late, I'm not close to hungry yet. The brief visit to one of the domains that flanks mine barely took the edge off the tensions coiled inside me.

I sink into my preferred chair, willing some of that tension to seep out of me. Everything is in order—as much order as I could manage. It will play out however it will. There's nothing to be gained by dwelling on events still in the future, beyond my grasp.

And yet my mind keeps attempting to leap forward to tomorrow morning when that pink-haired Seelie woman will step across the border with me.

I've reined my thoughts in for the dozenth time and

am just straightening up with the intention of going to dinner now—because although I still don't feel particularly hungry, at least it'll give me something else to focus on—when a trace of sensation trickles through the empty space inside me. I freeze at the edge of the chair and then reach out tentatively. *Talia?*

She doesn't respond. I'm definitely not experiencing the rush of twined experience I did the few times her connection has gone unguarded before. She must have whatever walls she's put in place against me still up.

But they aren't perfectly solid at the moment, and whatever *she's* experiencing is intense enough to seep through. Another tendril of it reaches me—a whiff of pleasure that teases through my abdomen right to my groin as if drawn by the lightest of fingertips. Then a whisper of a sigh released from hitching lungs, a deeper jolt of carnal bliss—

Even as my own breath catches, my throat constricts with sudden understanding. In our shared dream, she mentioned another man, a prospective mate, that she hesitated to leave. She's with him now. *He's* touching her, summoning pleasure in her, so much that it's filtering through her defenses.

My hands clench at my sides. A maelstrom of emotion surges inside me: fury that any other being is enjoying that much intimacy with the woman who is *my* soul-twined mate, pain that she's turning to him even after agreeing to come to me, and tangled through it all, a sharp twinge of arousal that has my cock half-hard where I'm sitting braced in the chair.

I should be the one drawing those sighs out of her,

sparking those pleasures in her. And oh, how it would feel to come together as we're meant to, to drink those shaky breaths from her lips, to feel her around me and know every flare of passion and delight is thanks to me—

I shut my eyes and set my jaw, resisting the flood of feeling. Throwing into place a crystalline wall within me like the one I used to shut *her* out during the conversations with my colleagues it was best she wasn't privy to.

Even the faint impressions of her ecstasy fall away. There's only blankness within now, echoing with the thud of my heart and the throb of my cock.

It doesn't matter. Tomorrow she will be with me and leave this intruder to our bond behind. Why shouldn't I want her to get him out of her system as much as she can? Better she does that than come to me regretting that she didn't get one last chance, isn't it?

Yes—yes, it is.

I stand up, perfectly steady, and grimace at the brush of my trousers against my still aching groin. The impulse flickers through me to head to my bedchamber to release it, but I'm no wolf to be led by my basest desires. I inhale and exhale slowly, once and again and three times, and the flow of blood slows. The pressure recedes.

There. It need not mean anything at all. I am master over myself.

I'm even less enthusiastic about dinner now than when I first meant to go, but starving myself certainly won't help matters. Keeping my steps light, I make my way to the smaller dining room where I eat when I don't have visitors.

The silver dome covering the plate is still warm to the touch. I haven't let it sit too long.

I get to enjoy the meal, however much I can, for two bites of curried fish and one of braised frost kale. Then there's a knock on the door, and one of the servants from my flock peers around it at my answer.

The stout fae man dips into a quick bow. "I'm sorry, my lord. Arch-Lord Terisse has arrived to speak with you. I can tell her you'll be with her shortly?"

Well, there goes what little appetite I recovered. I nudge my chair back. "That's all right, Oswald. I'll come now. Thank you."

I'd expected this. Perhaps some part of me hoped that when one of my colleagues responded to the brief message I sent reporting that my soul-twined mate would be joining me, it'd be while I was away from home. But I do have to speak to them about it eventually.

It could have been worse. I'd appreciate Laoni's questioning even less—although naturally the self-styled leader of our quintet of arch-lords would see making such a visit as beneath her. If she'd felt that she needed to handle the matter directly, she'd have demanded *I* come to her.

Terisse is waiting in the entrance room just off the terrace, which tells me she flew here—and it appears she did so alone. I'm not sure how much of this unusual situation my colleagues have shared with their coteries so far.

When I enter the room, she turns toward me. Only faint lines on her otherwise smooth, coppery face show she's well into middle-age. The tufts of dark, greenish hair that fan out around her head like shadowed shards of emerald contain no traces of gray yet. She considers me with no hint of approval or concern revealed in the even line of her prim lips.

I dip my head slightly in acknowledgement, no subservience due between equals. "Welcome to Heart's Cadence, Terisse. What brought about this visit?"

She offers a small bob in return. "I apologize for the abrupt arrival. I'll keep this quick so as not to interrupt your night any more than I already have. We simply wanted to get a more extensive report on the new development with your soul-twined mate."

We, because naturally my colleagues conferred before deciding she'd be the one to approach me. I'm speaking not with her but all three of the others through her as soon as she reports back, no doubt.

I snuff out my momentary irritation and nod. "Of course. Everything is settled. I'll go across the border shortly before noon tomorrow with the shielding spell to ensure my security, although my mate honestly believes her pack intends me no harm. I'll take an oath to ensure *her* security in the winter realm and bring her back with me. She's agreed to a trial stay of ten days, but I expect once she's had time to adjust to the bond, all will be well."

"Have you considered that the visit might be a gambit to allow her to commit some treachery against us while she's here?"

"Of course." Of all the things my colleagues might accuse me of, carelessness is certainly not one of them. "Besides the fact that she could hardly lie while so close to the Heart, I have her thoughts from right inside her head. I've sensed no ill intentions from her."

Talia is wary and perhaps even frightened, defensive of her people and the violence that's been committed against them, but I couldn't expect anything less. I didn't glean the smallest bit of vengefulness from her.

"You'll want to keep a close eye on her nonetheless, knowing how… unpredictable the wolves can be." Terisse sucks in a breath just shy of a sigh, and I can't help wondering if my colleagues would have preferred it if the Seelie had refused to hand over my mate after all. If they were bargaining on getting to wage war with that point of leverage.

It wouldn't surprise me. I'd be more startled to learn they gave a feather about my marital success. Other than how that success might suit their ends, now that their first goal is no longer viable.

"See if you can't win her over quickly, then," Terisse goes on with a flick of her hand. "Derive whatever you can about their plans and defenses through your bond. We can't waste this opportunity."

My hackles rise for the fleeting instant before I shake off the instinctive reaction to how callously she's speaking of my mate. Her perspective is a logical way to look at the situation. No doubt I'd be thinking of it exactly the same way if I agreed with my colleagues' larger goals.

I can't ignore her point completely, though. Even if I'd rather we didn't find ourselves at war, we do need *some* kind of a solution. My loyalty to my flock and my people has to come before any devotion to an uncertain mate.

"You can be sure I'll be alert for any information that

could aid us in our difficulties," I reply. "I do ask that the rest of you give us our privacy during her visit. If you wish to speak to me, I'll come to the rest of you. It may be stressful enough for her adjusting to the thought of living here without the pressure of more watchful eyes." And Heart only knows what skeptical remarks they might make in front of her, regarding both her and me.

"We can respect the complexities of your uncertain bond." Terisse turns as if to go, but pauses in mid-swivel to glance back at me. "But do keep a close eye on your own heart, Corwin. We wouldn't want *her* to be the one to win *you*. I'd imagine you'd agree that one such catastrophe in your family line is more than enough."

I fix my mouth into a stiff smile, biting back the cutting remark that leapt to my tongue. None of my colleagues would have resisted getting in that jab to drive their disdain home. "Naturally. You have nothing at all to fear there."

She makes a short sound that's barely agreement and steps toward the doors. A moment later, the dark shape of her raven launches into the air from my terrace.

She's gone, but they'll be watching me these ten days —far more closely than they have ever before.

And the worst of it is, I can't even blame them.

10

Talia

I hesitate just outside the partly constructed castle, looking toward the temporary pack village. The early morning sunlight paints the landscape with soft golden tones and shimmers off the haze of the border beyond the eastern forest. Just looking at it makes my gut knot tighter.

I probably should have done this sooner, given her more time to decide—but the plan fell into place so quickly, and *I* hadn't quite decided I was going to make this request until I woke up this morning.

Maybe I still haven't totally made it. I waver on my feet before pressing onward to the house I know Harper is staying in.

The summer fae tend to be early risers unless there was a revel the night before. My friend answers my knock already alert and dressed—in a relatively simple gown by her standards. She looks me over, her initial smile faltering. "What's wrong? Has there been more trouble from the ravens?"

I guess that's one way of describing the situation, but it's not at all what she means. I shake my head. "No attacks or anything. I wanted to talk with you about something. Can I come in?"

"Of course." Harper steps back, her brow still knit with worry. I'm not totally sure she *shouldn't* be worried.

The temporary homes the pack-kin are using while the full castle and village are being built contain just one large, circular room with a few basic wooden furnishings. The table in the corner has only one chair. Harper perches on the edge of the narrow bed, and I grab the chair, turning it to face her.

Once I've sat down, it takes a moment for me to find my words. We've been keeping my connection to the Unseelie as quiet as possible—Sylas is hoping to have my visit there stay essentially secret—and talking about it still unnerves me.

I clasp my hands together on my lap and drag in a breath. "Something happened the night of the coronation celebration. When the Unseelie arch-lords came to talk to ours. I—I've formed a soul-twined bond with one of their arch-lords."

Harper's eyes grow so wide there seems to be a real risk they'll fall out of her head. "*What?* But… you're not even fae." Her pale cheeks flush red. "I mean—"

I let out a choked sort of laugh. "It's okay. I know I'm not, and I know how crazy it sounds because of that. But obviously whatever tied my blood to the curse connected me to the world in other ways we didn't expect too." I'm hoping this is the last of those surprises, but at this point, I'm not counting on it.

"So what are you going to do?" She bites her lip, and I assume she's thinking of what my absence would mean for the Seelie and their curse, but I've misjudged her. "I suppose you have to go to him? I'll… I'll miss having you around. We won't be able to see more of this domain together after all."

The fact that she's more bothered by losing my company than my blood reassures me of my choice. I manage a crooked smile. "I'm not committing to anything yet. There are a lot of things and people I'd miss here. And I don't know how much we can trust any of the Unseelie. But I've agreed to stay with him for ten days just to get to know him a little, so that if"—*when*—"I decide to come back, the Heart will know I gave it a try."

Harper nods slowly. "That makes sense. I wouldn't trust them either, after all those attacks. Are you going today, then? You came to say good-bye?"

"Kind of." I rub my mouth. "I was actually wondering… how would you like to explore an Unseelie arch-lord's domain instead?"

She blinks at me, and I swear her eyes nearly do fall out this time. "You—you want me to come *with* you?"

My fingers curl into the skirt of my dress. "I know it's a big ask. It could be dangerous. The Unseelie arch-lord has agreed that I can bring one companion with me, but we had to promise it wouldn't be anyone with much warrior training or experience. It'd be nice to have someone I know that I can talk to while I'm there, someone who can be a second set of eyes in case the winter fae have any ulterior motives… It's okay if it's too much. I won't be upset if you say no."

Not with her, at least. The thought of crossing the border into totally unfamiliar territory with no one I can count on to support me over my Unseelie hosts makes my skin crawl.

Harper is simply staring at me now. "And you'd trust *me* to be that person?" she says in a small voice.

"There isn't anyone else I'd want to ask." With my men and Astrid out of the equation, Harper is the only member of the pack I've talked much with, shared anything personal with. Being in Corwin's home with a companion I barely know might feel even worse than being alone.

She made an awful mistake, but she's done everything she can to make up for it. If she's willing to brave the winter realm to support me there, then that's really all the proof I need that she deserves my trust again.

Her hands twitch at her sides. The idea obviously scares her.

I get up. "You can take some time to think about it. This is coming together quickly—I'm supposed to leave in a few hours—but you don't have to decide this exact moment."

"No." Her chin lifts. "I can decide now. I'll come with you. I'm glad you asked. You need someone there with you, and I won't be happy without my friend here, so it works out for both of us." A hint of a smile crosses her lips. "And it might be a little exciting seeing the winter realm. As long as the ravens don't try to peck us to death or anything."

"I'm pretty sure Sylas is going to make that one of the conditions of the visit," I say dryly, and then a giggle that's as much anxiety as amusement tumbles out of me. Harper laughs too. Right then, I have no doubts at all.

She folds her arms over her chest and gives me a once-over. "You're not meeting your soul-twined arch-lord mate in *that* dress, are you?"

I'm not surprised that would be where her attention goes next. I'm wearing a simple blue knee-length smock like the type most of the female pack-kin wear for their day-to-day lives, airy but plain. "I don't have anything fancy here. I wasn't sure I should make a big deal of it…"

Harper's huff tells me how much she disagrees. She jumps up and grabs the small trunk she brought with her. "You need to make a statement—that you're someone just as special as any bird-brain arch-lord. It's a good thing I came prepared just in case. Let's see… Yes, this one should do it. Just give me a little while to adjust it so it'll fit you properly. I'll have it ready in an hour."

"You really don't have to—" I start to protest, but she tuts at me and shoos me out so she can get to work.

"Go have one of August's breakfasts," she calls after me. "You're getting too skinny again; I'll have to adjust all your other dresses too if you keep that up."

I've actually already eaten, but it's true that my appetite hasn't been great the past few days. I make a silent commitment to eating decent portions of whatever Corwin's going to serve us, because I can't let myself get weak while I'm on Unseelie territory, and head back to the castle to await whatever gorgeous gown Harper is getting ready for me.

I reach the door just as Whitt comes striding out at a much more urgent pace than I'd expect from him first thing in the morning. My pulse stutters with the thought that we're facing yet another calamity, but the moment his eyes land on me, his expression relaxes. "There you are, mite."

"I just went to talk to Harper," I say. "She agreed to come."

He hums to himself. "An interesting choice after what she almost put you through, but I know better than to argue with your judgment. She's shown a fair bit of grit in the past couple of weeks, I'll give her that." He brushes his hand over my hair, careful not to make it too much of a caress while the pack-kin who only know of my more intimate involvement with August might be looking on. "Take a short walk with me?"

Maybe there is unfortunate news after all. I limp alongside him past the temporary village, across the broad field of twinkling flowers beyond, and into this domain's forest. It's less ominous than the thick brush and towering trees of Hearthshire. The trees are more stout than looming, with only small patches of flowers and ferns here and there where the sunlight streams through the canopy. The pulsing energy of the Heart tickles over my skin.

As we walk, Whitt scans our surroundings. Before we've gone far enough for my warped foot to start to ache, he stops at a massive log in a small glade. As he sits, he tugs me into his lap, enveloping me within his arms and beneath his chin as if he never means to let me go.

His breath tickles over my forehead with his voice. "I'd give anything to be the one to go with you, you know.

And not just to get a direct eyeful of what those blasted birds are up to. It doesn't matter how mighty you are—you shouldn't have to take this on."

The vehemence in his words brings a fresh ache into my heart. I lean into his warmth and his scent, summery as a sun-baked beach. Whitt doesn't often let much deeper emotion show, even when we're alone. Knowing more about his past, I can see why—and I treasure every moment of open affection he offers me.

Especially when I know it'll be over a week before I'll feel his embrace again.

"I survived nine years in Aerik's cage," I remind him as well as myself. "The next ten days *can't* be worse than that."

"If I thought there was any chance they'd come close, I'd be fighting tooth and claw to keep you here," Whitt mutters.

I reach up to touch his gorgeous face, and he takes the opening to steal a kiss. It lingers on, so tender the ache spreads through my whole chest. Then he nuzzles my cheek. When he speaks again, his voice is raw. "You have been *so*… I was such an idiot to think your presence would hurt us somehow. I wish I could do as much for you as you have for us. For *me*. The thing that kills me the most is that you'll be just across the border but completely beyond my reach."

I swallow hard. "You can't help that. And you *have* been here for me, in so many ways… I hate how much trouble I've brought—"

He catches my cheek before I can go on, dropping his forehead to mine. "Don't. None of that was your doing.

From the moment I came after you in the woods that night after I told you off, I've never once regretted having you with us. This doesn't mean much yet, but…"

He lets that sentence hang for long enough that I start to think he's changed his mind about whatever he was going to say. Then he dips his head farther to murmur by my ear. "Wye."

I peer up at him, confused. "Why what?"

His mouth pulls into a slanted grin. "Not the question. It's the first syllable in my true name."

His words knock the breath from my lungs. "But— you're telling *me*? You said—"

Whitt draws me close again, his voice still low. "I've never given it to anyone. It still doesn't do you any good, just having a piece. I can't risk the whole thing now when we don't know what that wretched raven arch-lord might try to ferret out from your mind—it's not just my own security but the entire pack, and Sylas as arch-lord… But I want you to have it as my promise that if there comes a time when that connection doesn't threaten us, I'll give you the rest. Even if we can't be bonded the same way you are to him, you'll be able to reach me somehow or other wherever I am, whenever you need me."

My throat squeezes tight. Having his true name would give me as much power over him as I can summon with my magic—the ability not just to delve into his mind and project my thoughts to him but to order him around if I wanted to do that. I probably *don't* have enough power to overcome his will if he resists, and from what I've heard whatever connection I could form would be only a pale shade of the innate, vivid shared awareness that binds me to Corwin, but still, it's an immense show of trust.

"If you still *want* that connection with me after all of this," Whitt adds. When I start to protest, he quiets me with a quick peck. "I know you would now. But you can't be sure—I've been alive for more than four centuries, and *I* can barely comprehend the power of a soul-twined bond."

He pulls back far enough to hold my gaze. "You need to know that we'd understand if something happens between you and him. The Heart gave you this bond. If you end up feeling more than you expect to and you want to act on those feelings, none of us—Sylas or August or me—will blame you, I promise you that. We all realize it's a possibility. We're prepared for it. I'll consider us *lucky* if what you feel for us overcomes even the Heart's blessing."

I blink back the tears forming in my eyes. My voice comes out thinner than I'd like. "I can't imagine wanting anyone other than the three of you. Thank you—for the beginning of your true name. For wanting to give it to me."

I don't know what else to say, so I settle for kissing him, hard, pouring all my love into our embrace in the hopes that he can sense it all even though no magic ties us together yet.

"It'd be for me as much as for you," Whitt says roughly, tucking me against him again. "Anything that will keep you close in whatever way, I'm all for." He pauses, and his voice drops. "I love you, Talia."

Joy quivers through me, bright and giddying. Maybe I should have assumed by now, after all the devotion he's offered me, after his brothers had made their own declarations, but Whitt's never said it out loud before.

I throw my arms around his neck, and he squeezes me tight. "I love you too," I say, choking up. "So much."

But in a few short hours I'm going to have to leave him and the other men I love behind.

11

Talia

As I walk onto the field around the Heart, the dress Harper fixed up for me whispers against my legs. The soft, ivory fabric with its pearly sheen covers my arms from wrists to shoulders and flows down, gently hugging my chest and hips, to my ankles. Panes of lace show peeks of my collarbone and my calves. The intricate patterns shine like frost against my skin.

I look every bit a winter princess, and I'm not sure how I feel about that.

I could see the same hesitation in my lovers' eyes when they took me in, mingled with their appreciation. Harper knows what she's doing—I look *good,* at least. Like a woman who can stand on her two feet, even if one of those feet is a bit wonky, and who won't be cowed by whatever the Unseelie throw at me.

Here's hoping that's actually true.

When we stop several feet shy of the border's

shimmering gray haze, Sylas positions himself next to me. Whitt and August flank us, August holding a trunk with some changes of clothes and a few other belongings I quickly packed. Harper stands off to the side, still in her casual dress from this morning so she doesn't upstage me but with her own trunk clutched in her hands.

I want to spin around and claim one last kiss from all my men, but Corwin is due to step across the border any moment now. I might have mentioned my heart's other commitments to him, but starting off this trial run with him seeing me in another man's arms seems like a disaster waiting to happen. So I stand still and straight, my arms at my sides, my heart thudding so loud I suspect all my fae companions can hear it.

My wall of light is still glowing inside me, shored up a few minutes ago. I don't want Corwin seeing just how nervous I am. I don't want to risk him catching glimpses of other, dangerous thoughts that might slip through my mind while I *am* so nervous.

The other arch-lords asked to be present as well, but Sylas managed to dissuade them. I guess it'd be pretty obvious that something big is going on if they were all here. What would the rest of the Seelie think if they knew the cure to their curse was about to cross enemy lines?

I inhale slowly, squaring my shoulders and steadying myself, and the mass of haze quivers. A figure comes into focus through the fog just before he steps out onto the grass on our side.

Corwin is dressed in the formal jacket and slacks I remember from the night of the coronation, though he hasn't brought out his wings. A thin circlet crown gleams silver amid his blue-black curls. His dark gaze shoots straight to me, and my heart stutters harder despite my best efforts at staying calm.

Looking at him, I can't read his emotions at all. His expression is even more impenetrable than Sylas's can be.

At least he seems relatively relaxed about the whole situation, though he stays within a couple of feet of the border as if he thinks he might need to dive back through to the winter side at any moment. He nods to me, his gaze flicking down over me for an instant before returning to my face. His voice comes out cool and even. "Talia. You look lovely. You're ready?"

"Yes." I motion to Harper. "This is my friend Harper. She's the one who'll be joining me. The dress is thanks to her."

He nods to my friend as well. "It's exquisite work." He turns his attention to Sylas, and his frame, equal to the other arch-lord's in height if slimmer, draws just a little straighter. "I'm sure you can understand that I'd prefer not to linger in your realm any longer than necessary. I'm prepared to take the oaths we discussed."

It's really happening. In just a few minutes, I'll be walking with him through that haze into the total unknown. Even Sylas and his cadre don't have much idea how the winter arch-lords live.

My pulse kicks up another notch, and my hand twitches to my hair before I can catch the nervous gesture. As I tuck the stray waves behind my ear, Corwin's gaze slides back to me—and his posture goes totally rigid.

I freeze with my hand still by my face, startled by his reaction and the sudden bewilderment that's crossed his previously implacable face. A flicker of hostility breaches the glowing barrier inside me. What have I done?

Corwin strides forward abruptly. I stiffen, my nerves jangling with alarm. He stops just a few feet away from me with a flare of his nostrils and a widening of his eyes. "You…"

"Arch-Lord Corwin?" Sylas says with a hint of a growl.

Corwin spins to face him. "What's the meaning of this?" he demands, his voice gone flat and outright cold. "You thought you'd pass off an imposter as my soul-twined mate? If you put some magic on her that you thought would disguise her nature, it's failed. She's obviously human."

Oh. Oh, no. A ball of ice forms in my stomach. He didn't realize. He was startled before only because he thought I was a Seelie woman—a *true-blooded* Seelie woman. Of course. It never occurred to him just how unlikely this bond was even beyond that. I didn't make a point of mentioning what I am because I assumed he'd simply know, and he's never gotten that close a look at me before.

"Corwin," I say quickly. "There's no trick. I'm Talia. I —I don't know how it happened; none of us do. It's just—"

My words are only deepening the offended curve of his mouth. I stop talking and do the only thing I can think of that could possibly convince him beyond a doubt: I let the wall inside me drop.

Emotions flood through the space between us: anger and betrayal and a jab of fear, so sharp-edged and swift I flinch. But a second later, all those sensations retreat behind a chilly wave of shock. Corwin stares at me, and I see myself through his eyes in the back of my mind, tense but standing firm.

I'm sorry, I think at him, hoping he can pick up on the honest regret I'm feeling. *I would have told you—I thought you'd already realized.*

For a moment, we all stand there in taut silence, my lovers braced, Harper hugging herself. Corwin's jaw works, but I can't imagine there's any magic that could create an illusion of a soul-twined bond where there wasn't one. He has to know it's true.

"Is there a problem?" Sylas asks, his low baritone unusually terse. "You wanted the chance to meet your soul-twined mate. Here she is. If *you're* rejecting her—"

"*No*," Corwin interrupts, before I can feel more than a dash of relief at the thought that this bizarre situation could be put to rest that easily. He tugs at the base of his jacket and seems to gather himself. As the glimpses of his emotions filtering to me settle, I get the impression of confusion and curiosity, but no more sense of anger.

"No," he says more smoothly. "I was only surprised. It is… rather irregular."

Whitt snorts. "Yes, we're quite aware of that."

August folds his arms over his chest in a subtle but implicit threat. "It shouldn't mean you treat her any differently than if she was the truest of true-blooded fae."

Corwin takes him in, and I catch wisps of recognition and defensiveness—and a renewed quiver of anger. Then it all fades away as he must reconstruct whatever wall he's used to keep me out of his awareness before.

Can he tell that August is one of my lovers? How

much does he care that there may be less of a place for him in my heart rather than seeing me as a possession that's been stolen?

The Unseelie arch-lord raises his chin at a haughty angle. "She's my soul-twined mate. That puts her above any other being in my consideration automatically."

"Then we can proceed with the oaths?" Sylas asks pointedly.

Corwin glances at me. His bronze face has become an unreadable mask again, but I think there's still something puzzled in his gaze. Well, why wouldn't there be? I've known how impossible this bond is from the start, and I'm still unsettled by it.

But I agreed to give it a try anyway, so the least he can do is not be a jerk about it. I raise my chin too, gazing back at him.

The corners of his lips curl upward with the faintest hint of a smile. Enough to melt a little of the icy panic that's been trickling through my veins since he figured out what I am.

Maybe this will be okay. Ten days. I can manage that. I've already seen that he isn't only the cold, impenetrable front he's presenting.

"Yes," Corwin says, still watching me. "Proceed with the oaths."

As Sylas lays out the phrasing previously agreed on, the thrum of the Heart's magic rises, lacing through his words. It resonates through Corwin's voice repeating the oaths. He swears that I will be free to return in ten days' time, that he will do everything in his power to ensure my and Harper's safety from any type of harm, and that he'll keep secret anything he learns from me that relates to the Seelie. He doesn't halt or hesitate once.

Then it's done. Corwin takes my trunk from August. I force myself not to look at my lovers. If I do, I'm afraid I won't be able to hold back the sob prickling at the back of my throat.

My soul-twined mate holds out his hand to me. "Shall we go, then?"

My arm balks at my side, the memory racing through my mind of his touch and the electric impact it had even in a dream. Before I can decide whether to face that intensity or risk offending him, he turns the gesture into a simple beckoning. As I step forward, he lets his hand drop without complaint.

Harper moves to join me. We have to make our own vows to cross the border so close to the Heart.

"By the Heart, I swear to do no harm to the fae beyond this boundary. May I pass in peace and amity," I say. A tingle shoots through my chest straight to my toes, its energy wriggling through my nerves. Harper makes the same declaration.

Then, with Corwin leading the way, we walk into the haze toward the lands of the winter fae.

Talia

It only takes a few steps into the border area before a chill seeps through the hazy air. The whisper of grass beneath my boots hardens into the crinkle of frost and then the crunch of a thin layer of snow. My dress may cover most of my body, but the silky fabric is so thin that the cold licks right through it. I shiver, and Harper grabs my hand, leaning close to me for both reassurance and warmth.

I stay focused on Corwin's tall, lean form just ahead of us, his pale clothes blending into the fog but his dark hair clearly visible. It's only a couple more strides before the border's haze falls away. I suck in a breath, staring at the landscape around us.

The winter realm couldn't look more different from the warmth and rich colors of the summer lands. We're standing on an icy plain which glints with the sharp sunlight falling from the clear blue sky. To our right, near where the Heart keeps up its rhythmic pulsing, looms an immense ivory tower with turrets jutting from its sides like tusks. I guess that's the Unseelie arch-lords' equivalent to our Bastion. Beyond it, I can make out one other building in the distance: a castle of gleaming silver.

That's not where we're heading, though. Just a little to our left, across the vast plain, rises another palace that seems to not so much reflect the sunlight off its translucent stone walls but absorb it and bounce it around in a boundless twinkling. The spires towering high above the main rooftop have the shape of crystal growths, dappled with facets. I can tell from the satisfaction that crosses Corwin's face, taking it in, that it's his home.

There are forests here too—ice-laden, leafless trees in a cluster farther to our left. And at a vast distance, craggy snow-capped mountains stretch toward the sky.

It's all beautiful in a cold, impervious sort of way. Corwin glances back at us and catches my next shiver, partly awe but partly the chill that's biting deeper into my skin. His eyes flicker with concern.

"My apologies. I didn't think—I'm unaccustomed to Seelie guests. Here, we all have warming enchantments woven into our clothes. I can put one in place for both of you quickly… if that's all right?"

My nerves twitch at the thought of him casting any kind of magic on me, but I'm not keen on freezing to death either. "Just that, no other magic?" I say quickly, afraid my teeth with start chattering if I open my mouth for too long.

"Only the warming charm," Corwin promises, and I nod.

He murmurs a few syllables with a brisk gesture of his hand, and heat unfurls over my body, chasing away the chill not just where my dress brushes against my skin but up over my face as well. I restrain another shiver that has nothing to do with the cold this time. The wash of warmth felt too close to being touched in a way much more intimate than I'm comfortable with from my theoretical mate.

At least I'm no longer on the verge of frostbite. Corwin casts the same spell on Harper's clothing, and she lets out a sigh of relief. He motions for us to follow him to the sparkling crystal palace. "I'll have one of the folk of my flock see that the rest of your clothes are similarly prepared."

"Flock?" I say, and then wince at myself. Of course raven shifters wouldn't refer to their people as a "pack." "Never mind." I wave toward the palace. "So that's yours? What did you call your domain—Heart's Cadence?"

His lips form a slight smile as if the fact that I remembered pleases him, but not so much that he's going to make too big a deal of it. He's kept our bond closed off —I can't read his emotions through it. Obviously trust is going to take a while on both sides.

"Yes, this is where you'll be staying," he says. "If you listen closely, you'll already be able to hear how the palace honors its name."

I don't understand what he means until I tune out the rasp of our feet over the icy terrain. Another sound slips through the air, soft and quavering but forming a clear melody once I've latched onto it.

Harper, with the extensive experience with music she

has thanks to her parents, must pick the tune up even faster. Her thin eyebrows rise. "That's coming from the palace?"

Corwin inclines his head. "The crystals were sculpted so that they'd resonate when the wind passes over them to form a sort of song. You're never far from music in Heart's Cadence."

The line sounds rehearsed, but the pride in his voice is unmistakeable. I study the palace, thinking about how lords design their homes back in the summer realm. "Are you especially strong in magic to do with crystals, then?"

"Stone of all sorts. Although I can't take credit for more than a few minor renovations to the palace. It's been standing for well over a thousand years. My great-grandmother chose diamond for the hardiness as well as its beauty."

That whole building is made out of *diamond*? I manage to snap my jaw shut before I'm outright gaping. It mustn't be that big a deal when you can summon as much as you want just by saying a true name, but still. The kings and queens still in existence back in the human world would faint over that kind of riches.

And that's where I'm going to be living for the next ten days.

Harper grasps my hand again, but there's a spring in her step now. The flush in her cheeks looks more excited than nervous. I'm sure it's easier to see this as a fantastic adventure when you're not wondering whether you can trust a total stranger whose soul has inexplicably merged with yours.

Corwin is watching me. My sense of the connection

between us shifts as he lowers his own barrier, allowing a few impressions to filter through. He's evaluating my reaction, hopeful but cautious. "What do you think?"

I instinctively summoned my own inner wall when I noticed his relaxing, but the tickle of hope sets me more at ease. I let my gaze rove over the palace, the forest, and the mountains beyond again, doing my best to take them in as if I was a traveler simply here to explore with no other pressures on me. Another wave of awe ripples through me, and I don't mind if he feels it. "It's very different from the parts of the fae world I'm used to, but it is beautiful."

Will I get to see much more of this place, or will Corwin want to keep me shut away in his home until he's sure of my loyalties and affections? I don't know how to ask that without it coming out badly, so I push the question away for now.

I expected more of a welcoming party, but only a couple of fae emerge from the palace to greet us. Both are dressed in well-constructed but simple tunics and trousers that make me suspect they're staff rather than anyone in a position of power.

Does Corwin have a cadre like all the Seelie lords do? Don't they want to meet his supposed mate? For that matter, where's the rest of his flock? I don't see any smaller buildings around. Surely they don't all live in the palace with him?

I don't vocalize any of my confusion even mentally, but Corwin must pick up on some of it through our bond. He points to a sheer edge several feet beyond the farthest reach of the palace where the land appears to fall away completely. "My flock has their homes along the cliffside on either side of the falls. There's something to be said for a view that gives you the impression of soaring even when you have your feet on the ground."

If you're used to having full control over any "soaring" you do, I'd bet there is.

When we reach the grand entrance with its onion-dome-topped arch, the two fae who came out to meet us usher us inside. "The rooms are ready, my lord," one says to Corwin. The other offers his hands to take Harper's trunk.

She hesitates and then hands it over. "Thank you."

The interior of the palace sparkles nearly as much as the exterior. Muted sunlight radiates through the high ceilings and the walls, which are thick enough to hide any view of the objects or figures that lie beyond them. Sleek blue-gray rugs cover the floors and muffle our footsteps. The faint melody continues rising and falling around us, easier to make out now that we're right within the palace.

After a couple of turns, the staff stop. Corwin opens a door to a vast bedroom with a pale, marble-framed canopy bed and matching furnishings. "This will be your room, for the time being," he says to me, bringing the prickling awareness that I'd be expected to eventually share *his* room with him. "And your companion will be staying right across the hall."

The man with Harper's trunk has already carried it into the room opposite. Harper walks in after him, gasping as she looks around.

Leaving my door open, Corwin sets my trunk at the foot of the bed and pauses. "I'd appreciate—could I have a few moments to speak to you alone? I feel it might be easier to settle into getting to know each other if we at least begin without an audience."

He might be right, and I don't get any sense of ill intent through the bond, only an honest desire to understand more about me. I have plenty of questions I want to ask him too, and it makes sense that he wouldn't necessarily open up as much with Harper there.

"All right," I say. "But—not in here." Having a private conversation with my soul-twined mate in a room that features a bed seems like it'd raise expectations I'd rather not have on the table. "Is there somewhere else we could talk?"

"Yes, of course."

Harper has overheard the whole exchange. "I'll be fine," she calls from the other room. "Just come get me if you need me."

Corwin steps back into the hall. "You both can venture anywhere you'd like in the palace that's available to you—and most of it is, other than a few rooms that require more discretion. I'd recommend you don't leave the palace without me until I've had a chance to introduce you to the full flock, so I can be sure of their reactions." He stops, maybe not totally sure of his *own* reactions yet, and then motions for me to follow him.

The halls we walk through feel even more empty without the company. I don't spot any other fae or any human servants, if he keeps them. The palace is vast and breathtaking in its spectacle, but somehow that only makes the emptiness feel lonelier.

He doesn't have a mate, of course, but neither does Sylas, and there was always a bustle of energy in and around *his* castle, especially once we were back at Hearthshire.

Corwin leads me into a sitting room with tall windows that look out over a wide diamond terrace with an even more epic view of the mountains. For all the glinting hardness of the palace itself, the sofas and chairs look comfortable enough, their marble seats, backs, and arms set with leather cushions. I sink down onto one end of a sofa, tucking my legs up beside me, and Corwin takes an armchair that he pulls over so he's facing me.

"Why don't you start?" he says mildly. "I can't imagine how many questions you must have that you hesitated to ask through the bond."

I have plenty, but I don't know which might get me into trouble. I go with the most immediate. "Do you have a cadre? Relatives or friends who are like… advisors, and the main people you turn to when you're guiding your— your flock?"

"Cadre is a Seelie term. We refer to our close associates as our coterie."

"So, you do have one then?" I glance around. "Do they live here in the palace too?" *Where* are *they, and why aren't they here for something like this?* I think to myself behind the partial wall I'm still holding against the full force of our connection.

Corwin's mouth twitches as if that idea is amusing. "No, they have their own homes—by the top of the cliff so they're close at hand when I need to call on them. You'll meet at least a couple of them while you're here, but they're mostly off conducting business and handling other matters for me throughout the realm."

Whitt and August often leave on Sylas's instructions, but rarely for more than a day or two, and they spend at least as much time with him. I restrain a frown, sucking my lower lip under my teeth instead as I decide whether I want to push farther. "I guess you don't... socialize with them all that much, then?""

"No. I suppose the wolves do?" His tone suggests he finds that amusing as well. My hackles rise automatically, but Corwin goes on without noticing. "I trust my coterie, and they're a great help to me, but our association is strictly professional. Nothing good comes from blurring the lines between colleague and friend."

That's definitely a very different attitude from the Seelie's. After spending so long in the company of my men, witnessing how well they support each other in both personal and official ways, I have trouble believing he's right and that the way he lives doesn't get lonely. But I guess he's never known anything else.

"What about—do you have family?"

A flare of uneasy emotion passes into me and then fades away. No outward sign of distress shows on Corwin's face. "I am an only child, and sadly my parents have met dire fates before their times."

"Oh. I'm sorry." A lump forms in my throat. I extend my sympathy to him through our bond so he'll know I mean that. "I lost my family too."

"Yes." He cocks his head, a thin furrow creasing his brow. "How did you come to be among the Seelie? You weren't working for Arch-Lord Sylas as a servant."

"No. I—" I want to say it's complicated and leave it at that, but I probably owe him more of an explanation, especially when he wasn't expecting a human mate in the first place.

I brace myself, narrowing it down to the facts and avoiding the panic-provoking memories as well as I can. "When I was twelve, my family was attacked by Seelie roaming in the human world as wolves. They killed my parents and brother and brought me back to the fae world with them. That lord kept me in a cage for nine years, until Sylas happened to find me and rescued me. He's allowed me to become a full member of his pack—well, as much as I can be."

The disbelief in Corwin's expression sends another prickle of irritation through me. He might have been willing to roll with the idea of a human as his mate, but he clearly has trouble imagining me as an equal to the fae. Or else has trouble imagining that any summer fae could accept me as one, which isn't much better.

"That first lord," he says. "He treated you quite badly?"

Isn't telling him I was in a cage enough to establish that fact?

Despite my best efforts, a shudder runs through me, dredging shreds of the past with it. The glow I was holding in place thins even more. Corwin must catch glimpses of the hard floor, the filthy blanket, the jabs of my captors' bodies shoving mine, and the snap of my foot. The best I can do is keep my breaths even though shallow.

"Yes," I manage in a rough voice. "It was horrible."

The arch-lord's eyes flash darker and his jaw clenches. If he were Seelie, I suspect his fangs would be coming out. Disgust flows from him back into me. "And this is how the summer fae see fit to treat other beings?"

Why does he have to make this about all Seelie kind rather than those specific monsters? Am I supposed to believe that all *Unseelie* handle humans with kindness and respect after what I've heard about how they treat other fae?

I outright bristle, sitting up straighter. "No. Not all of them. Sylas and his pack have welcomed me as their own."

Even as I say that, my errant mind summons a memory of my first couple of weeks with Sylas, of his former cadre-chosen Kellan who insulted and pushed me around, of my fears that even Sylas wouldn't let me be more than a prisoner. Corwin's mouth flattens. "I see even that isn't completely true."

"It wasn't—he dealt with Kellan—there was so much at stake—" I cut myself off before anything I don't want to reveal spills out, but I don't have as much control over my thoughts. Something in the jumble of recollections makes Corwin stiffen in his chair.

Oh, crap.

"What?" I say, crossing my arms over my chest, dreading the answer.

He stares at me. "Their curse. The savagery their wolves descend into under the full moon. *You* can heal it in them?"

I bite back several choice swear words. This was the thing we least wanted him to find out, and he's pulled it out of me less than an hour after I got here. "You can't tell the other Unseelie, *any* of them. That was part of your oath."

"I know." Corwin blinks, but he can't quite manage to break out of his stare. "Your position among the wolves makes more sense now. Perhaps even why the Heart might have blessed you so. But… for Arch-Lord Sylas to let you come here when all the Seelie are relying on you—what on earth was he thinking agreeing to this arrangement?"

As if the man in front of me hadn't been pleading to have me here. "Your people were threatening full-out war, in case you've forgotten."

Corwin shakes his head. "I'd have thought a boon like what you offer would be worth going to war over. Although I suppose thinking straight isn't exactly the wolves' specialty…"

A jolt of anger spurs me onto my feet. I'm not going to sit here and listen to him disparage the people who saved me and protected me any longer.

"There isn't any problem with Sylas's thinking," I snap. "He agreed to have me come here because he's so honorable he does whatever seems to be the most right even if his own people might suffer in the meantime, and that's exactly why I fell in love with him."

I know those last words were a mistake the instant Corwin's face hardens. Without waiting to hear his response, I spin on my heel and stalk out of the room as quickly as my uneven steps will take me.

Talia

I'm not sure how long I've been lying on my bed —which is annoyingly cozy, as much as right now I want to hate everything in the winter realm—when a knock sounds on the bedroom door. Corwin's voice carries through, low and a little stiff.

"Talia, dinner is being served, if you would accompany me."

My stomach, the traitor, chooses that moment to rumble. Corwin probably heard the sound with this sharp fae ears. I close my eyes, summoning another swell of the glow inside me that feels more like a shield than a simple wall now.

I promised to give him a chance. I'm stuck here for ten days either way. It's not as if I can starve myself for the entire time—and being that defiant would reflect pretty badly on my pack back home too, wouldn't it?

Besides, I have more questions that I haven't gotten

answers to yet that could benefit all the Seelie back home. Like why the heck the raven shifters have been so intent on stealing territory from them. Even if Corwin is kind of a jerk, I can tolerate his attitude if it means I find out something that could stop all the fighting.

I am going to lay down a new ground rule, though.

I push myself off the bed and go to open the door, staying inside the room while I study the Unseelie arch-lord. The slight stiffness in his tone is echoed in his posture, but he manages a small smile that doesn't look too forced.

"I apologize for earlier," he says. "It's a poor host that disparages his guest's associates. I hope we can put that misstep behind us?"

I'm sure he hopes I can put the whole falling in love with Sylas thing behind me too. I give him the steeliest look I can manage. "While I'm here, I don't want to hear any more insults about my pack-kin or the Seelie in general. There's a whole lot I could say about the winter fae if I wasn't trying to make the best of this, you know."

He dips his head, his lips twitching into a brief grimace. "That's fair. I will… reserve judgment for now."

Or at least he won't say those judgments out loud, but I guess that's as much as I can ask for.

I step out, and his arm moves as if to offer me his hand. He catches it before he completes the gesture, maybe remembering my reluctance when he did the same thing before we crossed the border.

As I walk beside him, my limp steadied but not completely erased by the brace built into my right boot, his gaze falls to my legs. "You favor your right foot," he says cautiously. "That was—I caught a glimpse of something when you spoke of your… captivity…"

I brace myself, holding the memories at as much of a distance as I can. "One of that lord's cadre-chosen broke it as 'punishment.' They let the bones heal wrong, so the injury is permanent now. But I get along all right anyway."

His hint of a smile comes back. "Yes, you do."

I glance over my shoulder. "What about Harper?"

"Oh, I had one of the servants escort her already. I thought it would be better if I spoke to you one-to-one."

Corwin says that, and then he lapses into a silence that stretches until we reach the dining room, so he mustn't have had all that much to say after all. He doesn't mention my declaration about Sylas, and *I'm* not going to bring up the other men I love if he'd prefer to sweep the subject under the rug for now.

We arrive at a smaller room than I was expecting with a table of mottled white-and-gray marble that couldn't seat more than eight. Harper is the only one already there. As we come in, she beams at me. I sit across from her, and Corwin takes the head of the table.

It's apparent from the crystal goblets and polished clay plates laid out in front of us that this dinner will be for only us three. Presumably Corwin's business-only coterie eats in their own homes. Do they have families or are their lives totally dedicated to their lord despite the distance between them?

I've already asked so much about Corwin's companions, though, and that's not even what's most important. For a little while, I let myself get diverted by the dishes brought out by the kitchen staff: a middle-aged man and a girl who looks a few years younger than I am, with similar enough bushy pale hair and snub noses for me to assume they're related. I don't know if they're the ones doing the cooking as well, but the creamy soup and delicately spiced steak would have August demanding the recipes.

A twinge of homesickness runs through my gut at the thought of him. Maybe a trace of that feeling seeps through my wall, because Corwin's gaze snaps to me.

I shore up the glowing barrier again and refocus on the present. Despite my best efforts, complimenting Corwin on the meal he's arranged and answering a few careful inquiries he makes about Seelie cuisine, the conversation stays stilted. He doesn't seem to know what to say any more than I do.

The plentiful food only makes me more certain that the Unseelie aren't facing some huge catastrophe, though. Corwin's domain has appeared nothing but peaceful since we arrived, and he's given no indication of any troubles here. But surely his people haven't been attacking and killing mine just for the fun of it?

I try to figure out a way of getting at that subject without asking him point blank why the Unseelie have been so awful, since that approach seems unlikely to go over well. "What sorts of things keep you busy on a usual day?" I ask. Presumably he cleared whatever would normally be on his schedule to make way for my arrival.

Corwin cuts off another slice of his steak with brisk efficiency. "There are always small matters to attend to in the running of the domain, of course, and regular meetings with my fellow arch-lords. When I can, I visit the farther domains to ensure everything is well across the realm. I like to stay aware of any significant happenings."

"Your coterie wouldn't handle that for you?" I say automatically, thinking of Whitt and his network of contacts.

"They keep me well-informed, but I like the other lords to see that I'm taking an active interest. And I trust my eyes and ears before anyone else's." He pauses. "It's possible I'll need to be away while you're here—never for more than half a day or so."

"That's all right. I wouldn't expect you to ignore your responsibilities." I pause, thinking of the wide variety of landscapes I've encountered in the summer realm, from dense forests to open prairie, swampland to towering hills. "Is most of the winter realm pretty rocky, like here and the mountains? Do all the flocks have their homes on cliffsides and places like that?"

Corwin's eyes light up a bit as if he's pleased that I'm taking any interest in his realm. "Not at all. Every lord and his subjects have their own preferences, and the winter realm is vast. You haven't even seen all Heart's Cadence has to offer yet. If you'd like, I'll make sure you get the chance to take in the falls and the lake beneath it—the spring that also feeds into it makes the water warm enough to swim— as well as some of the other unique features of this place."

I find I can smile back at him without too much trouble. "I *would* like that." It'd certainly beat staying cooped up in the palace all day. I had enough of staying homebound back in Oakmeet in the first month after Sylas brought me there, when my presence had to remain secret. "I'm sure Harper would love to see the sights too."

There's that twitch in Corwin's jaw, a subtle marker of his disappointment. He was picturing more alone time on these excursions, was he? Even though he doesn't say anything against having my friend join us, the fact that he just assumes I'd already feel safe on my own with him annoys me all over again.

Before I can think better of it, the one question sure to remind him of why I *can't* trust anyone here all that much tumbles out of me. "How about you also walk me through the reasons your people keep attacking mine?"

Corwin's fingers tense around his fork. "I told you, I don't agree with how that situation has been handled."

That's not an answer. I jab at a piece of steak with maybe a bit more force than is necessary. "*What* situation? Why did the other Unseelie arch-lords suddenly decide invading the summer realm is a good idea?"

A whiff of his own frustration trickles into me. "I don't think this is the time to get into such a complicated matter."

I raise my eyebrows at him. "So you're going to explain later, then? When should I expect that conversation to happen?"

The muscle in his jaw ticks two times in a row before he clenches it. His tone flattens. "I feel it would be most sensible to focus on our potential relationship with each other and how we're going to handle the mate-bond before getting into larger political issues."

"That sounds to me like you're saying you won't trust me enough to tell me what's going on unless I agree to accept the bond. What if I can't trust *you* enough to accept it until I understand?"

"Then I suppose we'll have to negotiate some sort of compromise. I'm sure that can be managed."

The strain creeping into his voice suggests he's not so sure after all. He can't really expect me to dive into life with the Unseelie without even knowing why they've been murdering all kinds of summer fae, can he?

"Are you even sure you *want* me to accept the bond?" I can't help saying. "You're perfectly happy to be tied to a mere human, especially one who's spent so much time surrounded by wolves?"

"Every soul-twined bond is a gift, however unexpected. I trust the Heart had its reasons, and that we will uncover them. It isn't as if the connection between us will go away whether we want it or not." His cool dark gaze holds mine. "*I* have been attempting to reach an understanding with you from the beginning. There was no running away on my side."

I glower back at him. "And you're being *oh* so open helping me 'understand' your side now."

Harper's gaze darts back and forth between us, her fork frozen in mid-air. The tension is broken by a figure appearing at the dining room doorway. It's one of the staff who prepared our bedrooms for us. He bows with an apologetic grimace.

"My lord, Verik has arrived with news. He wishes to speak to you with some urgency."

I'd swear Corwin looks relieved to have an excuse to leave the table. As he pushes back his chair, he gives me one last glance. "Verik is part of my coterie. This may take some time. Please, finish the meal and occupy yourself however you'd like within the palace until you wish to turn in for the night."

He stalks out of the room. I watch him go, chewing my last morsel of steak so furiously I can't enjoy the tenderness of the meat at all. Then I stand up, leaving behind my half-eaten roll and a few chunks of spicy carrot-like vegetable.

Harper scrambles to her feet too. "Where are you going?"

"I want to see what's so urgent."

I slip out into the hall, the dense rug swallowing all but a whisper of even my uneven footsteps. My instincts take me in the direction I think leads to the back of the palace with its vast terrace. It looked like an ideal place for landing or taking off—and it seems more likely that news from Corwin's coterie would come from farther abroad rather than from the other direction, within the Heart's domains.

Harper hustles after me, setting her feet carefully too. After a few turns and a bit of back-tracking when we nearly end up in the kitchen, I catch sight of a view of the mountains through a tall window up ahead.

As I hurry closer, I spot Corwin out on the terrace with an older man who has his wings out. They stand a few feet apart, the man I assume is Verik speaking with a few quick gestures, Corwin nodding and frowning. Their attention is fixed on each other, but I don't sense any of the comfortable companionship that Sylas shares with his cadre most of the time. Like Corwin said, they're all business.

Whatever news the coterie man brought, I don't get a

chance to hear it. As I venture closer, they wrap up their conversation—and in a blink and a sudden contracting, two ravens large enough that their wingspan could rival the reach of my arms are launching into the sky.

My shoulders sag. Harper comes up next to me, watching the dark forms soar into the distance. "Well," she says, "it's definitely… different here."

I choke on a laugh. "That's one way of putting it." I pull my gaze away from the sky. "Should we do some exploring in the palace?" Anything Corwin would want to keep secret, he's probably hidden well, but that doesn't mean it's impossible we'll stumble on something useful.

And having something to do definitely cheers Harper up. She grins. "Let's see exactly how an Unseelie arch-lord lives."

The proposal sounds like it could lead to some excitement, but the truth is, as we meander through the sprawling first floor of the palace and then climb a sweeping staircase to the second, I'm more and more convinced that an Unseelie arch-lord's life is pretty boring. Or at least *this* Unseelie arch-lord's is.

Every room is neat and clean with the same sorts of pale furniture and few objects that look remotely personal. Even Corwin's bedroom—what I assume is his bedroom anyway, since it's set apart from the hall of guest bedrooms where we're staying, even larger and with fancier furnishings—doesn't show much sign of a real life. I don't feel comfortable venturing into the inner rooms beyond the bedroom, though, and we do come across a couple of locked doors. Maybe he's simply very careful what pieces of himself he leaves in view.

We've meandered around part of the second floor when Harper stops with a jerk. Her head swivels as the rest of her stays perfectly still.

"What?" I murmur after a moment.

"I thought I heard— There it is again." She goes silent, watching me expectantly, but my human ears don't pick up anything. She turns again. "I think it's coming from… this way."

She heads down a narrower side hall, halting every few steps to listen again. "Yes. It's getting louder. What *is* that?" She shudders.

As we reach an alcove at the end of the hall, I understand her reaction. I can faintly make out the odd noises now—a thumping and then a grating sound like something jagged dragged against a smooth surface, so distant I can't tell whether it's coming from around us or overhead. And then the faintest of squeals, barely audible but so high-pitched I flinch.

I reach for the metal knob of the nearest door and twist, but it jars against my fingers. Locked. Harper tries the neighboring one, but it only opens to a linen closet, nothing disturbing there.

Meeting my friend's gaze, I see the same anxious question now running through my head reflected in her eyes. Just how big *are* the secrets Corwin is keeping hidden in this place?

August

I force an enthusiasm I don't really feel into my voice. "All right, pack. Let's see all those moves together now!"

The small group of my pack-kin living in our newly established Hearth-by-the-Heart run through the series of fighting techniques I've given them one after the other, lunging and wheeling, slashing out with their claws. Some are more hesitant than others, and none of them are on the same level as our official warriors, but a flicker of pride lights inside me despite my otherwise rotten mood.

If the Unseelie do come for us here, every one of my people will be prepared to defend us however they can.

When they're finished, panting but smiling, I give them a quick round of applause. "Perfect. I think you deserve a break. We'll pick things up tomorrow at the same time." Unless more urgent trouble rears its head, but I'd rather not think about that, let alone say it.

They disperse, and I drag the warm, mid-day air into my lungs. The air is lightly damp after last night's rainfall, but with the sky now mostly clear and the breeze rippling over me, it's refreshing rather than unpleasant. The weather is rarely less than ideal this close to the Heart.

I wish I was in a state to enjoy it.

I prowl around the temporary village as if I'm likely to find anything useful to do. I could make the trip back to Hearthshire to continue working with the pack-kin there and helping prepare for the move, but the thought of traveling even farther away from the border, of not being right here if something goes wrong in the winter realm and Talia manages to reach out to us, makes my gut contract into an uncomfortable lump.

She's over there with our enemies, risking everything that mattered to her here in an attempt to end the warring. The least I can do is be ready in case she needs me.

I've circled the new castle as well and am considering making a patrol of the border despite the sentries already on the job when Whitt finds me. He takes one look at my face and offers me a crooked grin. "It doesn't matter how many imaginary Unseelie you battle in your head, whelp, you won't get her back any faster that way."

I've bared my teeth before I can catch my instinctive reaction. My older brother doesn't take offense. As I shut my mouth, getting a grip on my temper, he bumps his shoulder against mine playfully, like he might have when I really was just a whelp.

"It's only been one day. All I'm saying is pace yourself."

He glances toward the border, and the dry humor fades from his voice. "I'm worried about her too."

Somehow having the acknowledgment that I'm not alone in my agitation makes it a little easier to bear. "I still think it's ridiculous that she had to go at all."

"Of course it is. But we all know the alternatives were worse." A glint comes back into his eyes. "I have faith that she won't pick some bird-brain over what's waiting for her at home."

"*That's* not what I'm worried about," I growl.

He cocks a skeptical eyebrow at me, which is fair, because it might not be the *only* or even the main thing I'm worried about, but I definitely don't like the idea of how her bond with this feathered arch-lord might be developing and what feelings could grow alongside it. But honestly… if she decides she'll be happier with him, as hard as I find that to believe, I'll have to live with it. I just need her to be happy. And not torn to bits by raven talons.

That thought must bring the storminess back into my expression, because Whitt gives me another nudge, this one gentler. "She's proven to be far stronger than any of us would have imagined to begin with. Let's not forget to give her credit for that."

"I know." I shoulder him in return and realize it's not just our shared fears that have soothed my spirits. Even though he's clearly concerned about Talia, there's an easy companionableness to his demeanor that was once familiar but hasn't seemed to come so easily to him for the past few weeks.

Our lover had to leave us, but maybe she left us more whole than we were before.

I shouldn't discuss the private frictions between lord and pack where our kin might overhear, but I allow myself a vague, "You're doing all right otherwise?"

As I expected, Whitt is sharp enough to pick up on what I'm referring to. His grin gets both wider and more crooked, but he sounds as if he means it when he says, "I think the past is laid to rest."

"Good." Sylas hasn't filled me in on the details, and I'm not sure I want to know exactly what went on a century ago between Whitt and Isleen. The one thing our lord made completely clear was that the fault in the betrayal was all Isleen's.

I don't have enough words to express how glad I am to have *that* woman out of our lives. Heart save Talia from a soul-twined mate so selfish and ruthless.

Whitt swipes his hands together. "Well, I'm off to oversee some negotiations with our new neighbors down the hill. I'll see you at dinner."

He lopes off, leaping forward into wolfish form after his first few strides. As I watch him go, my gaze trails from his tawny form disappearing down the slope over to the obsidian walls of Ambrose's former palace—and lands on a hesitant-looking figure who's just emerging between the standing stones of the wall I expect we'll soon dismantle.

One of our sentries comes up behind the newcomer, urging the man along. Her dagger is still in its sheath, but her mouth is set in a wary line, her muscles tensed defensively.

A prickle of alarm runs down my spine. I hurry over to meet them, reaching them just as they come up on the palace.

As soon as I'm closer, I recognize the newcomer. He's one of Ambrose's pack-kin, the healer who helped Donovan recover from his poisoning and testified during the hearing to confirm the justice of Ambrose's death. Even so, the sight of him sets my teeth on edge. He might have acted and spoken against his lord in the late arch-lord's death, but as far as we know, he stayed loyal to the man until then.

What can he be doing here now? The last thing we need is another problem.

The sentry tugs the healer to a halt and bobs her head to me. "I found this one skulking around by the standing stones, August."

"I wasn't *skulking*," the healer protests, and fixes his gaze on me. "I came on an urgent matter to speak to Arch-Lord Sylas."

Sylas is off in a meeting with the arch-lords that I balk at interrupting. "The arch-lord is otherwise occupied at the moment. I'd prefer he stayed that way until I know you actually have something useful to put to him. So you'll just have to take a cadre-chosen instead."

The healer cuts a nervous glance toward the sentry. From the looks of his slim frame, I could beat him in a fight in either form in five seconds flat. The back-up is hardly necessary.

I motion her off with a gesture of thanks. As she trots away, I study the healer. "*What?*"

He rubs his mouth, his gaze twitching around us again. "Could we step inside the palace? Ambrose's—the one that was his? I'll need to show you, and I'd rather no one overheard this."

I look him over once more, but I can't see any signs of threat. By all appearances, he's a lot more scared of me than I am of him. It isn't really his fault I'm so on edge.

I sigh and wave him toward the door. We step inside, our footsteps ringing out on the obsidian floor. The healer doesn't appear to be any more comfortable in here than he was outside. He crosses his arms over his chest with a shudder.

Before I have to press for answers, he heaves a ragged breath. "You know that my lord was aiming to go to war against the Unseelie. He spent much of the past two decades gathering weapons, many of them enchanted and highly dangerous, that he expected to use in that crusade. Some of them aren't even acceptable by fae law. He has a vault of them hidden in the lower levels of the palace. I didn't know about them until I overheard some of my pack-kin talking about it a few days ago."

A stash of horrible and illegal weaponry? Yeah, that sounds like the Ambrose I knew. But I still have to ask —"Why are you telling *us*?" And why with such urgency? We'd have discovered it when we demolished this palace anyway.

His mouth twists. "Many of us accepted Lord Tristan's offer to take us on after Ambrose's passing. The cadre-chosen who knew about the weapons told him—he's planning to come while your full pack isn't yet here to claim them for himself."

Of course he is. Just what we need. I swallow a growl and resist the urge to narrow my eyes at the healer.

He came to us over his new pack. He obviously isn't all that loyal to Tristan. And I know Sylas would say that right now in this period of transition and escalating tensions with the winter fae, we can use all the allies we can get.

Wouldn't it be nice for Talia to come home to a fuller pack than before, all the more ready to defend her from enemies both around us and across the border?

I rein in that hope along with my initial defensiveness and jerk my chin toward the healer. "Can you show me where this vault is and how to open it?"

"I know where the entrance is—I'm not sure I have the magic to unseal it quickly."

"Good enough for now. Lead the way."

As he heads along a side hall and down a narrow flight of stairs at the far end of it, I keep a close watch on his movements. I may not be a master of subtle observation like Whitt, but I know how to evaluate an enemy in combat. The healer has gotten more relaxed since he spilled the secret to me, as if he's relieved to have it off his chest. I don't see any indication that he's gathering his nerve to launch any kind of assault.

After everything that's happened, I guess it isn't all that hard to see that he's better off being on Sylas's side than Tristan's, powerful illicit weaponry or not.

In the passage below, the man slows, scanning the walls as he walks. We pass a dusty tapestry that I have to suspect might hide some other secret space and stop where a shallow crack mars the smoothness of the dark obsidian. He taps that spot.

"The entrance is here. There's a locking spell on it, tied to the castle. I don't have much skill for stone work."

"That's all right. We'll get it open." Stone is far from

my specialty either, but both Sylas and Whitt are fairly adept in that area. If we need someone who's mastered the true name for obsidian, which I'm not sure either of them has, there'll be someone among our and the other arch-lords' packs.

I turn to the healer. "Thank you for this. You've done us a great service. Do you expect to go back to Lord Tristan now?"

He makes a face. "I... I was hoping that I could trade this information for the opportunity to pledge myself to Arch-Lord Sylas. My former lord rarely consulted me in his plans, and I'd certainly have advised against them if he'd ever asked. I'd be happy to do whatever—"

I hold up my hand to stop him. "You can make your appeal to my lord. I'm sure he'd be willing to listen and consider your case—and that of any others who are uneasy in their current situation under Tristan."

"Oh, there are a few more of those," the healer mutters, and then flushes as if he wishes he hadn't said that out loud.

I chuckle and wave him back toward the stairs. "Arch-Lord Sylas expects loyalty and commitment, but you'll find he's more agreeable to be around than either of your masters so far. He should be finished with his business before much longer, and then we'll get all of this sorted out."

We emerge from the palace to find Sylas already striding across the fields toward us. My pulse hiccups at the severity of his expression. I grip the healer's forearm, bracing myself for the news that I misjudged him, that he's brought some disaster down on us while distracting me, but my lord barely glances at the man.

"There you are," he says. "There's been news from Copperweld—the Murk have made a fatal nuisance of themselves."

Talia

By my second dinner in Corwin's home, I've figured out that the middle-aged man and the girl who serve us our meals aren't faded fae but human. When the man burns his hand on the steam as he takes the lid off a pot of still-bubbling curry, Corwin tends to the injury with a quick murmur of magic that's clearly beyond the man's powers. His daughter watches with the eager delight of someone who doesn't expect to ever wield powers like that herself.

Corwin hasn't spoken to them any differently from his other staff, but then, he's pretty distant with all of them, so it's not like he's friendly either. I smile at the girl in thanks when she pours juice into my glass—I've been clear that I don't want anything alcoholic or otherwise inebriating—and study Corwin as he ladles some of the creamy curry onto his plate.

"Do you have many human servants?" I ask after they've left the room.

He blinks as if that's a question he never expected and then gives a subtle shrug. "Those two, a couple of the housekeeping staff, and one in the stables. I inherited them from my parents or took them on from colleagues. I don't make a habit of stealing away citizens of the human world, if that's what you're concerned about."

"They don't have the opportunity to go home if they wanted to, though."

His dark gaze lingers on me for a long moment, and I get the sense he's testing the wall I'm still holding up between us, wanting to gauge my emotional state. "I treat them well—well enough that there's no need to drug them or physically confine them as some of my brethren might. I've gotten no indication that they'd *want* to leave. As you've clearly discovered, the faerie world can hold much appeal even to those not born here."

That's a fair point. I nibble at my lip and then decide I don't really have any basis to be annoyed about it. Even Sylas has acknowledged that he used to have human servants before Kellan came into his domain.

And I can't say I'm not enjoying the food those two make either. The curry has a delicate spicing that mixes perfectly with the creamy texture, the bits of meat perfectly tender. Corwin is definitely keeping us well fed, at the very least.

When we get up from the meal, Corwin glances from Harper to me and asks in a careful voice, "Would it be possible to have some time to ourselves, just the two of us?

I thought I might show you my favorite part of the palace."

I start to balk, but Harper is already ducking her head. "I'll be fine," she says. "I don't want to get in the way. You *are* supposed to have a chance to get to know each other."

We are, and I guess I don't need to be nervous about my own safety with Corwin after all the oaths he took. I nod, but the memory of the unnerving sounds we heard yesterday sticks with me as I join him walking down the hall.

Maybe he'd be more inclined to tell the truth about them when it's just me, no extra company.

I hesitate, but Corwin glances down at me, reading something in my mood or an impression that's slipped through our connection despite my best efforts. "If something is on your mind, you can speak it, Talia. I'd rather know than not."

I open my mouth, close it again, and gather my nerve. "Harper and I wandered around the palace for a while yesterday after you left with the man from your coterie. There's a locked door in an alcove on the second floor—we heard some odd sounds that seemed to be coming from somewhere beyond it. Like something moving around up there."

Corwin's lips purse with a slight grimace. "Ah. That was—Let's just say that sometimes restless spirits linger on in this world as they do in the human world as well. I believe you'd talk about ghosts? Better not to disturb them, as they can be unpredictable."

Oh. He's got a ghost in his attic? I'd find that funny if

I hadn't experienced how creepy it was even at a distance. "It can't pass through the locked door?"

"No need to worry about that. The problem is contained." He motions to a door we've come up on, murmuring a quick word that must unlock it. "This is where I enjoy spending time on the relatively rare occasions when I don't have any duties to attend to."

I step past him into a room that's small by the palace's standards, but brightly lit even in the evening from glowing yellow sections in the crystalline ceiling. As seems to be Corwin's preferred style, the furnishings are spartan: only a tall marble cabinet against one wall, a cushioned settee across from it, and a massive, elegant harp standing in the middle of the room between them.

The harp's frame looks as if it's made of pure ivory, the strings gleaming with a silvery sheen. It rivals the apparently famous instrument Arch-Lord Donovan showed off during a banquet at his castle. I don't know anything about harps, but even I can tell this is an exquisitely crafted one.

A softness I've never seen before comes into Corwin's face as he looks at the instrument. "My family has always loved having music in our lives in every way we can. There's a particular pleasure in creating it from my own hands. Perhaps I could play for you?"

The suggestion feels like a peace offering, a tentative gift. I'm not sure I'm ready to accept it. I cock my head at him. "Is this supposed to distract me from finding out why your people have been pushing mine to the brink of war?"

I get a full grimace for that question, but Corwin

doesn't stiffen up like yesterday. He swipes his hand across his narrow jaw. "I suppose I deserve that jab for my reaction yesterday. I hadn't expected—I clearly should have—" He lets out a quick breath. "What I ought to have told you is that discussing those matters is more complicated than simply answering whatever questions you ask. I have oaths I've taken to my office and my colleagues as well, that restrict what I can say about our political dealings and when."

Oh. That does make sense. "If you'd said so in the first place, I wouldn't have been as frustrated."

"I realize that. I was startled, and then Verik came—" He shakes his head. "I'll be able to tell you more when our situation is more certain, which may take time."

"Okay." I pause, and then, because the disappointment creeping into his expression tugs at my heart more than it should, I move to sit on the settee. "I *would* like to hear you play in the meantime."

He smiles then, reserved like Sylas's but bright enough that I know it's genuine. I relax the barrier of light within me enough to get a taste of his happiness as he sits down on the stool by the harp.

That joy only grows, coursing between us, as he sets his slender fingers against the strings. They move with seeming effortlessness, stirring a stream of notes into the air that reminds me of the sparkling spring tumbling down the rocky waterfall in Whitt's favorite glen.

The music tingles over my skin and into my lungs. As the melody swells, Corwin's hands flitting faster, the vivid tones meld together into a blissful harmony. It's nice seeing him so relaxed, doing something purely for the sake of enjoyment. If it hadn't been for this demonstration, I might have thought he never did anything that didn't have some constructive purpose.

He has his own pleasures. He wanted to share this one with me. A smile crosses my lips, and I close my eyes. I don't think Corwin has cast any magic, but the sound is enough to sweep me away—into more memories of my own happiness in the realm I've left behind.

Golden sun beaming through bright green leaves. The softness of the grass and the warm breeze twining around me. August laughing with me as we assemble pastries together in the kitchen, then sweeping me into his solid arms. Whitt carrying me on his back through the forest to his glen, the rhythm of his wolfish muscles echoing his trust into me. Sylas, standing within the glinting walls of the Bastion as he received the crown he deserved so much.

A pang of longing and loneliness shoots through me. Tears prickle behind my eyes—and the music falls away.

I look up and find Corwin's gaze fixed on me. His mouth is tight. Abruptly, I register the new current of emotion carrying through our connection: an anguished mix of pain and jealousy.

He manages to keep his voice even, but a thread of frustration runs through it. "Even now, you're thinking of them. There are *three* you'd prefer over me?"

Did he think it was only Sylas? I tense on my seat, not sure how to respond. I told him how I felt when we first talked in that dream. Can he really expect things to have changed so quickly?

I curl my fingers around the edge of the cushion. "I hardly know you. They've been there for me from the first moment they rescued me. Did you think I'd simply fall out of love the second I stepped into your palace?"

He drops his hands to his sides, the knuckles flexing. "Our souls are *bound*. You're meant for me as I'm meant for you. The Heart has decided so."

I frown. "Well, I think I should get a little say too."

"That's not how this works."

"Maybe it should be." The good will his playing stirred in me fades away. I raise my chin. "I know you said you only care about what the Heart intends, but having me as your mate doesn't make any sense. I can't give you true-blooded heirs. I bet none of your colleagues would ever respect me—they probably hate me enough just thinking I'm Seelie."

"The Heart has willed it—none of my colleagues can argue with that. The bond wouldn't have formed if we couldn't overcome whatever problems might arise."

"I don't know why you're so sure of that. I've heard about some pretty horrible soul-twined pairings." I motion vaguely toward the world beyond the palace. "Wouldn't it be better for all of us if we could find some way to break the bond so we can get on with our lives the way we want to live them? Most fae never have anything more than a regular mate. You could find some true-blooded Unseelie lady who I'm sure would be happy to have you."

Corwin's eyes flash. "This may not be what I anticipated, but it *is* what I want. I have waited centuries to encounter the one my soul would call to. I can be patient as we navigate whatever difficulties our unusual partnering brings. It'll be worth it to have a mate who's joined with me more truly than any 'true-blooded' fae now could be."

A lump rises in my throat. "What about me? Doesn't it matter what *I* want?"

I catch a twinge of sympathy from him then. "You only want the others because you never knew you might find a deeper bond. You allowed your affections to grow that much without realizing how much pain you were setting yourself up for. I wish the Heart had been kinder to you. But if you can start to let them go—"

I stand up with a jerk and a lurch of my pulse. "You've clearly never loved anyone in your life if you think it'd be that easy. I shouldn't *have* to let them go. I didn't ask for any of this."

"It'll only be more pain if you cling to what you thought you'd have instead of accepting where you've found yourself."

"And if I don't know how I'll ever accept it? If I'm not sure I even can?"

A brief shimmer of anguish slips into me—and then Corwin closes off the connection on his side. His face forms that cool mask I've seen so often, all the joy of the music gone. He gets to his feet too.

"I'm certain the Heart would not have shone on us like this if it were impossible," he says, his voice so calm it sets my teeth on edge. "We simply have to find our path, and I'll help you in every way I can."

I don't want his help, but I'm tired of arguing. I'm just plain tired, really. I rub my eyes, my shoulders slumping. "I'm sorry. I didn't mean to turn this into a fight. I liked hearing you play—thank you for inviting me here. Let's just leave it for now."

We have eight more days to get through. I'd rather they weren't any more agonizing than they need to be.

Corwin seems to agree. He gestures toward the door, not even attempting to offer me his hand. "I'll see you to your room. Tomorrow will be a new day."

We walk through the halls in silence. When we reach my bedroom, I consider going across to Harper's and venting to her, but what would I even say? She probably wishes she'd have the chance to make a soul-twined match. I'd sound like a jerk complaining that I have *four* highly eligible fae men who want me for a mate, even if one is Unseelie. Also, she doesn't even know about two of those men.

Instead, I go into my room and flop down on the bed. I can't work up any enthusiasm for the books I brought with me. After a while, as exhaustion creeps over me, I change into my nightclothes and crawl under the covers, hoping tomorrow's new day will bring a little less pain for both me and Corwin.

How can I make him understand?

With that question running through my head, my mind drifts into sleep. I'm lying on soft grass under a clear blue sky, a dreamy haziness surrounding me, and a soft voice murmurs from somewhere beyond my view in words I don't understand.

A quiver passes through my mind, and then I tumble deeper still to where even dreams won't follow.

Talia

When I open my eyes to my bedroom in Corwin's palace, the space feels somehow different. I sit up, peering around me, but I can't pick out anything that's changed. There's a faint mugginess in my head as if I haven't completely shaken off sleep just yet, or maybe it's because of our argument…

What did we argue about? I remember snapping at him, frustration twisting through me, but the exact words we spoke, the things I was upset about, escape me.

Obviously it wasn't anything that important. I've just been on edge since we got here.

As I clamber out of bed and get ready for the day, the mugginess doesn't totally fade. I rub my eyes and go to the window in the hopes that the sunlight will wake me up more. Beams of it streak through the fluffy clouds, tiny snowflakes dancing between the streams of light. It reflects off the snow and the icy plain below toward me, but my head doesn't feel that much clearer.

My gaze slides to the hazy border. Flickers of images pass through my mind—greenery and golden light, and something… something I left behind.

My pack. Always there for me. I'll be back to them soon. If I can bring them news that the Unseelie are backing off on their attacks, even better.

Corwin is moving through the palace, a tentative but steady presence in my awareness. The barrier inside me has faded overnight, and I find I don't feel the need to rebuild it just yet. The thought of him sensing me the same way I'm aware of him provokes a quiver of anxiety, but only for a moment.

We have to learn to trust each other. That's why I'm here, isn't it? That's what will be best for everyone. He's figured out the secret of my blood and the Seelie's curse— what else do I have to hide?

He's giving the kitchen staff instructions for breakfast. I catch the gist of his intention but not the exact words. He must be able to tell I'm paying attention, because a moment later his voice travels through the connection between us, gentle and even.

The food should be ready shortly—it won't be anything elaborate. Shall I walk you to the dining room?

My first instinct is to balk, but why? He's trying to be hospitable, to show me how much he appreciates my being here.

He's my soul-twined mate. I should be giving *him* a real chance too, shouldn't I?

Something about that thought nibbles at my gut, but I

can't figure out why. *Thank you*, I say in return. *I'll see if Harper's up.*

I remember belatedly that Corwin hasn't been enthusiastic about my friend's company, but maybe he's gotten over that frustration. I don't sense any discomfort from him over it now. If anything, he sounds pleased. *I'll come and collect you both, then.*

Something about our argument last night or the talks before then must have gotten through to him. He's trying his best too. I have to smile as I head across the hall to knock on Harper's door.

Harper answers with a yawn but somehow not remotely sleep-rumpled. I'm not sure her hair is capable of falling in any way except silkily straight across her shoulders. She stretches her neck and peers into the hall. "Breakfast time? Has the arch-lord stopped insisting on escorting you?"

"He's on his way."

She takes in my smile and offers one in return. "Everything's okay? I heard you coming back to your room last night—you were walking fast, and you closed the door pretty hard. I would have gone over to see if you needed anything, but I…"

She's still not sure how much I really *trust* her. My heart twinges, and I grasp her forearm with a quick squeeze. "I think everything's okay now, and I'll come to you if there's a real problem. But I wouldn't mind you checking in on me either."

"Okay." Her smile widens. She darts a look up and down the hall and lowers her voice conspiratorially. "I'm glad Arch-Lord Corwin hasn't done anything too horrible.

August would make him regret it if he really upset you, that's for sure."

As she giggles, I blink at her in momentary confusion. Well, August is very protective of the whole pack—he's our head warrior, isn't he? And... I think he's been particularly quick to come to my defense.

Wasn't there—I have a vague sense of his brawny frame stepping in front of me to shield me, of wolves tumbling together in combat... The memories are foggy and distant, though, as if they happened a long time ago rather than just in the past few months.

I rub my forehead, and Corwin's voice reaches me again. *Is everything all right? You seem a bit unsettled.*

I think maybe I just didn't sleep all that well. I'll probably feel better once I've gotten some food into me.

Well, we can see to that right now.

The last words filter through the bond just as he rounds the corner at the other end of the hall. His lips are curved in the same soft smile I saw when he played the harp last night—*that* memory has stuck with me perfectly clearly.

Have I ever really noticed before what a striking face he has in general? Maybe he seemed too cold before for me to appreciate it. But now, as he walks up to us with those traces of affection in his smile and his eyes, his tall lean frame so measured in its obvious strength, my heart skips a beat. I find myself thinking back to that moment when we dreamed together and he touched my arm. To the thrilling sensation that passed through me.

It scared me at the time. Because... it was unexpected. And—there was something else, wasn't there? I have a sense of waking, of being comforted, but not why I needed the comfort.

Corwin has reached us, his warmth starting to dim behind the same concern he showed earlier. I shake off my confusion and aim my smile at him. "Let's go get that breakfast."

The Unseelie arch-lord might have asked for a simple meal, but the spread is still extensive, and everything from the fried eggs to the berry salad tastes as delicious as everything his chefs prepare. I wonder if he always eats this well or if he's going to special lengths to pamper me. He doesn't seem to linger over the food that much himself, mostly watching my reactions. I catch traces of satisfaction as he observes my own enjoyment both with his eyes and through our connection.

"I'll make sure we have those every morning for the rest of the time you're here," he says when I practically swoon over a pastry so buttery the flaky dough melts in my mouth. I'm starting to think the whole bond thing might not be so bad after all.

I scratch my arm absently, pulling the long sleeve of my winter-appropriate dress higher over my forearm, and a flicker of dismay passes into me from Corwin. He's studying the pale scar along the inside of my forearm. "What happened there?"

A shiver passes through me, thinking back. "A tuskcat. I don't know if you have those here in the winter realm, but they're like big cats with a boar's head. Our enemies cast a spell on one to make it attack me, but one of the pack warriors killed it before it could do more damage than this."

Harper's jaw tightens for a second, probably remembering that those enemies were the ones she briefly made plans with. As if meaning to offset that tension, she lets out a little laugh and says, "Lord Sylas and August looked so furious running to help that I'd be surprised if there are any tuskcats left in our domain after that."

Sylas and August… running to help. Those words don't *sound* wrong, but I can't quite fit them into the version of the scene in my head. It must have been August who healed the wound, right? Because… he's the main healer in the pack too. I'm pretty sure he looked after me other times. And Sylas has always watched over me—he knows how valuable I am.

Why does my head feel so fuzzy when I try to think of anything after Astrid stabbed the beast? I managed to dismiss the weirdness before, but I've been awake for a while now, and at this point I can't blame my fogginess on hunger either.

A chill passes through me. I glance at Corwin, swallowing hard. *He* swore not to harm me, but what if one of his fellow arch-lords managed to cast mind-altering magic on me somehow?

"I think something's wrong. I can't seem to focus on certain memories, like parts of them are blurry or just missing… I only just started feeling like this when I woke up. Could someone have come into the palace and done something to me last night?"

Corwin tenses—just slightly to my eyes, but I can feel it through the bond too, along with a jolt of… guilt? Then it's all gone, shut away like the slamming of a door. He's closed himself off.

"I'm sure no one could have entered without my permission," he says firmly. "It could be that the difference in environment is catching up with you? Perhaps you could use some more rest if you didn't sleep well, and I could have my healer speak to you."

I study him, more apprehension prickling through me. He's hiding something—why else would he shut me out? But *he* couldn't hurt me. He shouldn't even be able to order someone else to. That was part of—the oaths—we talked about—

My memories of those discussions have gone all muddled too. My heart thumps faster, panic swelling inside me. What's wrong with me? Why is so much—

It's all things to do with the three men I know I had those discussions with. Sylas and August and… and Whitt. When Harper mentioned the new arch-lord and August just now, and August before. The argument last night in the music room that I still can't focus on either—was that about them too?

My gaze darts to Harper. "Why did you say what you did earlier about August? Why would he be so worried specifically about me?"

She stares at me and then looks at Corwin, her shoulders stiffening. Corwin makes a brusque gesture as if he can dismiss the question. "I think it's best if we don't exacerbate whatever—"

"No," I say, my voice shaking. "I need to know."

"You've—you've been with August since you came to the pack," Harper says quickly, bracing herself as if she expects Corwin to attack *her* for mentioning it. "I mean, as… as lovers. He'd never let anything happen to you if he could help it."

What? How can that sound so obvious and yet—and yet when I try to even picture August's face—

Horror claws up through me. It's gone. Something *precious* has been warped in my head, and I don't know how to get it back.

"Talia," Corwin is saying, and I see the way he's gripping his fork, the whitening of his knuckles. I remember the flash of guilt. Understanding rushes through me.

"*You* did this." I spring to my feet, wobbling as I set my bad foot wrong, my fingers clamping around the edge of the table to hold me steady.

Corwin leaps up to help me, but he stops in the face of my glare. I hurl the full force of my anger and distress at the bond between us, willing at least a little of it to crack through his wall. "You changed my memories. Blurred them. You wanted me to forget—forget that I was with someone else? How could you—you swore—"

The undertone of Corwin's bronze skin has gone a faint, queasy green. "I think you should go," he says to Harper.

I smack one hand on the tabletop, rattling the dishes. "No. She's the only one here who actually cares about what *I* want. Whatever you did, you're not hiding it from her either."

Harper stands, but she stays there across from me with her back straight and her jaw tight. Corwin frowns at her and lets out a huff of breath as he turns back to me.

"I swore not to harm you, and I didn't. I was trying to

help. I could feel how it was hurting you, being apart from them, having your loyalties divided, when you never should have been put in that position. So I... attempted to set things right, as if you never had been."

He falters in the face of the pained fury I have no doubt he can sense now, even if only because my eyes must be shooting daggers at him. I didn't think I trusted him, but I did enough that this violation feels like the worst betrayal.

"That wasn't your choice to make," I snap. "I am who I am, and my life is what it is. Were you going to try to make me forget that I'm human next? Or how my foot got broken? Or why the Seelie need me, in the hopes that it'd be easier to convince me to stay? Messing with someone's head like that is—it's *sick*. The only people who've ever done that to me before were the monsters who left me in a cage for nine years, and even they only did it temporarily with fairy fruit."

Corwin winces. "Talia, I swear, I was only trying to spare you—"

"I don't want to hear you try to justify it." Maybe it's true, maybe the oaths ensured he'd only have been able to work his magic on my mind if he meant well, but the fact that it didn't occur to him that I had a right to my memories is almost worse. "Can you fix it? Can you get the fog out of my head? I want to remember everything the way I should."

He nods. "I apologize. I didn't realize it would cause you so much distress. I promise you my intentions were only the opposite. Will you—will you come here?"

I'm so keyed up I flinch at the suggestion, and

Corwin's stance turns even more rigid. I force myself to step toward him. "Do it quickly." I don't want to be in his presence any longer than I have to be.

He raises his hands to either side of my head, hovering an inch from my hair, and murmurs several unfamiliar syllables. A rush of tingling energy washes through my mind—and everything is clear again.

I inhale sharply and choke on a sob. August and Sylas and Whitt. All the devotion they've shown me. All the love I've felt for them. Every moment of affection and desire—the warmth of *that* bond wraps around me like an embrace and fills my chest with an ache so poignant my eyes flood with tears.

The man in front of me tried to take all that joy away from me.

I shove myself away from Corwin and march unsteadily to the doorway. "Stay away from me," I say without looking back. "I don't want to see you or talk to you or *anything* with you until it's time for me to go home."

Talia

A tapping sound outside my bedroom door tells me that Corwin has brought my dinner. He's set the tray down on the floor in the hall outside so I can retrieve it after he's gone.

He doesn't just leave, though. Even with all the light I can summon into my body shored up against our connection, I can sense him standing there, watching the door as if he can see me through it.

"Talia, please," he says quietly. "What can I do? What do you need from me? Tell me, and I'll make it happen."

I need for him not to have worked magic on my mind, to have tried to bend me to his idea of how I should be and what I should feel. But he can't give me that, so I say nothing. He's already apologized a few dozen times since yesterday morning. He's offered to swear a new oath before the other arch-lords to cast no magic at all on me so I know it won't happen again.

He even suggested he'd let me in through the bond so I can see that he honestly thought it would help and only regrets it now, and anything else I might need to know to trust him, although I'm pretty sure he'd be able to wall off his thoughts about things like the war with the Seelie out of professional discretion.

None of it feels like enough. None of it has eased the ache still clenched around my gut. I just want to go home and forget all of this ever happened, but he hasn't offered me *that*. I don't know if he even can.

"All right," he says finally. "I don't want your dinner to get cold. I'll keep coming back, but if you're ready to speak to me sooner, reach out through the bond. I'll stay open to you."

I wait until I'm sure he'll be out of sight, and then I open the door to collect my meal. As I bend down to pick up the silver tray with its covered plate and goblet of juice, I freeze.

A sprig of flowers lies next to the plate, bright blue petals around a pinkish center, the leaves a vibrant green. As I touch it tentatively, a faintly sweet perfume reaches my nose.

I've seen flowers like this before, but not on the chilly terrain around this palace. These are summer flowers.

Did Corwin risk going across the border again just to get these for me?

To bring me a little piece of the home I'm missing.

It still isn't enough, but it's the first thing he's offered that feels like he might really understand why I'm so hurt. Unexpected tears well up, and I have to swipe at my eyes a few times before I'm collected enough to pick up the tray.

I don't want to open myself up to Corwin from the inside, but tomorrow—tomorrow, when he brings breakfast, I'll at least thank him. That doesn't mean I'm going to *forgive* him, though.

As I straighten up, Harper opens the door across from me. She's holding a similar tray—she's been refusing to eat in the dining room out of solidarity. "Do you want some company?" she asks, looking meek, as if she thinks she's somehow been tarnished by simply being there when I realized what Corwin did.

I hesitate, but I've done so much wallowing in my frustration and hurt over the past two days that I'm honestly tired of it. And Harper *hasn't* done anything wrong. If it wasn't for her comments, I don't know how long it'd have taken me to figure out what I was missing.

I give her a weak but genuine smile. "Yeah, that'd be nice. Come on over."

There's a small table in my bedroom, but it only has one matching chair. "If people can do breakfast in bed, why not dinner too?" I announce, and set my tray on the blanket before hopping up to prop myself against my pillows. Harper's lips twitch with amusement. She tucks herself against one of the posts at the foot of the bed and crosses her legs so she can balance her tray on them.

Thankfully the kitchen staff haven't prepared anything too messy. There's a tart leafy vegetable that's been sautéed and some kind of fried meat in thin strips that look almost like bacon but have a smokier flavor. Back in Hearthshire, I'd probably have known exactly what these things are and how they were prepared because chances were I'd have been in the kitchen helping August make them.

That thought comes with a fresh pang of longing that tightens my stomach. I force down a few more bites, but despite the deliciousness of the food, I've lost my enthusiasm.

"Maybe we should take over the kitchen sometime and show Corwin just how much *you* can do," Harper says with a glint of mischief in her eyes. "I'm not that handy, but I'm sure you've learned enough from August that you could boss me around."

I have to smile imagining it, even though the idea also sharpens my homesickness. I wave my fork at her. "I'm not doing any cooking for him anytime soon."

"True. He definitely doesn't deserve it after that awful trick he pulled. We'll have to sneak in and make midnight snacks just for us or something." She pauses. "Midnight snacks are a thing, right? I think I read that in a book someone brought from your world."

From the human world, she means, as distant as that place feels to me now after nearly a decade away from it. But I can confidently say, "Midnight snacks are *totally* a thing. My mom was always hassling my dad about leaving crumbs on the counter when he'd go down to sneak a cookie or a piece of toast in the middle of the night."

The pang that comes with that memory is duller but also deeper. I swallow hard, remembering Mom's teasing voice and the wag of her finger, Dad catching her hand and pressing a quick kiss to the tip of that finger as he apologized with a grin. They were so happy. *We* were so happy, as a family. Yeah, we squabbled and sometimes Jamie got on my nerves, but that's what little brothers are for, right?

No matter how much happiness I'm able to find here among the fae, I am *never* going to forgive Aerik and his cadre for destroying all those lives before.

When I come back to the present, Harper is watching me with concern in her overwide eyes. "It made you sad, thinking about that. I'm sorry."

I shake my head. "It's okay. I'd rather remember my family and be sad than forget. It just hardly feels real sometimes, like they should still be back there, even though I know they're not. The attack happened so fast, and then everything was so horrible after for such a long time... I couldn't really grieve when I had to focus on surviving and staying sane, and now I'm not sure how to."

Her mouth tightens with sympathy. "Well, I'm still sorry. Sometimes—sometimes I forget how much you went through before you came to our pack."

"That's not your fault. I don't talk about it much." I didn't even tell her or any of my other pack-kin the truth when Sylas first introduced me to them, because he was still hiding me from Aerik then.

Harper glances away for a second and then looks back at me. "I *should* remember. It's not fair to you if I don't. I..." She jabs at a stray bit of meat but doesn't raise her fork. "Pretty much my whole life, I've felt like I was useless to the pack, you know? I didn't take to music like my parents do, no matter what they named me, so I couldn't help them entertain during the revels, and I don't have much of a knack with gardening or animals or anything else that would really help."

"But you're *brilliant* with the clothes you make," I protest.

She shrugs. "Pretty dresses didn't do anyone any good while we were in exile. My parents never complained, but I know some of our other pack-kin thought I was frivolous. And it was hard for me to relate to everyone else anyway. They all had the weight of the banishment and the memory of losing Hearthshire hanging over them, and I couldn't fully understand it since I'd never known anything else."

It must have been awfully lonely for her as the only child born into the pack after their banishment. I grope for the right thing to say. "At least that's behind all of us now. And I bet a lot of folk in the pack will want those dresses now that we're having balls and banquets and all kinds of celebrations."

"Yes." A sliver of a smile crosses her face and vanishes just as quickly. "But it was— When you first came, I thought you'd be like me. You didn't share all that history, just like I didn't. And since you were human... obviously you wouldn't contribute the same way as everyone else. But then—"

She bites her lip, looking so agonized I can't be even a little offended by her words. I set my tray aside and lean toward her. "I get it. *I* don't even feel like I can contribute on the same level as the rest of you. At least you were nice to me from the start."

"But that's the problem. I mean, *my* problem, not yours." Harper drags in a breath and meets my eyes again. "You made a place for yourself in the pack so quickly. You showed how much you *can* do and how hard you'd try to help out, and soon no one really cared that you aren't even fae, and I—I was a little jealous. I think that's why those girls who came to visit from Ambrose's pack managed to pull me into their scheme. They talked as if I was *more* special than everyone else in the pack who focused on everyday things, and they said things about you…"

She winces. "There was nothing nice about that, or about me going along with it, even if I didn't know just how bad it was going to get."

Maybe I should be upset with her for what she's just admitted, but instead all I feel is a weird sort of relief. It makes more sense now why she backed off from me and got caught up with Ambrose's pack-kin. They spotted a weakness in her, a resentment she hadn't meant to act on, and figured out how to exploit it.

"I know," I say. "I wouldn't have asked you to come with me here if I believed you ever wanted to see me get hurt."

"And I'm so glad for that. When I realized what I could have helped happen—that Ambrose might have been able to take you away because of me—and maybe he'd have been even worse to you than the lord that had you before Sylas—" She shudders. "I hated myself. You and I—we're *not* the same. You've had it so much harder than I have, had so much stolen from you and so many people hurt you. But you keep trying and making a place for yourself anyway. I'm *proud* to be your friend. And if that bird-brain arch-lord doesn't figure out how well you deserve to be treated, then you're better off without him."

She says the last bit so firmly, her eyes flashing with the Unseelie insult, that it melts some of the pain I've been holding inside. She can't fix what Corwin broke, but it helps a lot to know that I'm definitely not alone here, not in a practical sense or in being angry about what he did.

I scoot over to sit right next to her. "Thank you. Maybe it's silly, but it means a lot to hear someone else say that, especially someone who's fae. Hard to know whether my human expectations would seem reasonable."

Harper lets out a huff. "More than reasonable. Trying to make you forget all the good things Sylas and August did for you? That's so selfish of him."

I don't think she's caught on that those "good" things involved Whitt too, or that they were romantic with anyone other than August. I might feel comfortable letting her in on that secret someday… if it even still matters after all this is over.

I rub my forehead. "I just don't know what happens if I do decide I'm better off without Corwin. Where do we go from there? The soul-twined bond won't just disappear because I don't like it." If it would, it'd have been gone days ago.

Harper frowns. "I wish I knew what to do about that. I'm sure Sylas is working on figuring it out right now. In the meantime… do you want to sneak over to the kitchen with me and see if we can grab a little dessert?"

I have to laugh at her conspiratorial tone, my spirits lightening more than they've been since I uncovered Corwin's betrayal. "Let's do it. Sugar makes everything at least a little bit better."

The rest I'll figure out when I have to.

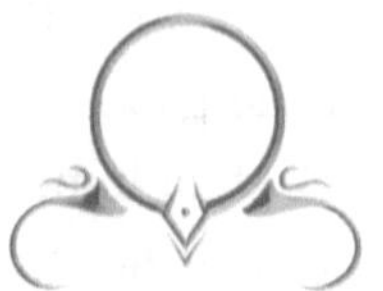

Corwin

Talia's bedroom door has appeared more impenetrable to me every time I've stood before it over the past two days. Looking at it now, I yet again grapple with the conflicting impulses inside me.

My soul-twined mate is on the other side of that door. Even with the bond between us dulled by her resistance, it tugs at my heart. The knowledge of how angry she is, how much I damaged her trust in me, has been searing into me like a burning blade from the moment she berated me in the dining room. If I let go of the tight grip I'm holding over my emotions, I might go as mad as those wolves she cares for so much do under the full moon.

It was a misstep, not a purposeful act of betrayal. I *couldn't* have harmed her with intent. She knows that, and yet reasoning it out, offering whatever is in my power to give her, hasn't been enough to bring her back.

Maybe that's fair. The Heart doesn't work through

reason, does it? What kind of madness is it already for me to be bound to a human woman who's already devoted herself to not one but three Seelie?

A soul-twined bond isn't meant to be a business partnership. It's about the deepest affection and intimacy. I didn't really think I'd be able to hold back as much as I do in every other area of my life. I just never expected it to turn out like this, with so many complexities and obstacles…

I close my eyes, my hands clenching at my sides. Every nerve in my body balks at the display I came here planning to make. I'm well aware of what comes with unchecked passions and how thoroughly they can ruin everything else around them.

But Talia needs to know how much this bond matters to me. How much *she* matters to me. She's come all this way, left behind everything she knew and cared about, to give me a chance. How can I say I deserve her if I won't compromise anything of myself?

These past two days knowing she's here and being unable to even see her have hollowed out my chest in a way I haven't felt since— Well, I'd rather not think of that. And truthfully, this is even worse.

The dining room where I once ate on my own at leisure now blares her absence. I can't sit at my harp without remembering her poised on the settee listening to me play for that brief, beautiful moment when we were utterly at peace with each other. When I try to sleep, her voice rings through my mind, sharp with the pain she showed when she discovered my uninvited spell.

This isn't how these ten days were supposed to go. And

with every passing hour, she's slipping farther away from me.

If I want to bring her back before she's too far for me to ever reach, I have to give her everything I can.

Girding myself, I sink to my knees and rest my forearms on the floor. I bow so low my forehead touches my clasped hands. The pose sends a prickle of shame through me, but I ignore the sensation. I ease back the tight lid I've been keeping on the turmoil inside me—not all the way, but enough that a rush of the grief and horror floods through me.

She has to feel it, at least a little.

"Talia," I say, loud enough to be sure my voice will carry through the door, "I've wounded you in an unconscionable way, and all I can think to do is humble myself before your rightful anger. I will remain here at your mercy until you see fit to speak to me, however long it might take. Nothing in my domain or elsewhere can come before making amends with you."

It's possible the security of not just my heart and soul but my entire realm as well rest on proving my commitment to her. Her tie to the Seelie's curse raises possibilities I'd never considered… but I can't use that information to persuade my fellow arch-lords while the oath I swore holds my tongue, and I can't speak to Talia about it while she's still so loyal to the fae who consider us their enemies.

So I stay as I am, prostrate before her door, not allowing myself to consider how it will look if one of the servants or even my coterie come by. I shamed myself by stealing into Talia's mind. Why shouldn't they witness the results of that? I have only myself to blame.

My back twinges, my wings itching to spring free and shelter me. I will away the urge. My remorse swells through me, but I get nothing back from the other end of the bond.

Then my ears pick up the faintest of sounds from beyond the door—the whisper of her feet brushing across the floor with her uneven steps. The thought of the beasts that shattered her foot summons a protective fury within me, but I shove that down too. This isn't the time for it.

But when my mate is fully mine, I will carve every wolf who hurt her into pieces with pleasure.

The violence in that idea unnerves me—*this is what comes of unleashing one's emotions*—but then the door is easing open and I can't focus on anything except the woman peering down at me.

My head is still bowed, but I hear the soft hitch of Talia's breath and the rustle of her dress as she leans far enough to glance down the hall. As if *she's* worried about who might witness my demonstration of regret.

"What are you *doing?*" she says, her voice shocked and possibly even horrified.

My throat tightens around the words, but I can't say they feel wrong coming out. "I kneel at your feet to beseech your forgiveness. I overstepped my authority so far —I failed to honor you as you deserve—it was not my place to alter your history or decide which parts of it should be valuable to you. I offer no excuses. I only mean to show I understand how horribly I erred."

Talia swallows audibly. "Don't you care if someone sees

you? What kind of fae arch-lord grovels in front of a human?"

I let myself look up at her then, as well as I can while keeping my back bowed over. Her mouth is pressed in a taut line, her eyes wide and starkly bright with uncertain emotion. She grips the doorframe, looking as if she might retreat and slam the door in my face at any moment—but she hasn't yet.

She's here. She's listening.

"Your being human matters no more than if you were fae," I say. "Even if you were simply my guest under the care of my household, my conduct would have been appalling. But you aren't simply a guest. You're my soul-twined mate."

"You didn't choose me any more than I chose you. And don't say you'll go along with it because of the Heart and all that."

I hold her gaze despite the awkward angle, hoping she can feel the truth of this statement as I say it. "I choose you now. Not only because of the Heart's will but my own as well. You're an intelligent, determined woman who I can see has earned every bit of respect your Seelie pack offered you. It will be my honor to have you stand beside me as my equal, and it sickens me that I have threatened that future with my actions."

Her lips part, but she hesitates, still deliberating. Still on the verge of walking away.

I was too distracted by all the surprises that came with her arrival and all the politics surrounding it to recognize her strength at first. She's endured so much— she's enduring so much now—and instead of appreciating the steely will and nobility it took for her to come here despite the love she feels for those other men, I treated her as if she were a broken thing I needed to fix.

What does it matter if she's mortal? I could imagine her standing up to every one of my colleagues in ways I've never dared. Removing those other lovers from her mind would be no more than a cheap ploy. If I'm going to earn her love or at least her dedication as well, I have to prove I can match them.

I have to prove I can accept them and what they mean to her.

I brace myself against the additional discomfort that comes with the offer I know I need to make. "You don't have to forgive me yet. I would only ask—will you share with me what I was unthinking enough to try to steal from you? I want to hear about the men you love and how they came to mean so much to you, so I can understand. So I can know you and everything about how *you* came to be as you are. They're important to you, so they're important to me too."

The barrier in our bond wobbles then. It softens, and a trace of her emotions drifts through to me: a tangled mix of pain and anger and the recognition of how hard that request was for me to make.

Talia wets her lips. Then she says, quietly but clearly, "All right. You can come in. Take the chair by the table. I'll think about where to start."

Relief rushes through me, so sharp it's almost painful in itself. I ease upright and follow her into the room, respectful of the distance she's keeping between us. As I take the chair she indicated, she perches tentatively on the edge of the bed across from me.

"How much do you want me to tell you?" she says, with astonishing tenderness considering how badly I hurt her and how fresh that wound still is. "I know it makes you uncomfortable hearing about it—about them."

A pang shoots through my chest, poignant and undeniable. This woman's resilience and will would make her a worthy partner for any arch-lord, but her compassion… That makes her exactly the partner *I* would want.

I could fall in love with her if I let myself. I know that beyond a doubt now.

I lean back in the chair, trying to appear relaxed so as not to concern her. "Everything. Anything you want to tell me. Anything you're willing to show me through the bond. You can leave out information you think they'd want to keep secret for the sake of their people, of course, but I want to know you as well as I can. That's the only way I can be the mate you deserve."

"Okay." She twines her fingers and rests her hands on her lap. Her gaze goes distant, a fond light glowing in her eyes that sparks a flicker of jealousy I can't totally suppress. "It was August I really fell for first. He's in Sylas's cadre, the head of the pack's warriors. But he's only ever been gentle with me. Right from the start, he went out of his way to make me feel like I could belong…"

As she goes on, talking about the first few weeks she spent with Arch-Lord Sylas's pack, more vivid impressions filter through the connection between us. She's lowering her defenses. Each jolt of joy and quiver of remembered pleasure pricks at me like a series of thorns, but I hold myself steady and still, taking it all in.

It *does* hurt, listening to her speak so affectionately of these men who won her heart before I ever knew she was meant to be mine. But I have to welcome every part of her and everything she's been through.

It's the only chance I have of winning my own place in that heart, for my own happiness—and perhaps the very survival of my people.

Sylas

"Well," Whitt says, surveying the ruined bins lying in disarray in the small storage hut, "the Murk couldn't have happened to a worse bunch of fae. And by that, I mean I fully approve of their choice of target."

August lets out a huff that sounds like agreement. I grimace, my fangs pressing against the inside of my mouth. As soon as I spotted the rodent footprints dappled in the earth around the hut and smelled their unmistakeable vermin stink inside, I couldn't hold them back.

"Better the Murk didn't harass any of our kin, even those we'd consider enemies," I mutter. "And regardless of what we think of their lord and cadre, the rest of the pack doesn't necessarily deserve our ire, including the poor fellow who met his end over this mischief."

It is difficult, though, to be in the presence of that

bone-white castle without thinking of the last time we were here, in the dimming evening light, carrying Talia away from her filthy prison. My fangs might be out even if the Murk hadn't worked their spite on Copperweld at all.

If it wasn't for the murder of the one pack-kin who must have happened upon the rat shifters at the wrong time, this mess would appear to be merely mischief. I wouldn't blame Aerik for wanting an arch-lord's attention on the matter regardless. Any overt activity from the Murk needs a careful eye, no matter how seemingly innocuous. They might mainly stick to aggravating us in minor ways, but I know with the twinge that creeps through my deadened eye just how vicious the rat shifters can be. That eye catches a ghostly flicker of scurrying forms cavorting amid the wreckage, there and then gone.

The Murk like nothing more than to bring us as low as they possibly can. I'm sure they wish they could drag us all the way down to their own wretched level. They certainly didn't show any respect to the man they left bleeding out under a sprinkling of dirt behind this small storage building.

Speaking of wretched figures… Aerik's shadow crosses the doorway. His arms are folded over his chest. I suspect he's no more pleased that I'm the arch-lord who took up this investigation than I am to be here. "Well, what do you make of it?" he demands.

Whitt replies for me. "It looks like their typical approach. Sneak in, wreak a little havoc, sneak out again." He glances around at the baskets of mushrooms gone black and mushy with rot and wrinkles his notes. "As much as your pack might have valued these delicacies, their loss is hardly catastrophic. My regrets to the family of your pack-kin who crossed their paths so unfortunately, though. If we catch them, you can be sure the mangy rats will pay for that."

"I don't like that they were so bold about it in general," I add. "Slipping into a building so close to the castle and the village. Did no one else see any sign of them?"

Aerik stiffens as if I've outright accused him of poorly protecting his domain. I'm more concerned because I assume he *has* been vigilant. He's probably been on guard against *us* ever since we brought him and his cadre to yield on Talia's behalf.

But perhaps his sentries were keeping watch against wolves and not taking enough care against rats. The mangy vermin are so small it isn't that difficult for them to lurk throughout our territory without being caught.

One of Aerik's cadre-chosen appears at his side. It's Cole, who I think frightens Talia even more than his lord, which means the sight of him brings my claws prickling to the base of my fingers. "They were as tricky about it as the pests always are," he says. "The rest of the pack didn't realize until one of the kitchen staff came to gather a few mushrooms for our breakfast."

Aerik appears rather mournful as he takes in his ruined stores, as if the loss of them bothers him more than that of his pack-kin. It *was* quite the collection of fungi, many rare species his pack must have gathered over time. I'm not above taking a minor satisfaction that he's being denied the delicacies I'm sure would have mainly been consumed by him and his cadre rather than the rest of their pack.

I step forward, and he draws back to let me pass,

leaving a careful distance that I know isn't just out of respect to my station. One wrong move, and I'd happily snap the monster's neck as I wish he'd given me provocation to do the other afternoon.

The warmth of the midday sun barely penetrates my skin. I study the tiny paw marks in the dirt around the building again and then consider the pale castle. There is no "wrong" magic in the world, but nonetheless, Aerik's affinity for bone and his use of it in his home send a quiver of revulsion through my gut. "This was the only resource they destroyed?"

Aerik nods. "That we're aware of, but as soon as we discovered this intrusion, I had my pack scour the domain. There's no further trace of them. No indication of how they made their way into or out of our territory either. The only signs of their presence are what you can see and smell around this building—and of course the wounds they left on my fallen guard."

They covered their tracks everywhere else. That's even more indication that the Murk didn't leave those signs out of negligence but because they were taunting us with the fact that they could pull off this trick so blatantly. August lets out a growl and scans the landscape around us as if he thinks he might spot one of the perpetrators right now and take a chomp out of them.

I restrain a sigh. "It doesn't appear there's anything else we can do at the moment, but I'll report their boldness to my fellow arch-lords and put out the word across the realm for all our brethren to be particularly wary. If you need any assistance setting down appropriate protections—"

"No," Aerik bites out in a tone that's just shy of insubordination. "I can look after my people perfectly well as I am."

I give him a steady look and watch him not quite hide a flinch. I overpowered him when we were on equal footing as lords. He knows how steep the consequences are for betraying an arch-lord. Even Ambrose couldn't get away with that kind of treachery.

"We'll be on our way then," I say. "Do inform the domains of the Heart at once if you find any further information about the culprits."

We've only just left the Copperweld's castle behind in our carriage when August gives a brisk shudder as if shedding the atmosphere of the place. "I can't be angry at his entire pack—none of them knew about what he was doing to Talia—but there's nothing I'd like more than to see that place razed to the ground."

I tip my head toward him. "I suspect you'd like even more to see Talia stepping back across the border to meet us."

A smile much smaller and sadder than is usual for my younger brother crosses his face. "Well, yes, there is that." He drags in a breath and squares his shoulders. "Nearly halfway there."

Assuming all goes well. Assuming Talia is still all right even now. I've never much cared about the separation between the summer and winter realms before, but now that what's happening on the other side of the border matters to me very much, the perpetual silence itches at my skin.

"No wars declared, no further skirmishes," Whitt

points out. "All in all, it can't be going too horribly." But his gaze is pensive as he gazes off across the terrain around us.

There are an awful lot of outcomes we'd hate to see that wouldn't involve outright war. But it doesn't do me any good to worry about those or whether the woman I love will even still be *mine* when she returns. I have duties to my entire realm to carry out.

When we reach the new Hearth-by-the-Heart, I take a little satisfaction in seeing the growing walls of our new castle, looking closer to its finished form by the day. Most of the pack will spend their first full moon since my coronation back in Hearthshire, but soon after we'll be able to bring them all here and be completely united again. I don't like having them at such a distance any more than I do Talia.

"I'll go check on the construction progress in the village and any new discoveries regarding Ambrose's weapons stash," August says, hopping out.

Whitt springs after him. "I'm expecting a couple of our sentries to check in. If they have word of Unseelie or Murk activity, I'll bring it to you immediately."

And just like that, I'm on my own. It doesn't take all that many responsibilities to divide me from even my cadre on a regular basis.

I can't join either of them, as I'm meant to report to my arch-lord colleagues on my observations in Copperweld. I stretch my limbs to work out the stiffness from the carriage ride and magic a quick message to travel to Celia and Donovan. Then I head toward the Bastion, where they'll meet me.

Before I've quite left the castle behind, Astrid catches up with me, moving at an impressively athletic lope considering her age. However many centuries she has behind her, it'll be a long time yet before she really slows down, I think.

She falls into stride beside me. "I just got in with the new group of workers from Hearthshire to handle the additional aspects of construction. The original crew are already giving them instructions and getting them started. Is there anything else you wish me to see to now, my lord, or should I take up my usual patrol?"

I pause, and Astrid stops next to me, her eyes darkening with immediate concern. This woman has known me since I was an infant, and she picks up on my moods faster than anyone outside my cadre. By this point, I doubt my own father knows me as well as she does.

But the thought that just struck me isn't a worrisome one. At least, I don't believe it would be.

I've been treating Astrid as almost like part of my cadre already, haven't I? When Whitt and August aren't available, she's the one I've instinctively turned to. I entrusted her with Talia's safety when we couldn't be there, and she saw that duty through without fail. I can't think of any task I wouldn't feel comfortable putting in her capable hands.

I've simply grown so used to relying only on myself and my brothers for our most fraught matters that I hadn't seen what was right in front of me. I *do* need more pack-kin by my side if I'm to rule as arch-lord effectively. If I have any secrets Astrid would think ill of me for, then no doubt I'd deserve it.

It seems like a bit much to spring on her out of the blue when she was asking for nothing more than basic orders. I grapple for a way to broach the subject—to make sure she wouldn't find the offer more of a burden than an honor. "Astrid, you've served me and my family before me for a long time."

Her eyebrows lift slightly. "I have, my lord."

"Have you ever felt you might want to step back from service to enjoy the rest of your life at more leisure?"

They rise even higher. "If you're suggesting that I haven't been performing adequately and it's time I put these old bones to rest, then I hope you'd speak to me more plainly than that. But I feel perfectly capable, and I'd enjoy continuing to know I'm of use a great deal more than sitting around getting mossy."

Her response is so unsurprising it seems absurd that I even asked her. The corner of my mouth curves upward. "So you wouldn't object to being of even more use than you already are, then?"

Astrid fixes me with a wry look. "I wouldn't chide an arch-lord, my lord, but you'll get an exact answer sooner if you say exactly what you're thinking. I can certainly take on more if you need me to. Honestly, having work to carry out on behalf of the pack is what keeps me feeling fully alive. With my mate's passing, my family got both smaller and larger. I consider all of Hearthshire to be it now."

Her words bring warmth into my chest. I couldn't have hoped for a better perspective, and now I'm completely certain of my choice.

"In that case, how would you feel about joining my cadre?"

Whatever Astrid might have imagined I was going to say, it clearly wasn't that. She stares at me for several seconds before she recovers her tongue. "I—your cadre—are you *sure*, my lord?"

I can't help chuckling. When was the last time I saw her startled enough to lose her composure? Possibly never. "I'm certain I wouldn't be asking unless I was sure."

"Of course. I only—" She shakes her head as if to clear it and smiles at me, crookedly but obviously pleased. "I never expected to receive such a lofty invitation. Or maybe I assumed if I was going to find myself in a cadre, it would have happened sooner."

"Well, if I've learned anything, it's that life rarely follows the patterns we'd expect." I expected to have my soul-twined mate's cadre to join with my own. I expected to rule over Hearthshire and not the entire summer realm. But here we are, and I can't say I'm sorry for it on the balance. "An arch-lord has much more to attend to than the mere lord of Hearthshire. I've realized it's time I expanded my inner circle. Only if you're willing, of course—"

"Yes, yes, that shouldn't be any question." She smiles more broadly, and I could kick myself for waiting so long to make this invitation. However many years she has left with us, she deserved more of them in a position that offered her all the respect she was due.

She pauses, and a soft twinkle enters her eyes. "There is one point I should probably clarify first, though."

"What would that be?"

"As far as certain, ah, arrangements exist between yourself and the current members of your cadre, I feel I should make clear that I have no desire to take on any further mates and am perfectly happy to leave all of that business to the three of you."

A laugh tumbles out of me. We've been careful, but there's only so careful one can be, especially with the one we asked to watch over Talia closely. "I'd imagine neither we nor Talia will expect anything other than a professional relationship from you."

"Excellent." She laughs herself and then lifts her chin. "Well, then—when do I start, my lord?"

Talia

"That's done with," Corwin says, stepping back from the crystalline stable building he just finished adding a few feet to with his magic. "I'm sorry— I'm sure that wasn't the most exciting work to watch."

"I'm not complaining." I hesitate and then ease back my inner wall a little more than I already had so he can feel more of my genuine appreciation of his skill. I may have gotten somewhat used to fae companions casting magic around me, but witnessing any of them bend the world to their commands still fills me with a sense of awe.

And it was kind of nice seeing the intensity of Corwin's concentration stripping away that coolly composed mask he puts on so often. The determined smolder in his eyes and the power ringing through his measured true words might have made my pulse stutter in a way that wasn't totally unpleasant. I'd rather he hadn't picked up on *that* subtle reaction, though.

If he did, he doesn't show it, only gives me one of his restrained smiles. "You'll have to come and meet the new steed once it arrives. I understand it's a rather impressive one."

I raise an eyebrow at him. "I'm still trying to figure out why you need any kind of steed when you've got wings."

The Unseelie arch-lord lets out a brief chuckle that seems to surprise him as much as it does me. His mouth twitches with a flicker of embarrassment, but his emotions settle quickly enough, his tone relaxed when he answers. "With multiple types of terrain, we need many options for optimal traveling. Neither wings nor conjured vehicles can navigate forests as well as our mounts do, should we need to attend to what's within the trees rather than simply soaring above them."

"Fair enough." I glance across the short span of icy fields to his towering palace. The sun is starting to sink, the deepening purple of the sky seeping across the diamond spires. Thanks to the warming spell on my clothes, the chill in the breeze barely touches me before it's whisked away, but the wintry area around Corwin's home feels even lonelier than inside its halls. "Where to next?"

"Now I'd typically consult with my kitchen staff about the dinner preparations. If you'd like, you can determine for yourself that Charles and his daughter are perfectly happy here among the fae."

Is there a hint of teasing to that suggestion? I study Corwin, but as usual his expression doesn't give away much, although I might sense a smidgeon of amusement through our bond. "All right. To the kitchen it is."

I don't know if I could say that I'm enjoying myself,

but the silence between us as we walk back to the palace does feel more comfortable than I'd have expected a couple of days ago. Since his desperate plea outside my bedroom yesterday morning, Corwin has been on his best behavior.

We spent all of yesterday talking about my history among the summer fae—well, mostly *me* talking and Corwin listening, taking in the memories I let him experience through me, even though I could feel his hackles rising here and there. But I can't blame him for his instinctive reactions. Something about the soul-twined bond gives *me* a jab of guilt thinking about men other than him, even though I know I haven't done anything wrong.

He didn't let any animosity out, didn't say one word against my lovers or the Seelie in general. I don't think he could have faked the gratitude I caught from him when he told me how glad he was that Sylas and the others have protected me so adamantly.

With every moment we spent together discussing the love I've already experienced, any fear I had that he might try to take it away again dwindled until that concern disappeared completely. So when he offered that today I could join him for some of his duties around the palace and get to know the servants a little better, I accepted. So far he hasn't given me any reason to shut myself back in my bedroom to wait out the rest of my time here, but I'm still wary.

The kitchen Harper and I snuck into two nights ago looks even vaster fully lit. The fading sunlight combined with the yellowish glow of the extra lamps make the diamond counters and the silvery shapes of the ovens shine.

The human girl is just taking a fresh loaf of bread out of an oven, its crisp doughy scent lacing the air. Her father—Charles—is talking with a fae woman who appears to have brought in some vegetables. He turns to Corwin as soon as we enter.

"My lord," he says with a much broader and warmer smile than the Unseelie fae typically produce. "We've got quite the bounty today. Is there anything in particular you have a craving for?"

Corwin nods to me. "Perhaps my guest should have some say about tonight's dinner. Talia, the meals we've enjoyed so far were all thanks to Charles and Beth's impressive talents. Anything you'd like, I'd imagine they could find a way to whip up."

Beth comes over, rubbing her hands together. "Absolutely. A challenge just makes it more fun."

Okay, these human servants definitely appear to be totally at ease with their jobs here. I think over the meals we've had so far, all of them delicious, trying to decide which of my favorite parts I could ask them to replicate. "Do you ever cook fish with that reddish sauce we had on the quail? And I really liked the braised vegetables that looked kind of like asparagus that we had at lunch yesterday."

Charles gives his daughter a playful nudge with his elbow. "She's got good taste, doesn't she? That sounds like a perfect combination. Why don't you go and fetch a couple of trout?"

As Beth hustles off to the cold room, Corwin thanks

his chef and moves as if to leave. Something deep within me balks. The arch-lord stops before I've said anything, picking up on my mood. "Is everything all right, Talia?"

"Yes. I just—" Will this request sound like a total imposition? Or simply ridiculous? I grapple with the impulse for a moment before spitting it out. "I used to help out in the kitchen a lot back... back home. Would it be okay if I pitched in with dinner?"

Corwin blinks, definitely startled, but he glances at Charles in question rather than denying me. The human man shrugs, his bright eyes twinkling. "Never hurts to have an extra pair of hands, especially if they know what they're doing. Do you think you can manage trimming the moss-shoots?"

I smile back at him, an unexpected lightness washing over me. "Show me with one and I'll remember for the rest. I'm a fast learner."

The moss-shoots turn out to be the asparagus-like vegetable I asked for. Charles demonstrates the preferred cuts, and then I get to work, carving the knife methodically through the pile while he prepares the sauce for the fish. Corwin watches from a short distance, our roles reversed for the first time today. A faint glow of satisfaction washes over me through our connection.

He likes seeing me find a place for myself here, even if it's among the servants for now—and I like it too. The rhythm of the work and the familiar bustle and clatter of kitchen activity around me settle my nerves more than anything else I've experienced since I came to the winter realm.

When I finish with the shoots, Charles hands me a

mortar, pestle, and a small bowl of spice seeds, trusting I'll know what to do with them. I drop a handful of seeds into the mortar and put my shoulder into the grinding, my mouth watering at the tart tang that rises up. The scent reminds me of the cloves August used in some of his cooking…

A wave of homesickness sweeps through me, too fast for me to suppress it. A week ago, I'd have been perched like this next to August's brawny form, warmed by his smile and his encouraging words. Assembling a meal together in the perfect harmony produced by months of mutual experience—and love.

A pang of pain and jealousy prickles into me from Corwin, and my first instinct is to shove down those memories as quickly as I can. But… wasn't the point of yesterday to prove that he could handle me and my emotions as they are? That he could accept the commitments I've already made, the joy I've felt with the lovers I already found?

If there's going to be any chance of trust between us, I need to know that acceptance wasn't just a one-day thing.

I've barely come to that conclusion before Corwin has gotten his own reaction under control. The prickling discomfort subsides. He extends a tendril of apology and then, his inner voice cautious, says, *If you wanted to bring some ingredients and recipes back to share with him, I wouldn't mind. If he wouldn't mind attempting Unseelie-style cooking, that is.*

I glance at him with a jolt of surprise and unexpected affection. *I think he'd enjoy expanding his repertoire. Thank you.*

There's definitely amusement in Corwin's tone now, understated as it is. *I should be thanking you. You're the one preparing our dinner.* He pauses. *And I should thank him as well, for giving you a place you could feel at home among the fae, no matter whose home you're in. Will he still be spending so much time in the kitchen, even now that he's cadre to an arch-lord?*

I laugh out loud. *Maybe not quite as much, but I don't think you could keep August out of a kitchen for long unless the Heart itself commanded it.*

I suppose his pack can be happy for that.

We lapse into silence between us as Charles and Beth bicker amicably about the exact size the trout filets should be, but in that moment, I do feel at home. As at home as I *can* be when my real home is out of bounds.

Then another fae servant slips into the room carrying a tray of empty dishes. He draws up short at the sight of his lord—and my awareness of Corwin becomes abruptly dulled, as if he's shored up his own walls against our bond.

"It's fine," Corwin says with a brisk motion toward the far end of the counter. "You're not interrupting. I trust everything is in order."

"Yes, my lord. As well as it ever is."

There's a stiffness to both their voices. The servant darts to the corner, sets down the tray, and bobs up with his hand reaching into one of the cabinets, but I don't see him take anything out. Odd. I give Corwin a questioning look, and the barrier between us fades again.

My apologies. An instinctive reaction to an unexpected arrival. I should have remembered not everyone in the palace eats on the same schedule.

Is he embarrassed that I'm seeing a reminder of his separation from his servants? That answer doesn't totally sit right with me, but I don't know what to ask. The fae man heads back out again without a sign of concern, so maybe I shouldn't make all that much out of it. Corwin and I are both still finding our footing with each other, after all.

Beth comes over to rub the spices into the fillets alongside me, and then Charles has me sampling the sauce, and in no time at all the meal is ready. Corwin sends a servant to summon Harper while the cooks portion out the meal across several plates, including two for themselves and a few I assume are for other staff.

Corwin, Harper, and I gather in the small dining room like so many times before—only this time, I'm not just a recipient of the meal but a participant in its creation as well. Somehow that knowledge brings a more vivid flavor to the combination of flaky fish and savory sauce. I bite into the moss-shoots I trimmed with a weird sense of ownership, even though Charles did the actual braising.

Harper finishes her last bite with an approving hum. "The food here is always delicious, but I think this was the best dinner yet."

Corwin's smile comes out. "It was Talia's choice—and she had a hand in making it as well."

My friend grins at me. "That explains it, then."

The arch-lord considers both of us with a contemplative vibe and then asks, "Would the two of you like to accompany me to my music room? Perhaps I should make use of my own meager skills at entertainment for my guests."

My gaze darts to him. He's balked at including Harper

in our activities before, but I don't catch any sign of resentment in his expression or through our bond. I send a whiff of gratitude his way. "I'd like that." I turn to my friend. "He's very good on the harp. I think even your parents would be impressed."

"Well, I can't miss a performance with a recommendation like that," she says. "Especially when it's the instrument that's my namesake."

I'm a little afraid I might have oversold Corwin's abilities, since I'm no musical expert, but it only takes a few notes pealing from the strings before Harper is beaming. She sways a little with the melody he produces, a more buoyant one than he played before. It brings images of the dancers at Whitt's revels into my mind.

Do the winter fae even have parties, or is that too wild for them?

We have plenty of ways of celebrating what we value, Corwin says, picking up on the gist of my curious thoughts. *Perhaps not quite so… boisterous.* He stops at the end of the song and swipes his hands over his thighs. *The Seelie who led those festivities—you showed me that he took you once to a spot you quite admired. Perhaps I can give you a similar gift.*

Before I can ask him what he means, he switches to speaking out loud. "I thought I might pay a call on a domain a couple of hours from here tomorrow. It has some impressive sights. If the two of you would like to make the trip with me, I'd be pleased to share one of the winter realm's greatest wonders with you."

For a second, I tense up at the thought of leaving the relative familiarity of this palace and venturing farther beyond with this man I've only just found myself capable of forgiving. But he's gazing at us so earnestly. No trace of jealousy came through in his reference to Whitt, nothing but…

Nothing but hope.

I did want to see more of this realm before I left. I think I might even enjoy seeing it with the relaxed, generous version of Corwin he's letting me get to know.

For the first time since I got here, I can truly believe that some kind of peace between my people and his is within reach.

Harper is watching me, waiting for me to answer first. I know she'd love to get out of the palace. So I smile, my own hopes lifting just a little. "Let's do it."

2 1

Talia

For all the differences between the winter and summer fae, when the Unseelie want to get somewhere without using their wings, they use methods pretty similar to the Seelie. The vehicle Corwin conjured for this trip looks like a wider and shallower version of a summer fae carriage, though with a clear crystalline wedge jutting from the bow to cut down on the cold sweep of the wind and no canopy to stop the bright sun from warming us. A darker wood than the juniper I'm used to forms the carriage's body, and the unpadded seats stand down the middle rather than against the walls.

Since this is my first time seeing the winter realm beyond Corwin's domain, I've spent most of the journey standing by the side of the carriage rather than sitting on those seats, peering at the passing terrain. A lot of it has been snowy or rocky or both, but I guess I can't complain about that when most of the summer realm is either forests or grassy plains. We did pass a vast field of twinkling flowers that spun at random intervals and a landscape where several rivers cutting through each other created a patchwork of islands.

Corwin glances over at me from where he's poised at the bow, and the warmth of his smile travels through our bond as well as showing in his expression. *I'm confident you'll like what I'm going to show you more than anything you've seen so far.*

You're setting high expectations, I can't resist teasing. *Tempting disappointment.*

The corners of his lips quirk a little higher. *If you aren't impressed by this, I don't deserve to be an arch-lord.*

Sitting on the bench near me, Harper nudges me with the toe of her boot and raises her eyebrows at me as if she can tell we've been having a silent conversation without her. Her own sly smile suggests she doesn't mind. She might have been willing to kick Corwin to the curb over how he treated me, but she's happy that we're getting along now.

And… we actually are getting along, aren't we? Over the past couple of days, we've reached our own kind of peace. He knows where I stand, and he hasn't made me regret my growing openness once since that horrible offense that he was willing to prostrate himself to make up for.

I haven't let him completely in. I'm still avoiding letting him see anything to do with my unexpected ability to wield true names, which his oaths wouldn't require him to keep secret from his colleagues. As accepting as he's become of my Seelie lovers, there are intimate moments

I'd prefer to keep to myself because they're too personal to share.

He hasn't pushed for everything, though. I'm sure he's keeping plenty to himself as well. He still hasn't told me what's behind all the Unseelie attacks on the border, after all, although if he's made other oaths to keep information like that secret, it's not his fault. In every way I can think of, he's been showing how important it is to him to make up for our rough start.

I can't imagine giving up the men I left behind. A pang of longing still runs through me when I think of home. But it *is* a relief to relax more, to not feel like I'm up against an enemy. Corwin approaches things in a different way from the summer fae and from any human I can remember, but... I'm even starting to like being around him. Maybe we would have been friends if we'd met in some other way without all these pressures on us.

Looking over at him again, at the sunlight bringing out the sapphire blue in his black hair and the bronze tones in his handsome face, I might have to revise that thought. When he offers me one of his rare wider smiles that reach his eyes, it makes my heart skip a beat.

My appreciation of him isn't *only* friendly. But the soul-twined bond is at least partly to blame for that.

I still don't know what I'm going to do about that problem. I'm hoping that by spending more time together, the answer will come to me, even if it's hard to figure out what solution there could possibly be that won't break my heart or his.

Corwin must sense the lurch of tangled emotion that worry brings. A waft of soothing reassurance flows through our connection. *You don't have to make any decisions yet. You don't have to decide anything at all before you go back to the Seelie. I just want whatever decisions you make to be based on a full and accurate picture about what your life here could be like.*

So this excursion is only for the interests of accuracy and not to prove that you can also arrange a fantastic day trip? I ask with a hint of amusement, remembering how he mentioned my memory of Whitt taking me out to his favorite glen when making the invitation.

I'm allowed to have multiple motivations, aren't I? You're clearly an explorer at heart, and far be it for me to deny you the opportunity. He pauses, pulling his gaze away for a second before returning it to meet my eyes. *And it gives me great pleasure to see you happy.*

The affection that wraps around those words and flows through my chest makes my pulse stutter again. This time, *I* look away. I can still sense myself through his sight, his admiration of the way the sunlight brings out the vibrance in my own hair and lights up my face, his awareness of my eagerness and awe at getting to travel so far.

If he had qualms about my being human at first, I haven't caught anything that would make me think they've lingered. The fae put so much trust in the Heart and what it creates.

It'd be easier if I just accepted whatever blessing it's supposedly given us too, wouldn't it?

A castle of pale gray stone comes into view up ahead, and the carriage slows. I pull myself straighter, grateful to be distracted from the direction my thoughts were heading in. As Corwin directs the carriage to land on the outskirts of the sprawl of stone houses that arcs around the castle, Harper stands up to join me.

A few fae come over to greet us. Corwin hovers his hand just over my shoulder, careful as he always is not to touch me. "I've brought a couple of guests to see the painted forest. They've never gotten to experience it before."

The woman at the front of the small group beams. "I hope you enjoy our work, then. I'll let our lord know you've come by in case he wants to join you, Arch-Lord Corwin."

They all dip into a bow and head back. Corwin motions for us to follow him toward a stretch of small, pale trees farther across the icy ground. I can't see anything about them that looks painted or particularly impressive.

Patience. We're not quite there yet, Corwin says with a fondness that feels almost like a caress.

A narrow path has been cleared amid the trees and the frost-tinged bushes. A delicate scent, like what candied pine needles might smell like, tickles my nose. We walk for about five minutes, Harper sticking close by my side. Then the smaller trees thin and disappear completely to make room for a stretch of taller ones that extend their high, spindly branches toward the sky.

The trunks of those trees hold a riot of color. As I step closer, my breath catches, understanding now why this is called the painted forest—and why the woman mentioned their "work."

From the roots to where the branches sprout high above my head, paint covers every inch of the smooth bark with a vast assortment of scenes. One tree shows some kind of festival taking place all across a castle's grounds. Another depicts fae battling magical beasts while others tend to the wounded. I stop at one on which the winter fae have taken to the skies, some in raven form, some men and women with only their wings extended, soaring here and there amid the clouds and other flying creatures. The strokes of paint nearly bring the movement to life.

"Wow!" Harper murmurs, gaping at a neighboring tree. "This pa—I mean, this flock, they painted all of this?"

"It's been a tradition going back centuries," Corwin said. "They consider it an honor when the flock decides someone is ready to claim their tree. But you haven't seen the best of it yet."

I cock my head at him. "What do you mean?" *It's spectacular already*, I add silently. *Thank you for showing me this.*

He flashes what might be the first full grin I've seen from him. "All we need is the wind to rise—you'll see." *And you'll thank me even more then, I promise.*

I step back, peering up at the branches, and just then a breeze ripples through them. A glinting dust, fine and pale as sugar crystals, shimmers down from the branches. I follow its fall—and lose my breath all over away beneath a rush of wonder.

The paintings *really* move. As the powder blown from the branches glides past the images, the figures come to life. The flying birds and fae swoop past each other, spin, and glide. I even make out faces shifting with exhilaration and laughter. On the next tree over, fae children scramble along a mountainside, leaping and sliding.

I glance from one trunk to the next, my jaw gone slack, my chest full of amazement. The impulse rises in me to jump and whirl alongside the painted figures, as if I can join in their magic. As if I wouldn't stumble after a few steps if I attempted to be so graceful on my warped foot.

That's all right. It's enough just to watch.

Corwin's voice travels into my mind laced with unmistakable delight. *That's the reaction I was hoping for.*

The powder wisps away. The air has gone still again. I step back to take in more of the trees. "How often does that happen?"

"The breeze is never totally still for long. Take your fill."

When the air stirs the branches again, I drift between the trees, wanting to glimpse every scene in the extensive collection. I'm not sure I've seen even half of the wonders this place holds when footsteps rasp along the path toward us.

"Arch-Lord Corwin?" a fae man says, dipping low. "My lord wishes to speak with you on a somewhat grave matter. There's been—"

Glancing back at Corwin, I watch him raise his hand to cut off the rest of the man's sentence. The happiness in his expression is already fading, an uneasy chill rippling from him into me. A second later, my sense of him falls away. He's put up a partial wall, muting almost all of my awareness of his inner state.

"I understand," he says to the man. As I tense, he catches my gaze with an apologetic grimace. "I'm sorry. Matters of politics. You'll be safe here. You can continue exploring until I can return, or make your way back to the castle when you're ready and the flock will ensure you're comfortable."

"If there's any way I can help…" I have to offer.

He shakes his head. "With luck, I won't be gone too long. Don't let this ruin your enjoyment of the forest."

His closing off and his departure kind of does, though. Harper and I meander among the trees through a few more dust-falls, and each painted scene provokes a fresh wave of awe, but my stomach stays knotted.

What was the man going to say that Corwin didn't want me to hear? What's going on inside the Unseelie arch-lord that he's decided to keep me shut out after all his work to gain my trust?

I shouldn't be wandering around gaping at pretty pictures, no matter how magical, if something important is happening here.

Harper is alert enough to pick up on my mood. "Time to go back?"

"Yeah. I want to know what this 'somewhat grave matter' is."

I'd have considered sneaking into the castle if I thought I'd have much of a chance at eavesdropping on whatever is so secret. But when we've reached the edge of the village, I spot Corwin just emerging, an older fae man in fine clothes who I'm guessing is the local lord walking beside him, his posture downcast.

I slip between the buildings as stealthily as my limp allows, Harper trailing behind me.

"I just didn't expect—it's the second one this year," the lord is saying in a rough voice. "Has there been any progress at all?"

"We at the Heart are doing everything we can," Corwin says, and then, to my frustration, the fae woman who greeted us comes bustling over to escort me the rest of the way to him.

As soon as the arch-lord sees Harper and me, the conversation dies. He turns to the lord, his mouth slanting at a painful angle. I might not have much sense of him through our bond right now, but his sadness at whatever the situation is rings through every word. "You have my promise I'll pursue every avenue until we come to a solution."

I hold my tongue until we've clambered back onto the carriage. "A solution to what?"

Corwin looks at me, the sadness I heard before etched all over his face. "It's a private matter. If there *is* anything you can do at any point, I will let you know."

"Okay," I say, believing him, but that's not enough to stop the lump from rising in my throat.

We're bound as tightly as any two souls can be, and yet there's still so much distance between us.

Talia

At first, I'm not sure what's woken me. I jolt into consciousness tangled in the sheets on my bed with a vague sense of dread creeping through me but no memory of any dream that stirred it up.

I'm no stranger to night wakings. It's been weeks since my last nightmare of my time in Aerik's cage, but those haunted my sleep for a long time after Sylas and his cadre rescued me.

My first thought is that the old torments have followed me here in a vaguer form. I try to shake off the uneasiness and press my head back into the pillow, but the dread gets stronger instead, swelling inside me into a sharper horror.

As I sit up, hugging my knees, my mind wakes up enough for me to realize the impressions aren't my own. The disturbed emotions are washing into me through the soul-twined bond. Corwin is the one feeling that dread and horror.

Images dart through my head, washed up by his anguish: figures I don't recognize, their skin pale and eyes staring glassily, their mouths contorted in obvious pain. My stomach lurches. The faces—the corpses?—fade in and out of a darkness that winds suffocating around both them and the awareness seeping into me from Corwin. No conscious thought comes with the images, no understanding that I'm seeing this too.

Corwin? I think at him. *Are you all right?*

He doesn't answer. The horror takes on a deeper chill even as the images waver. *He* must be dreaming—dreaming some gruesome nightmare that he isn't waking up from.

Corwin! I shout at him inwardly as "loudly" as I can pitch my inner voice, but nothing changes.

I shiver, gathering my imagined light to rebuild the barrier between us. As the images dull, guilt fills my chest instead. I've pushed the horrors away, but my efforts have done nothing for him. He's caught up in all that awfulness —how long will the dream go on?

All those times Sylas came to break me out of nightmares… He offered me that kindness before we were really anything to each other. Am I going to ignore my soul-twined mate's distress? I don't like the idea of Corwin tossing and turning while those horrible images haunt him.

I hesitate for a few moments longer and then shove myself out of bed.

I don't remember exactly which doorway leads to

Corwin's bedroom, but when I let the wall of light thin, it's easy to follow our connection to him. My sense of him tugs at me, leading me down the hall and to a door. I knock on it, and then, when there's no answer, twist the knob. It opens easily.

The room on the other side is dark. The sound of Corwin's breath reaches me, soft but ragged. The blankets shift with a jerk of his limbs. A jab of agony shoots through our bond despite my glowing barrier, and my own breath catches in my throat.

"Corwin," I say out loud. "Wake up."

He's wrapped so deeply in the nightmare that my voice isn't enough to shatter its spell. I limp barefoot across the floor to the bed. He's right by the edge of the mattress closest to me. The scent of him, cool and piney as a snowy forest night, fills my lungs.

Bracing myself in case he startles, I grasp his shoulder through the blanket. "*Corwin.*"

The arch-lord flinches. My vision has adjusted enough to the darkness for me to see his eyes pop open. He stares at me, another raspy breath hitching through him. His voice comes out hoarse. "Talia?"

"You were having a nightmare," I say quickly. "I didn't —I didn't want to leave you in it."

A mix of relief, shame, and gratitude hit me in the instant before he resurrects his own walls. He sits up gingerly, the covers falling to his waist. I can only make out the faintest shapes of the true name tattoos that mark his dark skin all across his chest and arms. His tone turns stiff. "Thank you. I'm sorry I disturbed your sleep."

"It's all right. I know what it's like—getting caught up

in nightmares." I hesitate, biting my lip, part of me wanting to flee back to my bedroom and the rest caught in a tangle of concern and curiosity. "You were dreaming about people… who died? Did that really happen?"

I think they were Unseelie. From what I remember of the fleeting glimpses, they all had at least somewhat pointed ears, so they were definitely fae, and I can't imagine Corwin being brought to nightmares over the deaths of the Seelie, even if he isn't exactly in favor of the attacks on them either. There wasn't any blood or obvious injuries in the dream, though. If those images were based on memories, what *did* happen to them?

Corwin swipes his hand across his face. "You know from your Arch-Lord Sylas that sometimes one has to make decisions where there is no happy answer. Some of my regrets come to me in human form. It's nothing you should trouble yourself with."

I think he's implying that the people in his dream weren't real, only representations of his emotions, but he's using that tricksy fae phrasing that avoids the subject without saying anything direct enough to be a lie. Whatever the nightmare was about, he clearly doesn't want to talk to me about it.

I pull back instinctively, meaning to go, but with the same movement my gaze falls to his hand. It's clenched against the pale blanket—his whole arm is tensed, the lean muscles taut from wrist to shoulder, tightly enough that it's obvious even in the darkness.

He may not want to tell me about the nightmare, but it's still troubling him—a lot.

Without any conscious thought, driven by the pang of

compassion that rings through me and the impression of closeness that hasn't totally faded even with our bond now walled off, I reach for him. My fingers graze his forearm—and sensations explode through my entire being.

It's ten times as intense as when he touched me in our shared dream. In that first instant, all barriers between us are blasted away. I see myself through Corwin's eyes, standing before the faint line of light around the ajar door, as clearly as I see his form on the bed through mine. I feel the lurch of his pulse, somehow both ecstatic and panicked at the abrupt intimacy, the claws of anguish still gripping his lungs tightly, the tension wound all through his body as he fights the conflicting urges to either bury all that emotion as deep as he can or to offer it up to me.

There's awe in him too, swelling through me as it expands in his chest—that I risked this physical contact after avoiding it for so long—that I risked it out of concern for him. It wells up inside me so swiftly and completely I almost choke on it.

I don't know what to do with that much emotion from him. I don't know how to answer it—

He reins it in. The effort it takes washes through me, but as it does the sensations dwindle. They're not gone completely, but it's as if the volume has been turned from blaring to a murmur.

I'm stripped bare, every nerve trembling. I can't seem to summon one particle of light to shore up my own defenses.

How much did he see in *me*? Have I given away—no, I can't think about anything I wouldn't want him to know—is he still seeing—?

My hand has slid to his wrist. I'm clutching him, and maybe it's our physical connection that's stopped the soul bond from being sealed completely. I can't quite will my fingers to loosen, though. Beneath the cacophony of all the impressions and emotions still whirling through me, a note peals out as clear as one plucked from the strings of Corwin's harp.

We're meant to be twined like this. The Heart bound our souls together, and as confusing as the experience is, something about it is perfectly *right*.

I close my eyes, mentally shaking that thought away. I only feel like that *because* of the bond. It's still my choice —the Heart doesn't get to dictate my life without any say from me.

Carefully, Corwin rests his hand over mine. When I look at him, his dark irises stand out against the whites of his eyes, intent on me. "Thank you," he says again, and this time his gratitude sweeps through me with the words. "I know it's been hard, trying to navigate the bond. I had no idea exactly how it would feel either. Perhaps I've kept you at more of a distance than I should have when I've wanted you to open up to me. Given my position…"

He trails off as if he isn't sure how to finish that sentence. But I understand. He's keeping things from me for the exact same reason I'm keeping things from him— because of our other alliances, because of conflicts we have no way of settling on our own, no matter how generous we are with each other.

Whether or not we accept this bond is our choice, but the tensions between his people and mine go far beyond that.

I'm pretty sure I already know the answer, but I find I need to hear it from his own lips, when I know he won't lie and when the connection between us hums so powerfully I'll even feel the truth of it within me. "You want me to accept the bond, to stay with you—is it only because you don't want to defy the Heart and you think it'll help stop the fighting? For the greater good?"

His gaze doesn't leave my face. The affection that emanated from him during our trip tingles through my chest, along with the unfurling of a more potent longing. Ever so tentatively, his thumb traces a line across my knuckles, sparking a quiver of sensation I'm afraid to focus too closely on.

"No," he says. "I have plenty of more selfish reasons too. You are… nothing I would have expected from any partner, and many things I wouldn't have let myself want. Things I'd like to have in my life." He swallows audibly. "I think I've managed to put aside any resentment toward your Seelie men, but I won't deny I still envy the bonds they've been able to build with you. I don't know how I can offer you what they have when our situation is so complex. But I will try, as long as you'll let me. I think I could be a good partner to you too."

That should be all I need to hear. To know he values me as a person, that he wants to build that kind of trust and devotion between us—and maybe it *would* be enough if I didn't have those other men in my life.

But I do have them, and as much as my heart thumps with the urge to embrace Corwin and throw myself into this fate I didn't ask for, it also aches from going without the love I already found.

I don't have to say any of that. Corwin must pick up on my inner turmoil through the bond.

He raises his hand to graze my cheek. "I don't blame you for being uncertain. I won't blame you if you choose them. The fact that you care for them so much is part of what I admire about you. I handled some things very badly when you first arrived here, and I still regret all of that. I am... honored that nevertheless my well-being matters enough to you that you came to help me tonight, that you haven't rejected me outright."

The hope that comes with those words ripples between my ribs into a blossoming of warmth. How can I *not* care when he speaks to me like that?

His fingertips linger against my skin so softly his touch feels like a breath, and I taste the impulse he's reining in, to lean across the short distance between us and kiss me. Heat spreads through my lips. The bond winds through me, tugging at my heart even more urgently.

Corwin simply watches me. If I went to leave now, he'd let me go.

I don't want to leave.

Whitt's reassurances rise up in the back of my head. He expected me to find out what I can make of this bond —all three of my Seelie men did. They knew how powerful it would be, how many urges it would provoke. How can I decide what's best when I'm holding myself back from experiencing so much of it?

I step closer and tip my head to bring my mouth to Corwin's.

It's only the lightest of kisses, a brushing of our lips, but the electric shock of the intimacy surges right through to my bones. The firm heat of his mouth melds with his awareness of the softness and sweetness of mine. Joy and pleasure crackle between us as if on a constant circuit.

Before I'm even aware of my intention, I'm pressing my lips even harder against his, absorbing the rush of sensation. Every part of me is lighting up with the sizzle of desire that only seems to grow as it races between us. I want—I want—If a simple *kiss* can feel this good—

The hunger dizzies me, overwhelms me—frightens me. All at once, I'm drowning in this wave rather than being carried aloft on it.

I wrench myself backward with a gasp, my skin still scorching, my body trembling. Corwin looks rather unsteady himself.

"I—I can't," I manage to stammer. "It's too much."

"I know," he says raggedly. "It's okay." The bliss he felt in the moment thrums into me, but his inner voice is tender carried with it. *Take whatever time and space you need. Just know that I'm in this with you, whatever you need from me. We'll find the path that's right.*

I want to believe that, but it's hard to even breathe with the memory of that kiss blaring through my mind. I take another step back, my wall of light coming to me easier now that I'm not touching him at all anymore. "I think—I should get some more sleep."

He nods without any hint of frustration, but as I flee into the hall, I can't shake the feeling that I'm somehow betraying him *and* my lovers back in the summer realm—and maybe even myself as well.

Talia

Breakfast is a relatively simple affair: hardboiled eggs and fresh-baked rolls, fluffier and fatter than August usually makes them, with cream, peach-like jam, and honey straight off the comb to spread on them. Corwin notices how much I'm loving the honey and offers another chunk of comb to me, and I find myself blushing as I hold out my plate to accept it.

I felt settled enough when I woke up this morning, but just being in his presence, being aware of him through the only partly walled-off bond, has put me off-balance all over again. My gaze keeps snagging on his lips with a tingling through mine when I remember our kiss.

He doesn't show any sign that he's noticed what I'm thinking about, but I can't believe he hasn't picked up on it at least a little. Every now and then a similarly eager warmth filters from him into me.

Like right now, as I bite into the roll I've just drizzled honey on.

My cheeks heat again, but I'm distracted from my embarrassment by Harper shifting on her chair. When she notices my attention on her, she shoots me a quick smile, but a moment later she's winding a few strands of her hair around her finger. She's not usually this fidgety. It reminds me of how she acted when Ambrose's pack-kin were cajoling and intimidating her.

One of the servants appears in the doorway just then. "My lord, Olander has arrived and is asking to speak with you when you're able to."

Corwin wipes his fingers on his napkin and looks at his empty plate. "That's all right. I'm done here—I'll come now." He glances at me. "Olander's from my coterie, but it may not take long. You can wait for me here—I'll let you know my plans as soon as I find out what this is about."

I nod, and he leaves. Harper tears the rest of her current bun into little chunks. Watching her, I swallow my current mouthful and ask, "Not all that hungry this morning?"

She gives a little twitch as if shaking herself. "Sorry. I just—I didn't sleep all that well."

She hesitates, and I give her a closer look. "If there's something else bothering you, please tell me."

"I just don't want to make it sound like something's wrong when things have started to go well for you." She rubs her mouth, her gaze darting around nervously.

I summon more of my inner light to make sure Corwin won't accidentally overhear what Harper has to say. "Go ahead. I can't make a real decision if there are things I don't know."

"Okay." She drops her voice lower. "I—I woke up early this morning and couldn't get back to sleep. It's just so different from back home. Anyway, I went out and wandered a little, and I ended up back by that spot where we heard the strange noises before, the alcove where the door was locked. At first it was quiet, but then as I started to walk away, I thought I heard an actual *voice* from up there. Like a person's. Mumbling something—I couldn't make out the words—but it definitely sounded almost like talking. I've never heard of a spirit that could hold a conversation. It's usually just, like, a ball of energy, bumping against things."

She looks at me as if worried I'll be upset that she's mentioned it despite my reassurances. I don't know what to say. She's obviously unnerved by the experience, but—

"I haven't gotten the sense that Corwin would want to harm anyone," I say slowly. "Or that he has prisoners here, or anything like that. We haven't opened up to each other completely, but I don't think he could completely hide it if he was the kind of person who'd shut people away in so much pain they'd make sounds like the ones we heard before. Maybe someone went up there to try to settle down the spirit or… whatever you normally do when you have one that's restless?"

"I don't know. It was earlier than I've seen servants up before. Whoever it was sounded pretty miserable and out-of-sorts. And I waited a while afterward, and no one came out through the door." Harper shivers. "But it was only for a moment. Then everything went quiet again. Maybe I made it into something bigger in my memory."

That seems possible too when she's said she hadn't gotten enough sleep and was uneasy here in the winter realm in general. I don't want to discount her distress completely, though. She has a lot less reason to lie to me about anything upsetting going on here than Corwin does. I can't remember his exact wording when he talked about spirits, but it might have been vague enough to avoid giving the full story.

"I'll pay even closer attention when I'm talking with Corwin, watch for any sign that there's something we should be worried about going on. Maybe once we're more comfortable with each other, I can convince him to introduce us to this spirit, and we can see for ourselves what's in there."

"All right." Harper laughs softly. "I'd actually be interested to see one. I've only ever heard stories."

A prodding sensation inside me tells me Corwin is reaching out. I let the glow inside me thin. *Sorry, I'm listening now.*

I'm afraid I need to go down to the village to consult with folk of my flock on some matters today, he says in an apologetic tone. *I'm not sure exactly how long it'll take—at this point I'd imagine I'll be returning by lunch.*

That's okay. I know I'm not your only responsibility. Far from it. I hesitate, sucking my lower lip under my teeth, and then venture, *Could I come along? I'm finished with breakfast, and I'd like to see the village and meet more of your flock. I won't interfere with whatever business you need to do, just hang back and watch.*

There's a pause. My awareness of him dulls again as he must close off our connection to consult with his coterie man. My heart sinks with the assumption that he'll brush me off like he has every other time I've tried to find out more about his actual work as arch-lord, but when his voice returns, it's cautious but not resistant. *That's a reasonable request. I've sent my people to get everything ready for the meeting. Can you join me on the terrace so I can escort you down?*

A smile springs to my lips. *Yes, I'll be right there.* I don't imagine this will unravel any of Harper's mystery, but maybe today I'll learn a thing or two that'll help me understand the conflict between summer and winter.

Harper sends me off with a wave, looking more relaxed now that she's shared her anxieties, and I find Corwin waiting on the terrace as promised. A light snow is falling, glinting here and there when the thin sunlight catches it. The flakes brush my cheeks with a chill before the warming spell in my clothes rises up to melt them away.

The Unseelie arch-lord turns to meet me, and his wings unfurl from his back in the same moment. I halt in my tracks, a strange mix of awe and uncertainty spreading through my chest at the sight of him.

I'm only just getting used to appreciating the dark curls of his hair and those burgundy-brown eyes I've now seen soften just for me. The black feathered expanses stretching out on either side of him give his tall frame a grandeur I haven't witnessed since back when I considered him an enemy.

It's… it's kind of magnificent. And kind of scary, how hard it is not to gape in wonder.

I manage to regain control of my tongue. "I—do we need to fly down?"

Corwin's mouth tightens with a hint of apology. "There are paths along the cliff, but they'd take much longer. I can carry you so that our skin doesn't touch, if you want to avoid the intensity physical contact brings to the bond."

The intensity I embraced for at least a little while last night. But I don't want to end up too distracted by our connection to focus on the actual business he's going to be attending to—and being carried by him in flight is bound to be plenty distracting on its own.

I step closer, taking a deep breath. "That sounds like a plan."

He picks me up carefully, one arm around my back and the other beneath my thighs, and gives me time to adjust myself against him so I'm comfortable. If comfortable is even the right word for it. Even without skin-to-skin contact, every inch of me hums at his nearness, the heat of his body washing over me from his arms and his chest where I'm leaning against him. His wintry forest scent wraps around me.

I swallow hard, keeping my gaze low, nervous of looking into his eyes when our faces are so close together. "I'm ready."

We sway with the first swish of Corwin's wings lifting us off the ground. My pulse hitches, and I grasp his padded tunic. But with a few more flaps, the steadiness of the rhythm eases my nerves. It's only a gentle rocking as he picks up speed and then totally smooth as he soars down over the edge of the cliff toward the homes clinging to its face on either side of a glittering frozen waterfall.

The houses we glide past look almost like ice themselves, formed out of crystal just like Corwin's palace, though many in different hues from his colorless diamond. They all have a small terrace of their own jutting out where it'd be easy for anyone arriving by air to land. A few of the members of Corwin's flock raise their hand to him as we pass.

He lands lightly on a terrace about halfway down, right next to the torrent of ice. The frozen waterfall looks perfectly solid, but a faint trickling sound tells me at least a little actual water is tumbling down the cliffside behind that mass.

Corwin sets me down at once and studies me as I straighten my dress as if checking for signs of distress. I'm simply gathering my composure. When I look up, my balance sufficiently regained, I smile at him. "That was kind of fun."

One of the rare, warmer smiles I can't help treasuring crosses his lips. He retracts his wings and beckons for me to follow him into the house.

Two men and a woman are waiting in the room inside, the woman and one of the men sitting on stools of pale wood, the other man standing across from them. Aside from a few other chairs set against the walls, the circular space holds no other furniture. It must mainly be used for meetings like this.

As we step inside, Corwin's expression reforms into his usual solemn mask. He motions for me to take one of the chairs by the wall and introduces me with the same gesture. "This is Talia, a guest of mine of some importance. Talia, meet Olander and Zelpha of my coterie, and Mithron, one of my flock's most dedicated sentries. He's been stationed to travel along the fringe domains of our realm."

The three all dip their heads, more out of respect for their lord than for me, I'm sure. I wonder if anyone in his coterie knows why I'm really here, but I can't help being grateful that he isn't revealing my real role. I can't imagine what kind of stares I'd get over being introduced as his soul-twined mate. If I end up deciding to see the bond through, then I'll be willing to deal with whatever chaos ensues.

As I sit down, Corwin folds his arms over his chest, focusing on Mithron, a slight, sinewy-looking man with a jutting chin that could almost be a beak in itself. "As I understand it, you've come to report an increasing presence of hostile beasts in those fringe domains."

Mithron nods sharply. "Yes, my lord, and other domains as well. At first it was just a few extra reports of maulings and other attacks in the villages nearest to the edge of the Mists, but there've been more every week for the past month, and what prompted me to come immediately was several in the past few days from domains closer inward where the creatures never used to venture at all."

"What sort of beasts exactly are we talking about?"

"It hasn't been just one but a few different sorts. The most deaths have been from chimeras and searmaws, as you'd probably expect."

Corwin frowns. "And *those* have ventured farther inward as well?"

"Yes, my lord." The sentry grimaces. "The warriors of those flocks have been culling their numbers as well as they can, but with—with the reduced situation nearly every domain is finding itself in… it's more difficult to keep the beasts under control than it used to be."

His eyes dart to me for an instant. A prickle runs over my skin. Reduced situation—fewer warriors because of those who've died fighting the Seelie? It's hard for me to summon a lot of sympathy when they'd never have been "reduced" if they hadn't attacked my people in the first place.

"The lords I spoke to asked me to come to the arch-lords for guidance and any other aid they can offer," Mithron adds. "I thought it best to speak to you first."

"And I appreciate that." Corwin glances at his coterie members. "What have we heard from the rest of the realm?"

The man on his feet—Olander—is stouter than the sentry but with a robust sort of grace. He doesn't answer, pacing slowly from one end of the room to the other, his pale eyes distant with concentration.

The woman—Zelpha—leans her muscular frame back in her chair, her chestnut-brown face drawn with concern. "Similar reports have come back from other areas along the fringes, although not so urgent that anyone brought it to an arch-lord's attention yet. My best estimation would be that they're struggling more than they've admitted, not wanting to add to the troubles already keeping us busy."

Olander hums. "I looked through the records ahead of

reaching out to you. There hasn't been an incursion of beasts like this since several centuries ago, and even then it wasn't on this scale. They were quickly driven back after their sudden arrival."

Corwin exhales slowly. "All right. Let's go over the strategies the affected flocks are already implementing and what we might add to those."

While they hash out the details, I simply sit and listen like I promised I would. I can't follow everything they mention, terms I'm not familiar with popping up here and there, but I get the gist of it. Now and then, one of the three shoots a glance my way with a pause in a sentence or the overall conversation. Wondering why I'm even here if all I'm going to do is gawk at them, no doubt.

What do I know about vicious faerie beasts anyway? My thoughts slip back to the tuskcat that attacked me. Astrid killed it with a sharpened stick—Corwin has already discussed the weaponry the winter fae are using.

But the tuskcat had strayed beyond its usual territory too. In that case, it'd come because Ambrose's pack-kin had drawn it into Sylas's domain through magic. I doubt this huge influx of creatures into all sorts of domains would be happening on purpose, but maybe...

I open my mouth and then balk, not sure how to insert myself into the conversation. Instead, I tentatively reach out to Corwin through our bond. *Would it be okay if I mentioned something?*

At the next natural pause, he turns to me, as if it was his idea—since the others don't know I could have spoken to him silently. "Do you have anything you can make of this matter that we haven't already covered, Talia?"

I send a tendril of gratitude his way. "Yes. I—are there any fae who've mastered the true names for those creatures? If those people are spread out across the domains now, maybe bringing them together and having them tackle one area at a time would be helpful so there are enough to get the beasts under control. If there's no way to simply discourage the creatures, they could draw them into a trap or at least a situation where it'd be easier to hunt them…"

My throat closes up with the pressure of four sets of fae eyes now trained on me. "I mean, probably you've already considered all that."

"No," Corwin says. "It's a good point, making more of a combined force out of those efforts. Olander, find out who remains with the appropriate true names for one or another. They *have* always played a role we took for granted in maintaining the borderlands, but their numbers may well have dwindled. We might want to take a longer-term approach, see about training more fae to master those names." He runs his hand along his jaw.

From the rest of the conversation that follows, it doesn't sound as if I've come anywhere close to solving their problem, but then, I didn't expect to. I get the impression that I might have made some small difference, at least. Better than sitting here like a lump the entire time, not contributing anything.

Flying back up to Corwin's palace is easier, now that I know what to expect. I still don't look into his face while he's carrying me, but he gives me a chance to take in the view across the winter realm from an angle I've never seen before. The mountains look even more sublime when I'm viewing them from mid-air.

It seems a little too soon that we're landing on his terrace. The snow is starting to thicken, but I'm not quite ready to go inside. I brush the cold flakes from my hair and offer Corwin a hopeful smile. "It wasn't so bad having me along, was it? I didn't cramp your style?"

He chuckles. "No. I—I rather liked it." His eyes catch mine with a sudden intensity. His voice softens. "I'd like to think there could be many more meetings like that, with you playing an even larger role as you come to know my people better."

If I accepted him as my mate. Picturing it sends a giddy quiver through my chest, but memories stir at the same time: the happiness I felt when Sylas let me in on his discussions with his cadre for the first time. The plans we built together, the challenges we've overcome.

I can't say anymore that I don't want anything to do with this place. But I know down to the depths of my being that I can't give up the men I've come to love so much. This situation is just… impossible.

A spark lights in my head with an even giddier rush of sensation. Unless—

Corwin cocks his head. "What's made you look so pleased with yourself?"

"I just—" I almost falter and then gather my courage. I'm only here for a few more days. I *have* to say it sometime. Better if he has more of a chance to let the idea sink in.

"I just was thinking, maybe I could have that with you…

without having to lose everything else. I don't know exactly how it'd work, and I'm not even saying for sure I'd want to go through with the bond yet—I'm not ready to decide that— but if I did… A lord like Sylas wouldn't normally have gotten involved with a woman who has other lovers as well, but he was able to adjust to the idea, even to appreciate what it meant. If he and his cadre would agree, and you'd agree— maybe I wouldn't have to give up on *anyone*."

Corwin stares at me. A flicker of shock and something pained passes into me and then fades quickly as he walls off his emotions. The warmth that filled his expression a moment ago vanishes. "A lord sharing with his most trusted advisors is hardly on par with some sort of arrangement between fae of different realms—arch-lords no less—*my* soul-twined mate no less."

The wind whips over me, tossing my hair, but I don't let myself look away from him. "If there's no arrangement, then you might not end up with any soul-twined mate at all. I don't care what the Heart thinks it's doing. I was theirs first."

His voice goes even flatter. "It isn't even about me. *They* would never agree to it. They were barely willing to allow you out of their sight to come to me as it is."

"That's different. They had no idea what you're like. They were protecting me." I set my hands on my hips. "You won't know unless you ask them about it."

"I assure you, I don't need to." Corwin spins toward the door to the palace with a jerk. "Consider the matter put to rest. No good can come out of discussing it, only more distress for both of us."

Corwin

I can tell from the moment I step into the Hall of the Heart that I'm not going to enjoy this discussion with my fellow arch-lords. Of course, I was already fairly certain of that from the moment they summoned me out of my chambers before I'd even had a chance to *think* about breakfast. Especially considering we only just spoke yesterday afternoon concerning the growing issues with roaming beasts coming in from the fringelands.

None of my colleagues have bothered to sit. Laoni, Terisse, and Uzziah all eye me with chilly expressions as I take my spot at the polished marble table. Only Neve looks unperturbed, but these days the frail elderly fae woman occasionally seems not totally aware of what's going on around her, so that's no guarantee she's on my side. If her hazy periods start to overtake her lucid ones, I expect her son will demand she let him take over her post.

I might not have been prepared when this position was first thrust upon *me*, but I've had plenty of time to hone my approach since then. The best way to hold my own among my colleagues, who are all centuries older and more established than I am, is to maintain the coldest and most impenetrable of fronts myself.

I fold my arms over my chest and draw my spine as straight as it'll go, which brings me a couple of inches taller than even Laoni with her ample brawn. "What is so urgent we had to gather so soon after our last meeting? Has some catastrophe occurred?"

"I'd say so," Laoni bites out with a toss of her turquoise hair. She considers herself the highest authority of us all on the grounds that she's held her position the longest, although that's not so much due to an excess of competence as the fact that her father had her late in life and passed when she was not much older than I was at my own coronation. That fact hasn't given her any sympathy for my situation, though. If anything, it's the opposite.

She continues in a brittle voice. "It's come to our attention that the Seelie woman you brought to your palace, the one you claim is your soul-twined mate, isn't Seelie at all. She's *human*."

Ah. I hadn't seen any need to inform my colleagues of that development until I was sure Talia would be remaining among us for a longer period. Mainly because I expected the news would be received with exactly the reaction I'm facing right now. One of the fae who observed us on our brief travels must have been gossipy enough for the fact to make it back to another arch-lord.

"I didn't consider the information immediately

relevant," I reply, reining in a flicker of annoyance and keeping my own voice perfectly even. "Either way, she has ties to the Seelie. Either way, the Heart's choice is unexpected."

Uzziah sputters, sending a ripple through the doughy flesh of his dour face, which sags as if gravity weighs on it harder than it does the average fae. "Unexpected? It's a travesty. It must be some mad trick of the wolves, making you hallucinate a connection. The Heart would never—"

"It has," I cut in. "I'm not some fledgling who'd be distracted by shiny tokens. I've been inside her mind and she in mine. We shared dreams before we even spoke in person. Do you know of any possible spell that could create such a bond?"

He doesn't, clearly, because all he does is glower at me in answer.

Laoni shakes her head. "It doesn't matter whether it's a true bond or not. You can't accept it. If it had been a true-blooded Seelie, we might have used that for leverage. Even a mostly dilute fae wouldn't do us much good, let alone some human who was likely no more than a servant as it was."

As if the only possible use of me having a soul-twined mate is to help us negotiate for our ends. Anger stirs in the pit of my chest. I have reason to believe that Talia could be the solution to our people's hardships beyond anything we'd even dared to hope for—but my oaths prevent me from saying anything about that to the four around me. I still haven't even risked saying anything to *Talia* for fear of the consequences if she tells her Seelie arch-lord what we've faced.

My mate wouldn't use our vulnerabilities against us. I've seen enough to know she's far too honorable for that. But the Seelie—no matter how much *she* trusts them, no matter how kind they've been to her—it's not for nothing that they shift into wolves. They can be as vicious as the beasts we need to push back to the edges of the Mists. And I can't see any reason that their hearts would soften for any of us in the winter realm.

I inhale slowly to steady my temper. "I can hardly dismiss her and ask the Heart for a different mate. She's the one it's seen fit to give me."

Terisse scoffs. "Better a regular mate than to be soul-twined to a dust-destined mortal. You can't seriously be considering binding yourself to that flimsy thing permanently, bringing it into your confidence—"

"*She* is a perfectly capable being in her own right." I cast my gaze around the table, more anger rising. "How thorough a vetting did each of you give *your* soul-twined mates before accepting them? What tests did they have to pass to prove themselves worthy? Or did you simply follow the bond because clearly it was what the Heart offered you?"

"When it's one of our own kind, there's no reason to be so concerned," Uzziah retorts. "It's hardly the same situation."

"I think it is. The question is what the Heart wills, and the Heart wills that I should be bound to this woman." I wave my hand in the direction of the glowing mass that sends its thrumming energy over us even as I speak. "Would you defy the very source of all our power?"

Laoni hums to herself with a patronizing air that sets

all my nerves on edge. "The Heart's first will is that we serve our people as well as we can. But perhaps you are letting sentimentality dictate your thoughts rather than logic. From the looks of it, you've already grown attached to this human girl. Taking her on romantic trips across the realm? Hiding her true nature from the rest of us?"

As well as I can, I resist the urge to bristle, which becomes even harder when Terisse makes a tsking sound. "It wouldn't be the first time in your family that emotions led one astray from one's duties to—"

"I'm fully aware of my duties," I interrupt, not quite a snap but with enough of an edge that I wince inwardly. The three who've been berating me look at me almost pityingly, as if I've proven their point and myself incompetent with that minor lapse. Even Neve studies me with a vaguely sad slant to her mouth.

And into that moment, Talia's voice reaches me. It's barely more than a whisper through the imagined crystalline wall I've conjured inside me to shield her from this discussion, but she's compelling her voice forcefully enough for it to filter through. *Corwin, is everything all right? You feel... upset.*

Dust and doom. I can't imagine how much more than "upset" the emotions she sensed must have been for them to have reached her at all and for her to feel she needed to reach out. I clench my jaw, about to tell her everything is fine, but the gazes still fixed on me with their accusations and their disdain make me hesitate.

Whatever they say, she isn't fragile. Not so fragile that hearing them talk about her as if she is would damage her. If she's going to make an honest choice about her future, she deserves to know at least this much of what she's walking into, doesn't she?

She deserves a mate who'll treat her like she has a real place here.

My fellow arch-lords have discovered that you're not quite the Seelie lady they assumed, I say, letting my inner wall drop. *I'm failing to appreciate their advice on the matter.* Then, squaring my shoulders, I address the figures before me. "My soul-twined mate is witnessing this meeting through me now. If you're going to disrespect the bond the Heart gifted us with, you may as well do it in the face of that bond."

Talia stays silent, but I can sense her awareness within me, taking in the room through my eyes with a prickle of irritation I know is directed at my colleagues rather than me. Terisse has stiffened.

Laoni's face goes absolutely rigid, as does her voice. "Allowing any other party access to the private meetings of this quintet is highly irregular."

"Challenging a soul-twined bond is highly irregular," I reply. "Can any of you honestly claim before the Heart that you've never shared aspects of our conversations here with your own mates?"

The silence that follows is answer enough. "That's hardly the same either," Uzziah begins.

I fix my sternest look on him. "It's *exactly* the same. She is my soul-twined mate as determined by the Heart, and no words you throw around can diminish that fact."

Laoni aims an icy scowl at me and steps back from the table. "You've heard our opinion on the matter. I expect you to think it over—and consider what is truly best for the people you've sworn to serve."

Oh, I already have. She hasn't the faintest idea.

The other arch-lords stride away from the table without so much as a farewell. I turn too, an odd rush of exhilaration sweeping through me even though beneath it my gut has tightened.

I've given them more ammunition for their stockpile against me, their justifications for never taking my views into as full an account as each other's. But I find I can't regret that. What I said needed to be said, or I might as well roll over in a much larger and more permanent way.

If I lose Talia, it'll be because *she* refused me, not because I let those sneering bastards dictate the terms of my life.

Talia's voice carries to me with a wry but tentative question. *I guess I broke up the party?*

Not your fault. They had a little taste of their own hypocrisy and found it unpalatable. I apologize for disturbing you.

No, it was fine. I… I like it better when you let me see what's going on with you. She pauses, and through my impressions of her I gather she's leaving her bedroom, already dressed. The emotions that seep through our bond are such a twisted mix of contrasting shades that I have trouble picking any one apart from the mass. *Are you coming back now? It smells like breakfast is just about ready.*

Yes. I'll see you in the dining room.

It doesn't occur to me to pay attention to her making her way there. I'm focused enough on my own surroundings, crossing the snow-clad plain between the

Hall of the Heart and my palace, that I'm taken completely by surprise when I stalk past the front door and find Talia in the entrance room waiting for me.

I stop in my tracks. She smiles a little shyly, and the hints of affection that shimmer through our bond make me even more uncertain on my feet. For a moment, all I can think of is the kiss we shared two nights ago, the delicate warmth of her breath and the subtle strength wound all through her body, the pleasure I managed to summon in her alongside my own—

As she steps toward me, I tamp down on those thoughts, hard as it is with that luminous face and those bright green eyes before me. She's chosen the same pale-pearl dress she wore when she arrived here, and though she looked a tad uncomfortable in it then, now she moves amid the folds of gleaming fabric as if it's a part of her. The only detail stopping her from looking like the loveliest of Unseelie ladies is the rounded tops of her ears, mostly hidden by the fall of her vibrant hair.

In that moment, I truly don't care about that detail one bit. This is my mate. And she *is* lovely, in much more than just her appearance.

She ducks her head. "I know they're giving you a hard time because of me. I—I just wanted to say thank you. For what you told them. For standing up for me."

As if she should be grateful rather than expecting it. I summon whatever reassurance I can gather to offer through the bond. "Of course. It had to be said. I may very well need to say it again many times."

"Thank you in advance for all those times too, then." She takes another step, bringing her close enough that she can slip her arms around me and lean her head against my chest.

My heart stutters, and the rest of me freezes up. I want *so much*—it's dizzying, like dropping into a freefall and finding you can't flex your wings. My colleagues' insinuations are still ringing in my head, and the memories of sobs and wails, and—

I close my eyes, and other memories that aren't mine drift through our connection: Talia's arms embracing other men who hugged her back with enthusiastic tenderness. Who didn't stand there rigid as a boulder the way I'm doing right now.

A stab of panic—that I'm failing, falling short—splits through all the other turmoil inside me, and I force myself to move. To relax into her hold. To ease my own arms around her and pull her just a little closer to me.

Talia squeezes me tighter, with a pang of affection that seems to match what's echoing through her memories. For all the envy in me that those men feature so large in her life, it's also an honor to find I might have a spot alongside them, however precarious it might be.

I don't know how to say any of that aloud, so I let as much of the feeling as I can coherently convey pass from me to her.

Is this sentimentality? Am I proving my fellow arch-lords right that I'm following my heart over my mind?

All I know is that this moment feels perfectly right. *Talia* is right, for me and for the people I serve.

Heart help me manage to convince her of that too.

Talia

I've just gotten out of the bath. The room around me is hazy with steam, and what I can see of it doesn't make much sense. These vibrant tiles on the floor belong to the sauna back in Hearthshire, but the crystalline walls are all Heart's Cadence.

I reach for my towel, and somehow Corwin is there, handing it to me. Looking at me, standing naked in front of him. A flare of heat courses through our bond and sparks something sharp and dizzying in me.

He's nearly naked too, a towel of his own wrapped around his lean hips, so much sleek, sculpted muscle on display above and below it. His eyes smolder as they meet mine.

Desire ricochets between us, winding through my chest, summoning a throbbing between my legs. Every pulse of it tugs me toward him. *Mine. Mine. My mate.* The call of it clangs so loudly I can hardly think.

"Talia," Corwin rasps, looking just as overwhelmed, a wildness in his expression I've never seen before. My pulse hitches harder, as if propelling me into him—and then our mouths have collided, his hard and hot against mine. His fingers tangle in my damp hair, his other hand tracing the curve of my waist and yanking me against him.

Yes. Every particle in my body cries out in eager relief, as if I've been waiting for this moment for years. His skin sears against mine, but it doesn't feel like enough. I ache to melt right into him, to merge with him bodily as thoroughly as our souls are twined. A matching longing careens from him into me.

I kiss him with all that pent-up hunger, and he groans against my lips. *Talia,* he murmurs through the bond. *Talia.* As if there's no room left in his mind for anything but me. He tips my head to kiss me even more deeply, cupping my breast at the same time. The swivel of his thumb over my nipple sends a jolt of pleasure through me that leaves me whimpering.

My hips grind against him with a mind of their own. That heated friction does nothing but intensify the ache in my core. I *need* him, need to be joined with him, to carry out our bond in every possible way—

Yes, he mutters, his tongue delving between my lips to stroke over mine. *Yes, all of you, now. Mine.* The words are barely coherent, but the same thoughts whirl in my head.

His hand slides to my bottom and he hefts me up against him, bracing me against a wall that's suddenly right behind me. The bulge beneath the towel presses between my legs, and I almost sob with the demand for release. I grasp at him, kissing him frantically, running my fingers over every inch of taut muscle they can reach, pulling him closer. My hips rock against him in a motion that's nothing short of begging.

The towel drops. The inferno of longing and lust spiraling between us burns hotter as his rigid length rubs against my most sensitive spot. I gasp, clutching him. With a groan, he lines himself up and plunges in to meet the place where I need him the most—

And I jerk awake, my heart racing, the sheet that's twisted around me damp with sweat. I'm in my bedroom, enveloped in darkness.

It was a dream. Just a dream.

But the feelings weren't imaginary, not entirely anyway. I squirm, and my hardened nipples graze the fabric over them with blissful quivers. My skin still feels hot enough to scorch my nightgown, and a torturous pang reverberates up from my core.

Not just from *my* core either. The heat that's flooding me tastes of Corwin too.

As my mind wakes up more, I sense him on the other end of our connection in his own bed, his body aflame with unfulfilled desire, his rigid erection pressing against the covers.

I can't help remembering what it felt like to have that length filling me for the instant before I woke up. Another peal of need quakes through me. Corwin's stutter of breath reaches me from the inside out—and then his hand dives beneath the blanket to curl around his hardness.

Oh. A real gasp falls from my lips at the surge of pleasure that gesture brings him—and me through him. He slides his hand up and down his length, spreading the liquid that's already formed at the tip, and the spot between my own legs grows even slicker than it already was from the dream.

Spurred on by my response, he picks up his pace, imagining the tight wet heat he thrust into in that imaginary sauna of the dream. The taste of my skin. The feel of my body against him and around him.

A breath shudders out of me. So much tension swells through me I think I'm going to explode. I shove my arm under the sheets and curl my fingers against my sex.

That first touch comes with a shock of relief and headier hunger—and a bolt of urgent lust that shoots straight to my core from Corwin. Clamping my teeth against a moan, grateful that the diamond walls in this palace are solid enough to dull any sounds that might escape me, I rock the heel of my hand against the tender nub that's aching for contact.

Oh, God, it feels so good. The blazing pleasure builds with each stroke of Corwin's hand over his hardness. I echo that bliss with the rhythm of my fingers now pushing right inside me.

It isn't enough, I'm not nearly filled, but I match his pace as closely as I can. My hips arch up, my whole body straining toward its peak.

The ecstasy flowing between us flares hotter and brighter with every electric jolt flowing between us. Corwin grips himself harder, and I work my hand against my sex faster.

With one final flare, we shatter together into giddying burst of sensation. A rush of shooting stars whites out my vision behind my closed eyelids and crashes through the rest of me, leaving me boneless.

I slump into the mattress, my fingers wet with my spent arousal and my nerves still tingling. My sense of Corwin dims. In the wake of our release, exhaustion rolls over me, and I tumble back into a sleep that's deep and dreamless.

When I wake up to morning sunlight, it takes me a moment to remember why my fingers are faintly sticky. A flush burns my cheeks. I scramble out of bed and clean up as quickly as I can at the wash basin.

As I get dressed, a twinge of guilt settles in my gut. I didn't *actually* do anything with Corwin. I had no control over the dream, and afterward… I'm not sure I could have fought the pull of desire through our bond no matter how hard I tried. Not once in there did I really touch him.

But the act we shared still feels incredibly intimate. Farther than I'd ever have wanted to take our relationship when I'm not even sure how much of a relationship we're going to have.

My men back home wouldn't blame me. I know they were prepared that our connection might be so strong I'd literally have sex with Corwin—consummate the bond, leave them behind for good. They wouldn't say I've betrayed them. But I can't quite shake the guilt.

Squashing it down as far as it'll go, I test my current sense of the Unseelie arch-lord. I'm vaguely aware of his existence—I think he's still here in the palace—but nothing comes through quite strongly enough for me to be sure of exactly where or what he's doing. I don't pick up anything particularly intense in his mood, so maybe he's taken this whole thing in stride? He might even have expected something like that to happen.

Is he going to want to *discuss* what we did? Even more heat floods my face. I swipe my hands across my cheeks and take my time lacing my braced boot around my warped foot, waiting for my emotions to even out.

By the time I step out into the hall, I don't think anything odd is showing on my face. Harper emerges at the click of my door, and she doesn't react to my expression. Of course, she looks kind of distracted herself.

"One more day," she murmurs, rubbing her arms as we head down the hall toward the small dining room. "I can't wait…" She trails off as if realizing I might not be feeling the same way she is about our impending return and glances at me more carefully. "Do you know what you're going to do?"

That's the big question, isn't it? I grimace, my stomach clenching for a totally different reason. "No. It's so complicated. And there's so much I still don't know." How can I decide when I'm not even sure why the Unseelie have been attacking the summer realm, whether Corwin agrees with that conflict or not? I have to convince him that he can trust me, to open up to me—there must be *something* more he can tell me that wouldn't betray his other loyalties.

But I can understand why he has to be cautious with that kind of information. He knows *my* loyalties are still mainly with the Seelie. Argh, it's such a mess.

"I'm not definitely refusing the bond," I add. "It seems like that would be kind of dangerous anyway. But I'm not ready to stay here either, and everyone back home still needs me to help with the curse. I guess I'll see how I feel once I'm back in the summer realm." Maybe I just need to spend more time going back and forth, getting to know Corwin as quickly as he'll let me.

I study Harper. "It's okay that you're looking forward to getting home, though. I think if I make another trip here, I'd be comfortable enough to come alone."

She shivers, but her jaw clenches defiantly. "No, I wouldn't want you to be stuck here with just the ravens around. I still don't know if even this palace is safe." She hesitates. "I went back to that alcove by the locked door again, earlier in the morning. I didn't hear any noises, but I did see a servant coming out with a meal tray. With a proper plate and goblet and everything—dirty like they'd been used. A spirit *definitely* wouldn't be eating regular meals."

A quiver of uneasiness winds around my lungs. "No. That does sound odd." And there was that time when I helped in the kitchen making dinner—Corwin got a bit awkward when a servant came in carrying a tray. Maybe it wasn't just because he was startled that he put up his guard, but something to do with who had eaten that meal. I frown. "I'll ask Corwin about it and see if I can figure anything out."

When we step into the dining room, the arch-lord is already there. He's holding a couple of empty goblets and appears to be debating the exact configuration he wants to set them in as if it's a complex puzzle. At the sight of us, he startles just slightly. Maybe he expected me to wait in my room until he came to escort us.

A wavering flash of heat rushes from Corwin into me, and I think I catch a hint of ruddiness beneath the bronze skin of his face. Then his composure snaps back into place, and he's the coolly dispassionate winter arch-lord I'm used to again.

Well, coolly dispassionate and a tad awkward. He fumbles with the goblets for a second before putting them down where I suspect they already were and seems to grope for his words before managing a basic, "Good morning."

I'm definitely not the only one uncertain about where we stand after last night, then. Somehow that sets me a little more at ease, even though my nerves squirm in my belly. "Good morning."

Harper gives me a more considering look then, so I quickly take my seat and fix my gaze on the platters the kitchen staff are bringing out. Corwin sits down too, his posture even more rigid than usual. I haven't quite decided how to bring up the issue of the locked door upstairs when a different servant hustles into the room.

She dips her head low. "Apologies for the interruption, my lord. You've been summoned to the Hall of the Heart at once."

Corwin exhales audibly and gets back to his feet. "Tell my colleagues I'll be there in a moment." He glances at me. "I'll try to settle matters with my fellow arch-lords as swiftly as I can, but don't wait for me."

Are they going to harass him about my presence in his life again? As he heads out of the room, I send a thread of sympathy and reassurance his way—only to slam into a wall between us so solid my head spins for a second. He's shut me off again, so completely I can't sense even a hint of him.

Whatever he thinks the arch-lords want to talk about this time, he doesn't want me hearing it.

Talia

I eat my breakfast on autopilot, barely tasting the buttery eggs or the crumbly pastry. Corwin let me hear what the other arch-lords said about me during that last meeting. What secrets does he think they might reveal now that it's so important to him to keep hidden?

Does he believe they're going to talk about the war with the Seelie?

The fact that I still don't know the reason for the attacks gnaws at me. But I don't see any way of convincing Corwin to share much more when he's restricted by his duties to the other arch-lords, who obviously aren't fans of mine. A restless urge tugs at me harder the longer we sit without his return, nothing but blankness where our connection should be.

There is something else I can do at least a little about. I

catch Harper's eyes from across the table, where she's just setting down her now-empty goblet. "Since I can't *ask* Corwin about what's behind that locked door right now… what do you say we go take a closer look ourselves?"

Harper's overlarge eyes light up with a gleam that's both eager and nervous. "All right."

Now that she's been to that part of the palace multiple times, she leads the way back to the spot easily, only stopping once to consider a branch in the hall. The alcove with the locked door is empty and, for the moment, silent.

I study that door, deepest into the alcove. Stepping close, I lean my ear against the thin gap by the doorframe. Harper waits quietly as I listen.

At first, there's nothing except the thump of my pulse. The seconds slip by. I'm about to pull away when a faint noise reaches my ears. A whimper and then a distressed-sounding mumbling. My body stiffens.

It's so muffled I can't tell whether the voice isn't saying any actual words at all or I just can't make them out, but it definitely has the quality of a person, one I'd assume was living.

I strain to make out more. The mumbling fades. There's a choked sort of sob, and then a ragged shout that's just loud enough for me to catch one bit of sense in it. "—Heart take me—"

My own heart lurches. I pull back, staring at Harper. "There's definitely someone up there. Are you sure spirits can't talk like people?"

She nods, wringing her hands. "My father loves getting any account he can about spirits and things like that. He's always said the reason they act out so much is out of the frustration that they barely even remember what they used to be and can't do any of the things they could before. 'Just a tangle of energy you wouldn't even know was there unless it collides with something.'"

"Well, whoever I just heard, they sound like they're upset or hurt." *What the hell is going on? Why would Corwin have someone locked away—why would he have dodged the question rather than telling me the truth if he has a good reason? Unless the winter realm has spirits that* can *talk... Of course, that wouldn't explain the servant with the meal tray.*

Harper hugs herself. "What should we do?"

Corwin is still keeping me shut out—and I'm not sure I trust him to give me any real answers anyway. I worry at my lower lip. "The servant you saw—how did they lock the door after they came out?"

"She had a couple of keys on a ring. I thought it was strange that they were using physical locks instead of magic. But maybe whoever's up there is fae and might be able to magic their way out otherwise."

Which means we couldn't magic our way in, even if we knew the right words. I hesitate, and another faint cry seeps past the door, pained enough to send a streak of ice down my spine.

"Let's go to the kitchen," I say. "If that's the main reason servants are going up there, maybe we can find the key and see for ourselves what's going on."

Harper looks even more anxious than before, but she hurries alongside me on the way downstairs. We peek into the kitchen.

It looks like Charles and Beth have already finished

washing our few breakfast dishes—if this place is anything like August's kitchen, Corwin's arranged for them to have that special faerie water that does most of the cleaning work for them. The gleaming space, all crystal and silvery metal, appears to be vacant now.

We steal farther inside, scanning the counters and the walls. Harper starts opening the drawers, shuffling through various utensils and cloths. I scan the room, thinking back to the other evening when the servant came in with the tray. He set it down at the far end of the counter—and reached up into the cabinet there.

But he came away empty-handed. If he wasn't taking something out… maybe he was putting something inside it.

It's too high for me to easily reach. I beckon Harper over. "Can you check inside that cabinet?"

She opens it and bobs up on her toes to peer inside. A triumphant smile curls her lips. Carefully, she reaches in and retrieves a silver ring with two keys that was tucked away next to the goblets. "Good guess! I'm almost sure this is the key ring I saw. I wonder why they keep it in there?" Her brow knits. "The goblets on that shelf—they're different from the ones we've been using. I think it was one with that pattern that was on the tray the servant brought out."

I peer past her at a row of crystal goblets with a pattern that looks like blooming flowers rather than pointed icicles. They might be styled differently, but they're equally fancy. Why would this prisoner get their drinks in special goblets as elegant as the ones the arch-lord himself uses?

None of this makes much sense.

I motion for us to leave before the staff can catch us—and before I lose my nerve. "Come on."

We hustle back to the alcove, Harper keeping the keys hidden in her hand. When we pass a servant who's murmuring a cleaning spell over the floors, her posture tenses, but the man doesn't give us a second glance.

The alcove is still empty. Whoever's upstairs has fallen silent again. Harper and I exchange a glance, her mouth set in a pale line. "What if the person up there is dangerous?" she asks. "The arch-lord might have a good reason for keeping them locked up."

That worry has already been running through my mind. I give her the same answer I came up with for myself. "They're not right on the other side of the door. We can barely hear them. They must be farther away, in another room or something quite a bit farther back. That's why there'd be two keys, right? We don't have to get too close." And if Corwin had a *really* good reason, he'd have told me the truth to begin with.

Harper nods, more daring returning to her expression. As she tries one key in the lock, I watch the hallway, alert for anyone coming this way. The first key doesn't fit, but the second slides in and turns with a soft click.

Anticipation prickles over my skin. Harper sucks in a breath, making a quiet sound as if preparing a spell to defend us. I smile at her, a little scared but abruptly so very grateful that she's here with me, that I'm not facing the possible horrors of the Unseelie realm alone.

She nudges the door open. On the other side, a

narrow spiral staircase winds out of view. Only a thin wash of sunlight penetrates the thick diamond walls.

We close the door gently behind us so it won't attract attention and creep up the stairs. We've only made it to the level of the first window when a low moan reverberates down to us, much louder now that we're inside.

"There must have been a quieting spell on the doorway to swallow the worst of the sounds," Harper says under her breath. She hesitates and then presses onward.

I keep pace beside her, shuddering inwardly at the rattling sigh that reaches us next. A mournful voice—definitely female, I can tell now—undulates down the stairs. "Oh, my heart, my heart." Then a string of syllables I don't recognize, true names maybe.

We keep walking until it feels as if we've traveled upward at least three more floors. This must be one of the palace's spires—one I wouldn't even have realized contained any rooms.

My warped foot is starting to twinge. I pause for a second to give it a rest, and Harper peeks around the next bend.

"I see the next door," she whispers. "What do we do now?"

I push myself onward with her to a small landing several steps farther up. It's barely large enough for the two of us to stand comfortably side by side. A single, solid door stands before us. A sputtering sound and a thump carry through it.

Corwin's prisoner is right on the other side.

We risked enough coming up here. I'm not reckless

enough to throw open this door and face whatever might be waiting beyond it.

I inhale slowly and pitch my voice to travel through the door. "Hello? Is someone in there? Do you need help?"

There's a hitch of breath and a brief silence. Then a scrabbling sound that's almost animalistic, like claws against stone. But the voice that follows is undeniably a person's. "Oh, please. Oh, please. I can't stand it any longer. I must get out. I must follow him."

Follow who? Corwin? My heart squeezes at the anguish that colors the words. "We'll do what we can. Who are you? How did you—"

The prisoner cuts me off, becoming more frantic by the second. "Please! It's been so long, so long I've— Oh, it's so wrong." Her voice rises to a wail. "I can't bear— You must let me go! Now!"

By the end of that broken tirade, my eardrums are ringing. Fists pound against the door, followed by the scratching of fingernails, and her voice careens even higher into a shrill scream. I stumble against the wall, my pulse stuttering—and footsteps pound up the stairs from below.

I spin around just as Corwin rounds the last bend. He stares at me, his bronze skin grayed, his eyes wide, looking so much more out of sorts than even at breakfast this morning. "Talia," he says in a tight voice. "You…" He doesn't seem to know what else to say.

"What's going on?" I demand as the scream trails off into a series of sobs. "Who *is* that? What have you done to her?"

A tremor runs through my body with the knowledge that if Corwin wants to cover up what we've found, neither Harper nor I have anywhere near enough power to fight him. He swore not to hurt us, but who knows if he might have some devious way to get around that. Harper steps up shoulder-to-shoulder with me all the same, her chin raised defiantly.

The Unseelie arch-lord stands there, his handsome face becoming increasingly pained by the second. He closes his eyes and seems to gather himself. "I suppose you'd have to know eventually. I'll introduce you to her."

He eases around us to the door, pulling a key of his own from one of his pockets. As he speaks a few words that thrum with potent magic, the sobs on the other side dwindle. There's a sigh that sounds more resigned than agonized.

"I calm her as much as I can, but it never has more than a brief effect, no matter what I try," Corwin says with obvious regret. "She should be subdued for a few minutes, at least." He unlocks the door and motions for us to step in just ahead of him.

I venture into a small round room that holds bookshelves—mostly empty—as well as a table and chair and various small objects strewn around, including a few of the books that must have been on those shelves at some point. At the far end of the room, another doorway shows more stairs leading to further rooms above.

The chair is tipped on its side. Crouched on the floor next to it, leaning a nearly skeletal arm on the wooden back, is an emaciated woman.

Her black hair, streaked with gray, hangs nearly to her waist, strewn wildly across her shoulders and back. Dark eyes burn into us from within her pinched brown face.

Her hunched body trembles with her breath. Her fingers curl where her hands are braced against the floor. A ragged dress hangs off her emaciated frame—the fabric looks clean enough, but it's been ripped all along the hems.

Corwin shuts the door and comes to stand beside me. He keeps his tone measured and gentle. "Hello, Mother. Talia and Harper have come to meet you."

Mother? My gaze jerks to him, and an ache of confirmation passes through our bond, which he's allowed to open just a little.

The woman just glowers at us. Then she presses her hands to her face with a quiet sniffling sound. She shakes her head as if refusing us, the room at large, maybe the entire world.

"It's all right," Corwin says in the same even voice, but I can hear the sadness wound through it. "It was good to see you."

I keep my mouth shut until he's ushered us out and locked the door again. My questions come out more tentatively than the first round. "What happened to her? Why do you keep her locked up like that?"

Corwin holds out his hand to Harper, who gives him the keys from the kitchen with a guilty twitch of her mouth. He looks at the key ring rather than me as he replies. "My father—the arch-lord before me—died rather suddenly in his prime about five decades ago. The death of a soul-twined mate is always hard on the surviving partner, but my mother was particularly... overcome with grief. At first she simply refused to leave her regular rooms and sank deep into mourning, but after a time she became obsessed with joining him in death."

Harper winces. I don't fully understand the magnitude of his statement until he explains for my benefit. "Fae don't die easily under normal circumstances, even when they wish to. Our innate instincts to preserve our own lives are nearly impossible to completely override. She made a few attempts that fell short of the mark, only causing her great pain and distressing the folk of our flock who witnessed her. If she's allowed to roam freely, she'll continue to harm herself. I keep her confined with only what objects have proven or been enchanted to stay reasonably safe and do my best to alleviate her distress."

The pang that echoes from him into me speaks of how much he feels he's failed at that goal. My throat constricts. I have the impulse to hug him like I did the other day after his previous meeting with the arch-lords, but he's holding himself so tensed I'm not sure he'd appreciate the gesture. Most of his emotions are still muted.

"I'm sorry," Harper says quietly. I'm not sure if she's apologizing for stealing the keys or for what happened to his mother or possibly both.

"We heard her again—Harper saw someone bringing down a meal tray—it seemed obvious it wasn't just a spirit." I pause. Do I really need to ask why he avoided the subject? It's obviously painful for him to talk about. But still...

"You came here to understand what being my mate would mean," Corwin says without any trace of anger. "Perhaps I should have been more open from the start. It's only—" He stops short with a flare of emotion that's oddly both frustrated and shamed for reasons I can't grasp. His wall slams back into place, cutting off that too. "Well, you know now. Let's leave her to whatever peace she can find."

We descend the spiral staircase without another word. When we come out into the hall, Corwin halts to lock the second door behind him. I waver on my feet. "Are you going to finish your breakfast?"

"It's been brought to my study. I have a few things to look over there." He nods to me, polite but distant—a distance that feels strained after the closeness we've shared both intentionally and otherwise.

The motion feels like a dismissal, but I don't like it, not after what we just saw. As he walks off, my legs balk for a moment. I glance at Harper. She's frowning, but she waves for me to go after him.

I hurry after Corwin as fast as my limp allows, and I think he slows just enough that he doesn't leave me behind, but he doesn't acknowledge me either, not until he reaches his study. With one hand on the doorframe, he glances at me.

When I first met him, I'd have taken the impenetrable mask of an expression he's wearing right now and the unyielding set of his shoulders as cold indifference. Now, even without the benefit of our connection, I can see how much effort it's taking for him to keep up that front. How much of a front it is.

Does he put up those walls because he doesn't want to show the rest of us what's going on inside him or because even *he* doesn't want to deal with it?

"Yes?" he says, a single syllable that somehow holds so much understated emotion. I can't tell whether he'd rather I leave or push on, but it's not only up to him.

My hands twitch with the urge to fidget. I tuck them under my elbows. "What you just told me—it's obviously a big deal. You almost said more about it. I don't know why—you could have told me more of the truth, at least, when I asked you before. That she was sick or something. If there's something else... I *do* want to understand what it'd mean to be your mate. But I can't if you shut me out about things that are so important to you."

Corwin's shoulders sag, just slightly. He opens the door and waits for me to walk past him inside.

His study is formed out of the same gleaming diamond as the rest of the palace, but the furniture in here is pale wood like the chair in his mother's room rather than marble. Everything on the sleek desk and the shelves carved into the walls is perfectly tidy, with a blatant sense of personal order. Even his breakfast tray is laid out with precision. I doubt there's one thing in the place that Corwin couldn't find instantly if he needed it.

Rather than sit behind his desk, the Unseelie arch-lord sinks onto one of the thinly padded chairs that encircle a low table at the other end of the room. Maybe he sometimes has meetings with his coterie there. I follow him, settling onto one of the other chairs.

He peers at the shelves in a detached sort of way, but at the same time he opens his end of our bond. Not all the way—just enough for a stream of tangled grief and shame to wash over me. His hands flex against the arms of the chair.

"You're right. There was no legitimate reason for me to keep this from you. It has no bearing on matters of politics and it offers no threat to my flock or the rest of my people." He sighs and drags his gaze to me. "It was selfish. I didn't want you to think less of me."

I blink at him. "Why would I think less of you for something awful that your mother has gone through? It isn't your fault. It must be awful for you too." Losing his father so suddenly, having to take over the arch-lord position sooner than he'd ever have expected, trying to help his mother or at least keep her from hurting herself at the same time…

Sympathy wells up inside me, and I convey it to him as well as I can through the connection between us.

Corwin's mouth twists. "I suppose it makes sense that you'd see it that way. I'm more accustomed to… My fellow Unseelie, and my colleagues in particular, consider the state my mother has fallen into to be a flaw in her nature. A rather serious one. And they're particularly concerned about that flaw having been passed on to me."

Flickers of memories that aren't mine dart through my head: the faces I saw around the table in his Hall of the Heart chilly with condemnation, fragments of sentences in sneering voices. *Over-sentimentality. Emotions out of control. Instability. How can we trust…?*

"She lost her mate," I protest, my hackles rising at the remembered specters of those haughty fae. "Isn't it normal for her to struggle after that?"

"It's always painful, and there's always a grieving process, but we of winter pride ourselves on our self-control." Corwin swipes his hand over his face, rumpling the glossy curls along his forehead. "To be completely incapable of functioning, especially when you have other responsibilities—to get to the point of wishing to cast yourself to the Heart before your time... I don't know whether that might be more typical among the Seelie, but it's rather unusual here. Enough to draw plenty of remarks."

"But there's no reason for them to assume it has anything to do with *you*."

He shrugs. "I was quite young when my father's responsibilities were passed on to me, and I couldn't let us lose the domain as well. I made a few of my earlier decisions hastily, misplaced my trust... let my temper get the better of me at least once." His pause speaks of even more pain. "If you and I are to fulfill our bond, I'll tell you more about that another day. Suffice to say, my colleagues found ample excuse to question my fitness for the position. I'm lucky I found my footing soon enough to avoid an outright challenge."

So many things he hasn't outright said hang heavily in the air, but I can put together enough of the pieces to see the full picture of the fae man in front of me as I never did so clearly before. I already knew he wasn't anywhere near as cool and emotionless as he likes to present himself. In that dream last night, he showed a passion that could match any of my lovers back home.

I thought he was holding back and keeping me at a distance because he didn't trust me yet, but it's so much more than that, isn't it? He doesn't even trust *himself*.

He doesn't believe he should have much in the way of feelings in the first place. He's *ashamed* of the fact that he cares as much as he does. His father died something like fifty years ago... How long has Corwin been training himself to suppress every feeling he has that goes beyond mild interest or annoyance?

How hard has it been for him to open up as much as he has at my coaxing?

A sharper appreciation rushes through me for the tender words he's managed to offer me, the declarations he's made on my behalf, even that hug he hesitated before returning the other day. I mean enough to him that he's willing to risk his fellow arch-lords' opinions of him—his own opinion of himself—to earn my devotion.

I get up and cross the short distance to his chair. Corwin watches me, wary but with a hint of welcome in the reactions trickling through our bond. I don't let myself hesitate as I extend my hand to graze my fingers across his high cheekbone.

Sensation jolts between us, but I'm better prepared for it this time. I *want* him to feel how much I mean this.

"I think it must have taken incredible strength to have held your flock together as well as you have, considering everything. Anyone who complains that you weren't absolutely perfect is a judgmental idiot. If I don't accept the bond, it won't have anything to do with expecting you to be impervious. If I do accept it, it'll be because you let yourself be more than diamond and ice with me."

Corwin's lips curve into the faintest of smiles. Something that was strung taut amid all his other emotions dissipates with my words. He takes my hand and presses a soft kiss to the inside of my wrist, and somehow that small token of affection ripples through me with twice as much heat as anything we did in our shared dream last night.

"So you are making me see," he says in a low voice. He turns my hand to kiss it again, on the knuckles this time, and releases my fingers. And it occurs to me that what I just said—what *he* just said—may be exactly why the rest of the Unseelie arch-lords would rather see me gone from their realm forever than united with this man.

Talia

 didn't bring much with me to the winter realm, and it should all come back with me for now, but the morning of my return to summer, I find myself pawing through the contents of the trunk, unable to decide on what to wear. I've left my clothes to wash and to tug at my hair in front of the mirror and finally to pace around the room aimlessly several times when there's a knock on the door. I sense before he speaks that it's Corwin.

"Talia, I… have something for you."

The words come with a whiff of hope and nerves. I look down at myself and decide it doesn't matter that I'm only wearing my nightgown. He's seen me in it before anyway.

He's seen me in much less, if we're counting dreams.

With the heat of that memory chasing at my heels, I open the door. Corwin stands a little stiffly on the other side, but my line of thinking has brought a hint of a smolder into his burgundy-brown eyes. I resist the urge to shore up my inner wall so he won't feel the tingle of attraction that races through me.

I'll only be with him for a few more hours. The least I can do is stay at least partly receptive to our bond for that time.

Because he's Corwin, he doesn't remark on either of our reactions. His gaze veers from my face to my shoulder, and his forehead furrows with a flare of concern. "You were wounded."

My dresses have hidden the scars from Aerik's jaws. It was so dark and he was so caught up in the aftermath of his nightmare the other night that he mustn't have noticed them then. I wonder if they even showed up in that other dream—we were both awfully caught up in other emotions during that one.

I brush my fingers over the hardened ridges of darker flesh. "A long time ago. When the fae who captured me attacked my family. It doesn't hurt anymore. It just… isn't pretty."

Consternation flashes across Corwin's face. "There is *nothing* that could stop you from being absolutely lovely," he says, meeting my eyes again. Anger trickles through the bond. "If I get the chance to venture farther into the summer realm, I'll happily return that pain to the monster who dealt it a hundred times over."

My mouth twitches, his vehemence dulling whatever pain does linger from the memory. "I know at least three Seelie who'd be happy to join you."

"Yes. Well." He looks down at the folded bundle of

fabric he's holding, abruptly awkward, and offers it to me. "This isn't as intricate as the work your friend does, but I had the craftsman who produces most of my own clothes create something for you. If you're willing to wear it. I wanted to give you something of the winter realm to bring back with you."

I can tell how much my response means to him. I accept the bundle, the cloth downy soft against my hands. He has solved one of my problems, assuming there's nothing objectionable about the outfit. "Thank you," I say. "I'll put it on now."

He gives me one of those tiny smiles. "I look forward to seeing you in it."

Before I can think better of it, an offering of my own tumbles out. "Wait right there. You can be the first person I show it to."

I shut the door—because I'm not at the point of taking *off* my nightgown in front of him, no matter what ideas get into my dreams—and change quickly. The dress Corwin gave me slips over my slim frame with a cozy warmth that makes me want to curl up and just snuggle it. But the gown still manages to be sleek and elegant. When I take it in, turning on my feet in front of the full-length mirror, a bittersweet pang forms in my chest.

The dress is designed in the Unseelie style I've seen various folk of the flocks wearing: more structured than the typical flowing Seelie dresses, with separate panels around the waist and across the bodice. The trimmer skirt hugs the line of my thighs almost to my knees and then expands with a subtle flare of fabric.

But Corwin has commissioned it in a color I haven't

seen any of the winter fae wearing. They all tend toward muted, grayish tones, whether pale or dark. My dress beams a vibrant green, almost the same shade as my eyes.

He's given me a winter dress in summer colors. Like the reverse of the airy, snow-pale gown I arrived to meet him in.

A little of the tension balled in my stomach releases. Maybe… maybe everything will be okay after all.

Uncertain anticipation seeps through me from the man waiting outside. I open the door again and then step back to let him in, not sure I want to put on some kind of fashion show in the hall where the staff might pass by.

Corwin steps inside tentatively. His uncertainty falls away with a flare of appreciation that ripples through me and gleams in his eyes, even though he doesn't let it touch the rest of his expression. "It fits you well."

"It does. I like how it feels, too." I smooth my hands over the skirt and glance up at him. "It's perfect. Thank you."

He lets his smile widen then, with a rush of relief that's tinged with sadness.

Because I'm leaving. Because he doesn't know when I'll be back—*if* I'll even be back.

But if I'd had any doubts about that still lingering, this gift has banished them. I don't know how we'll make our way through this tangled mess of interconnected lives and loves, but I'm not willing to give up on any part of that mess yet.

I rest my hand on his chest, the padded doublet he's wearing as soft as my dress, and hold his gaze. "I have to go to them. They need me, and—and I love them too much to let them go. But I'll come back. We'll figure out some kind of compromise for me to travel back and forth until we can decide on a more permanent solution."

The sorrow doesn't leave him, but a glow of happiness warms our bond in spite of it. "I hope your Seelie men will be as generous as you are."

I make a dismissive sound. "It'll be my choice. They don't rule me." If there's one thing I know for sure, it's that Sylas would never try to cage me in any way.

That thought brings up other concerns I can't totally avoid, as much as I might like to. I pause and force myself to say, "You know how I feel about them. How close I've been with them. I—I'm still going to be *with* them while I can. I'll close off the bond as much as possible so you don't have to—"

Corwin touches my arm, stopping me. His jaw clenches for a second, but I don't sense anything worse than a tremor of discomfort.

"Close yourself off from me if you feel *you* need to," he says quietly. "I can understand there may be moments you'd rather keep between yourselves. But anything you don't need to hide for your own comfort, don't shut me off for my sake. They're part of your life, and I want to experience as much of your life as you'll allow me to. I won't know just how much I can compromise if I'm pretending away the full truth of our situation."

Imagining him being aware of some of the particularly intimate moments I've shared with my lovers in the past brings a flush into my cheeks—and makes my gut twist guiltily. "Are you sure? Wanting them in my life doesn't mean I want to hurt *you*."

"I can take care of my own reactions. If it bothers me too much in the moment, I'll step back on my end." His thumb grazes my skin with a gentle sweep over the fabric of the dress. "I don't blame you for having trouble deciding, but I want you to know that I'm completely committed to you and whatever having you as my mate brings."

The determination in his voice makes me choke up a bit. I let instinct propel me onto my toes, my hand sliding up his chest to grip his neck.

Corwin bends to meet my kiss with a swell of emotion that's all delight. As our mouths meld together, that delight sweeps through me, leaving every nerve humming with it.

It isn't fair that I should be so deeply connected to a man who's so far apart from the others I love. Just this brief embrace brings out a tug of longing to join as completely as the bond demands, with a spark of heat shooting low in my belly.

I pull back before that spark can burn hotter, lowering my head and closing my eyes as I will down the crackle of desire. Of *need*. We might not have done anything outside of that dream, but it's made my body and soul so much more aware of the possibilities.

Corwin reins in his own flash of lust. When he speaks again, his voice is low and rough. "You know—I didn't direct that dream in any way—I found myself in it as unexpectedly as I'd imagine you must have. The bond draws us together automatically. I wouldn't have tried to force anything you weren't ready for."

"I know." But suddenly it's very hard to think about

anything other than the heated presence of the man in front of me, the connection intent on pulling me toward him, and the bed that's just a few steps away. "Maybe we should go get breakfast now."

He laughs with a bit of strain. "I'd be pleased to escort you to the dining room."

Harper meets us in the hall and exclaims over my dress. She beams even brighter when Corwin says it hardly compares to her skills with cloth and thread. For a little while during breakfast, I focus on nothing but the food and the easier conversation we've been able to fall into with most of the secrets between us stripped away.

But it isn't long before my eagerness for my return bubbles to the surface too forcefully for anything to distract me. It's been ten days since I last saw Sylas, August, and Whitt. I have no idea what's been going on in the Seelie realm during that time. Our greatest enemies on the summer side have already been dealt with, and I haven't seen any sign that the Unseelie have launched further hostilities while I've been here, but still…

It's been too long since I felt their arms around me, welcomed their caresses, heard their voices murmuring words of affection in my ear. Since I got to tell them how much I love *them*. Even if everything's been perfectly peaceful over there, they have no idea how *I've* been. Whether I might return only to say that other than giving my blood once a month, I'm devoting myself completely to my soul-twined mate.

Maybe sensing my growing urgency—and the twinges of guilt I can't suppress, knowing that he's sensing it— Corwin leaves me to Harper's company for the rest of the morning until it's time for me to leave. He lifts my trunk without a word, and the three of us walk across the chilly plain to the glinting haze of the border.

After eyeing the sun to judge the time, Corwin intones the words of the vow that will let him cross so close to the Heart unhindered. "By the Heart, I swear to do no harm to the fae beyond this boundary. May I pass in peace and amity."

My pulse hiccups at the thought of the risk he's taking, the trust he's putting in my people. "You don't have to come with me if you'd rather not take the chance. I can go through with just Harper."

The Unseelie arch-lord shakes his head. "I won't cower in the safety of my domain when it comes to my soul-twined mate. And I'd prefer to discuss the details of your next visit to the winter realm, should he agree to it, with Arch-Lord Sylas directly. I'm not unprotected. I'll cast the spell that will retaliate against any who cast the first blow."

I watch him as he murmurs the spell-casting words, the thrum of energy that carries from the glowing Heart rising alongside them. A faint glimmer settles over his clothes and sinks into him. He lifts his gaze to meet mine again. "Are you ready?"

I nod, my chest full to bursting with a weird mix of impatience and a little sadness of my own. I can't wait to be home, but I can already tell I'll miss Corwin's presence after I leave. The bond between us isn't going to let me forget I've walked away from him.

He offers me his hand, and I take it, not shying now from the sharper rush of sensation that comes with the contact. Mixing in with the sorrow and affection wound through him, I pick up on a trace of pride as well.

He's told me plenty of times before that he wants to make this work despite who and what I am, but until this moment I'm not sure I ever totally believed he was *happy* about the Heart's choice rather than simply accepting it.

Harper grasps my other hand, and we step into the haze of the border together. The chill in the air falls away with each step. The summery scents of fresh grass and sun-warmed earth reach my nose before I can see more than a faint impression of them. My homesickness overwhelms every other sensation in me, speeding up my uneven pace.

We step free of the haze onto the field where I left. My three Seelie men stand in a row several feet from the border, their stances tense but relief crossing all their faces at the sight of me.

Seeing them, my heart flips over with an even deeper jolt of longing. It feels like it's been a hundred years since I looked into Sylas's mismatched eyes, watched Whitt's mouth curve into that fond smirk, basked in the warmth of August's beaming face.

No power in the world could stop me from dropping the hands I was holding and darting forward. I barely even notice the wobble of my warped foot. Since I don't know who else might be watching from farther away, I can't fling myself at all of my lovers whole-heartedly, but I hurtle straight into August's arms.

His chuckle comes out a little choked as he sweeps me off my feet. I tuck my head into the crook of his neck as if it belongs nowhere else and hug him back with everything

I have in me. His musky scent with its hint of sweetness envelops me, and in that moment I'm nothing but joy.

I still have them. They're all here and fine—they came for me.

As the initial burst of happiness evens out, my sense of Corwin seeps back into my awareness: a prickle of discomfort, an urge to wrench me back. But there's also an unexpected thread of tenderness weaving through the rest.

August eases me to the ground, and I glance at Sylas and Whitt with a smile I hope conveys how happy I am to be here with them too, even if I can't express it as fully. "You can see I'm fine. Corwin kept his word. He was a very good host, even with everything being so... complicated."

Sylas inclines his head to the Unseelie arch-lord. "I appreciate your willingness to compromise on this matter."

"She's worth it," Corwin says from where he's hung back by the border. He speaks simply and quietly, but there's a power to the words that wraps around my heart as much as August's arms just encircled my body.

I reach for Sylas's hand and twine my fingers with his, deciding I can be allowed at least that much intimacy. His firm grip in response steadies me. "I still consider this my home," I say. "But... I'm not ready to reject the bond either. I don't know exactly how this is going to work in the long run, but I want to go back to the winter realm sometime after the full moon for another stay. There's still a lot we need to figure out."

Any fear I had about Sylas's reaction vanishes with his nod, though he squeezes my fingers a little tighter as if he'd rather not let me go ever again. "Of course there is." He pauses and then returns his attention to Corwin. "I'd imagine you might prefer to discuss the details of her next journey to your realm now, while we can speak face to face."

"Yes, I'd like that." Corwin ventures a few strides closer, his shoulders relaxing a tad from their previously rigid position. "I realize Talia has more of a commitment here than just the matter of the curse. Perhaps we could—"

Before he can finish that sentence, several fae bolt across the field from the sparse trees that frame it.

By the time a startled yelp has broken from my throat, they're already on Corwin. He heaves backward, jerking his arms up around his face as if bracing for his protective spell to blast them away—but they don't strike any blows. As most of them hurtle into a ring around him, the man who reached him first snaps two pieces of metal around his neck like a collar.

Corwin gasps raggedly, a jolt of shocked distress shooting through our connection. A stinging pain radiates from the collar all through his body, dulling his sense of the Heart's energy.

"What are you doing?" I cry, limping forward.

The other fae close tighter around Corwin, much less careful with him now. One whips a vine around his wrists to tie them. Another shoves him to his knees. And he can't fight back because of the vow he took.

The agony of his helplessness peals from him louder than the pain of their mistreatment. The spell he cast to defend himself mustn't be working.

"What is the meaning of this?" Sylas demands as he strides over to join me, his aura of authority radiating controlled fury. "This man is here on our invitation, and—"

"They're carrying out my orders, Sylas." A tall, stately figure steps out from the trees, her shimmering ivory hair rippling over her dark shoulders as if on its own breeze and her heavy-lidded eyes stern.

Arch-Lord Celia considers Corwin with a disdainful glance and then turns to us. "I'm afraid there's been a small difference of opinion in our approach to the Unseelie. He came on your invitation; now he's my prisoner."

Talia

My feet won't stay still, even though the warped one is beginning to ache. I pace from one side of Sylas's new office to the other in a restless if wobbly circuit. "How could she do it? To go behind your back like this…"

Sylas's mouth has been set in a frown since his conversation with Celia less than an hour ago. She insisted that he step aside with her to discuss the situation, Donovan coming out to join them, but I refused to leave the field even though there was nothing I could do to stop her warriors from hauling Corwin away to—to wherever she's taken him.

Our bond has been quiet since that first blare of pain and panic during the attack. Is he shutting me out because he doesn't want me to feel what they're doing to him *now*? Or because he thinks I was in on this plan?

Both possibilities make my stomach churn.

"She and Donovan decided it was too good an 'opportunity' to let it pass them by," Sylas says, his voice rough with barely veiled frustration. "I suspect it was almost entirely Celia's idea and she simply convinced Donovan to go along with it. Two arch-lords carry the trio—they didn't need my permission to go forward, although she acknowledged that it was 'unfortunate' that she blindsided me."

"You didn't even get a chance to say how you felt about it! They should have at least told you beforehand."

He sighs. "I haven't held the position for even a month yet, so they don't quite consider me their equal yet, I'd imagine. And they see my input as biased because of my connection to you."

Celia probably realized that not only would Sylas have argued against the plan, he'd have interfered when they insisted on going through with it anyway. But Corwin doesn't know that. Whatever he thinks about my involvement, I'm sure he assumes my Seelie men were partly responsible for his capture.

August steps closer to me, catching me before I can continue my pacing and hugging me tightly. I can't quite relax, but I slump a little into his embrace, leaning my head against his chest. "What do they think they're going to get out of this? Isn't holding an arch-lord hostage even *more* likely to start a war?"

"She didn't want to get into the details of her strategy with so many witnesses around," Whitt says, the caustic note in *his* voice not at all veiled. "We're to meet in the Bastion to discuss the matter more formally as soon as we get word."

A chill ripples through me. "They aren't going to kill him, are they?"

August strokes his hand over my hair. "I can't see how that would benefit the Seelie in any way." He glances toward his brothers.

Sylas shakes his head. "At this point, the most I've gathered is that she wants to use him, not destroy him. Her men treated him more roughly than I'd prefer, though. I don't understand how they were able to subdue his magic in the first place."

"It was one of the artifacts from Ambrose's secret stash," Astrid pipes up from where she's been observing the meeting near the door. When we headed to the palace, Sylas mentioned to me that he was taking her into his cadre, though they haven't had a chance to carry out the formal ceremony yet. "I got one of her people who helped sort through them talking. Apparently the band they fixed around his neck has an iron core. When the ring is closed, the iron shatters any magic the prisoner would try to cast —and any already cast on them, I'd imagine."

August winces. "That's against our laws of warfare—it should have been destroyed. I can't imagine even *making* something like that."

"Apparently Celia sees eye to eye with Ambrose in a few areas, one of them being illicit weaponry," Whitt says.

I turn in August's arms to look at the others. "What stash? What does this have to do with Ambrose?"

Sylas's frown shifts into an outright grimace. "One of Ambrose's former pack-kin defected from Tristan's pack to ours. He came with information about a storeroom full of weaponry—much of it in defiance of our standards of morality—that Ambrose maintained in his palace. I informed Celia and Donovan, naturally, and their packs have had a hand in sorting through what we found. I assumed everything we'd consider unnaturally cruel was being disposed of."

Whitt lets out a curt huff. "Ambrose was stockpiling for his intended assault on the winter realm. We know Celia balked more at instigating a full-out massacre than getting retribution in general. She simply made use of the tools he left behind for her own approach."

A leaf whips through the window, veering toward Sylas so purposefully I know it's enchanted before he says anything. He snatches it out of the air. "There's our summons. Whitt, come with me to the meeting—we can go over every possible argument against keeping Arch-Lord Corwin prisoner on the way. Astrid, survey the grounds around the Heart and alert me if you notice any other concerning developments. August, you stay with Talia."

Normally, the ease with which he commands his cadre reassures me. Now, it only reminds me of how serious this situation is.

I raise my head. "I want to come to the meeting too. I'm the only one here who knows Corwin. I can speak up for him."

"I'm sorry, Talia," Sylas says grimly. "There's no way Celia would allow that. She's aware that anything we say you could pass on to him through your soul-twined bond. But I know enough to defend him—and even if he *were* a villain, this isn't any way to go about resolving our issues with the Unseelie. I'll come straight to you as soon as the discussion is over."

As he, Whitt, and Astrid stride out of the room, I sink deeper into August's arms. "I feel like I should be doing *something* to help, but I have no idea what."

He rubs my back. "Sylas will argue Corwin's case in every way he can. Donovan's trusted his advice before—hopefully we can sway him if not Celia."

Right. Because if two is enough, then Sylas and Donovan could overrule Celia. I cling to that speck of hope. "I guess there's no chance they'd let me see him?"

"Celia wouldn't even let *Sylas* talk to Corwin. Can't you reach out to him through your bond?"

"I can't sense anything from him right now. Maybe that steel collar thing is interfering with our connection too."

August hums thoughtfully. "I wouldn't think so. A soul-twined bond isn't constructed magic, it's pure Heart energy. Nothing should be able to interfere with that. But I could believe him wanting to shield you from what he's going through." He ducks his head to nuzzle my temple. "You've come to like him."

It's a statement, not a question, but he says it without a hint of accusation. I swallow thickly. "Yes. He's—he's a good person, even if he thinks about some things differently than you would. We *didn't* get along all that well at first, but when I stood up to him, he listened, and he really tried to make me feel at home. And he's the only one out of the Unseelie arch-lords who I think wants peace with the summer realm. I don't see how holding him hostage is going to do anything except make things worse."

"Celia has contributed a lot to fending off the attacks —she's lost plenty of her own pack-kin to the winter fae. It's possible she's not being all that rational about this plan. But if that's the case, then Sylas should have no problem showing it." August scoops me right off the floor. "Let's go to the kitchen. I know you're worried, but you haven't had lunch yet. You'll feel even worse if you're starving."

"Always looking for a chance to put food into me," I mutter, but I don't complain about him carrying me down. At the moment, I'll take all the comfort I can get.

We're in the kitchen, August slicing a fresh-baked loaf of bread to create sandwiches, when the first flash of sensation I've felt from Corwin in ages shivers through my nerves. I freeze on my stool, focusing on the impressions that reach me as closely as I can.

There's a stinging pain, mild but radiating all through his body. A sense of a hard floor beneath him where he's sitting. I can't see anything—I think his eyes might be closed. The weight of the iron collar presses against his throat.

My hands clench with a mix of anguish and anger. I propel my inner voice with as much force as I can give it. *Corwin? Can you hear me?*

Talia. His response sounds weary but at least not accusing. *I didn't even realize I'd shut you out at first. I was so out-of-sorts...*

It's all right. I'm just worried about you. I'm so sorry. I had no idea anything like this would happen.

It's not your crime to apologize for. I could feel how upset you were—I know you weren't involved.

I shift forward on my stool, bracing my elbows on the kitchen island. August glances at me but stays quiet, probably able to tell how hard I'm concentrating and guessing why.

Sylas didn't know either—it was the other arch-lords acting without consulting him. He's trying to negotiate your release right now.

Corwin's first, wordless reply is a wash of doubtful resignation. *He wouldn't tell you anything else, would he? Having me out of the way would certainly solve plenty of problems for him.*

This isn't *how he solves his problems. And he respected our bond enough to let me go to you in the first place.* I stop, shaking myself. I don't want to argue right now. My distress over Corwin's capture swallows up everything else inside me. *Are you okay, other than that collar thing that's stopping your magic? They aren't hurting you?*

They haven't been what I'd call considerate, but they haven't roughed me up particularly. So far. He pauses with a quiver of emotion I can't identify. His tone goes wry but quiet. *I'd have thought you might be relieved if the Seelie happened to dispatch me. It would make your situation so much simpler.*

There's no holding back the surge of horror that floods me at the idea of him being "dispatched"—of losing him to some violent act. Tears spring up so quickly they trickle out even when I squeeze my eyes shut against them.

Of course not. I don't care how complicated things are—I don't want you gone. I... My mind trips back to the morning when he prostrated himself in front of my bedroom door in his palace, to the way he looked at me as he explained why he was willing to humble himself before a mere human, as if it shouldn't need any explanation at all. The words slip into my inner voice as easily as if I've said them a thousand times before. *You're my mate.*

And he is, in the most important way that matters to the fae and others besides. Even as I sit next to the first man I've ever loved, I know that with a fierceness that winds through my chest and quivers through my bones. I don't understand why the Heart chose us for each other or what will come of it, but Corwin is *mine.*

Corwin startles, but his shock fades into a swell of happiness that seems totally out of place with his current situation. *Yes, I am*, he says, with a tendril of intention as if he's grazed my cheek with his fingertips.

We'll keep doing everything possible to get you out of there quickly, I tell him. *There isn't much—I don't have any real authority there—but it's only a few days until the full moon. I have power there even if I don't anywhere else.*

I can survive this. I don't want you doing anything that'll put you at odds with your pack, Talia.

I won't be. If Sylas can't settle things by talking it out, he might even suggest that tactic.

Corwin doesn't answer with words, but I can taste his skepticism. He might have held back his less-than-complimentary thoughts about the summer fae after I argued with him about it and accepted my affection for my three wolfish lovers, but he still doesn't trust the Seelie.

Maybe I can't sway the arch-lords' opinions, but I can do something about *that* problem, can't I?

Exhilaration trickles through me at the possibility of having something concrete I can put my mind to. August nudges my sandwich toward me, studying my expression. "You were talking with Corwin? Have you figured something out?"

"Not—not exactly." I dig into the hearty bread, butter and smoked meat mingling with its flavor into a delicious combination I can now appreciate at least a little. As I chew, I mull over my options. I'm not going to be able to pull this off on my own—that much seems obvious.

August polishes his own sandwich off in less than a minute. I glance over at him as he drops his plate into the sink of wash water. Is he going to be offended that I'd ask this?

I gulp down my last mouthful. "August, I want to hear what's happening at that meeting in the Bastion. I know Sylas said Celia won't allow it. Is there... any way you could get me in there without them realizing? Just to watch?"

Through our connection, I feel Corwin stir with renewed attention, but he doesn't comment on my request. I let the bond remain fully open. I'm doing this *because* I want him to see how all my men will stand up for him.

August rubs his mouth, considering. He looks me up and down. "You're not quite the tiny thing you were when we first found you, but you're still small enough that I do have a trick I think could work."

He hasn't balked or tried to talk me out of it, even for a second. I beam at him. "Then let's try that. As long as you don't think you'll get into trouble."

He grins back at me. "I don't plan on getting caught, but if we are, we'll just say the Heart compelled you and I felt a duty to respect that."

August ducks out of the kitchen and returns with a sheet of thick cloth. Once he's motioned for me to stand, he drapes the cloth around me and then scoops me up in his arms like he did to carry me downstairs, except tucking me into a tighter ball with my knees close to my chest. I nestle against him, closing my eyes in the darkness beneath the fabric. "Won't they realize what you're carrying even if I'm covered?"

August chuckles. "I know a spell or two that can help me shift the look of a thing. The guards should see me bringing a sack of 'evidence.' I can't see them turning away one of the arch-lords' cadre-chosen."

I stay crouched and motionless in his hold as he heads out of the castle. Only a faint whiff of the fresh outside air seeps through the cloth, but it smells familiar, like the wood that all Sylas's homes have been constructed out of. I focus on that and the solid strength of August's arms, tuning out my nerves as well as I can.

Whatever you hear, I'm not going to resent him for it, Corwin says. *I tried to wipe them out of your very mind, as much as I regret that now. I can't blame Sylas if he'd want to be rid of me.*

I convey my certainty through the bond. *I'm not at all worried about that. You'll see.*

I only know we've reached the Bastion when August comes to a halt and speaks. "My lord expects that any useful new evidence in the Unseelie matter will be brought to him."

It's a perfect lie that's not really a lie—Sylas *would* expect that, but August never said that what he's carrying *is* that evidence.

The guard at the entrance must wave him in. His footsteps thud louder on the stone floor inside. He turns, and we ascend a staircase.

August murmurs a few more words under his breath—other spells or true names to help conceal us? Finally, he stops again and carefully lowers me to the ground.

He eases the folds of the sheet aside so that only my face is uncovered. We're huddled in an alcove with a narrow opening that overlooks the main room of the bastion below. "I don't know that anyone will look this way," August whispers. "But keep any movements slow just in case. We'll just have to make sure to leave before the meeting's over."

I nod, squeezing his hand gratefully, and tip forward just enough to make out the figures on the floor below.

I've missed quite a bit of the discussion, but the archlords are still at it. Celia is sitting on her throne, her posture regal. Sylas and Donovan stand in front of her, Sylas looking from one to the other as he speaks. "—past weeks since the soul-twined bond was formed have been our most peaceful yet. Threatening one of their leaders seems much more likely to turn those attitudes back to blatant hostility than to end the conflict."

"It's been nearly thirty years of constant attacks and raids," Celia retorts. "Finally we have some real leverage to force their cooperation. How many more of our brethren would you have die instead?"

"I don't believe those are our only choices." Sylas turns

to Donovan. "You've seen how far I'll go to protect our people. But this isn't the right way. How can we stoop to the depths Ambrose was willing to plumb? We win this fight by keeping our honor even if the Unseelie haven't, not by throwing it away."

Donovan's expression is pained. "I don't know, Sylas. Celia's arguments are sound. We *haven't* been able to end the attacks in all that time, for all the higher ground we've kept."

Celia sniffs. "What would *you* have us do with the feathered villain then?"

"What we should have done in the first place," Sylas says. "Let him return to his home and continue to foster whatever understanding we can between the winter and summer peoples now that one of their leaders is invested in one of our own. *That's* an opportunity we've never had before—"

"And what makes you so sure you can call that human girl 'one of our own'?" Celia cuts in, so sharply I flinch inwardly. "She owes no real loyalty to us, and now that by some strange act her soul is twined with one of them, no doubt it's only a matter of time before she's completely devoted to the Unseelie. I'm not waiting around to watch that happen."

Sylas doesn't bristle visibly, but I can hear the growl in his voice. "Talia has more than proven herself a loyal member of my pack."

"And that's precisely why I can't indulge your thoughts on this subject for very long, Sylas." Celia stands up, as haughty as any of the winter fae arch-lords. Funny, she'd probably get along well with them if they hadn't been battling the past three decades. "You're fond of the dust-destined girl, and I don't fault you for that, but you have to see it's clouding your judgment."

"Celia, we're hardly done discussing—"

"I say we are." She strides off, and August lets out a soft curse. While he bundles me back up in the cloth, the last voice I catch is Donovan's, apologetic but unyielding. "I'm sorry, Sylas. I have to think of what's best for all our people. The Unseelie have already threatened outright war. If this is what it takes to ensure a fair negotiation… then I have to side with her." His footsteps rap against the floor as he too walks away.

As August hefts me up, my heart sinks. I got what I thought I wanted—Corwin saw that my men will fight for his freedom. But now I'm even less certain that the fight they can offer will be enough to win that battle.

Whitt

As we come up on Donovan's glazed clay castle in the dwindling daylight, Sylas lets out a rough sound. "I'd rather we were coming invited than turning up unexpectedly."

I make a face at the smooth brown walls, one I'd never aim directly at their owner. "Oh, I'm sure he expects a visit like this sooner or later, and most likely sooner. He knows he's the deciding vote, especially when Celia's gone rigid as a slate-tree. He's probably waiting for us to turn up and put on a song and dance for his entertainment."

Sylas still has enough good humor somewhere under the day's grimness to raise an eyebrow at me. "How much dancing are you planning on doing tonight? Should I have brought our musicians?"

I snort and elbow him—lightly, because he is still my lord, after all. But with our brief banter, a renewed sense of certainty settles over me.

We still have a potential disaster to untangle ourselves from, and a great many things hang in the balance, but the fissure between the two of us seems to have sealed. I'm not sure we've ever understood each other quite so well as we do now. The resentments I tried to bury extended much farther back than Isleen's entrance into our lives. They don't prick at me at all now.

Perhaps there was even a tiny bit of good amid all the havoc Sylas's mate wreaked, forcing those fault lines into the light where we had to address them. Not that I intend on giving her credit for anything.

While I assumed Donovan anticipated our visit, I'm surprised to have him greet us as we reach the castle's main door. One of his servants must have alerted him to our approach. His youthful face looks weary, the wayward strands of his fiery hair arranged in an even more erratic configuration than usual. I don't think he's taking his opposition to Sylas lightly.

And well he shouldn't. He wouldn't be *alive* if it weren't for Sylas putting his own life on the line.

"I'm not sure there's anything you can say that'll change my opinion on the matter," he says without preamble, "but I'll listen."

Sylas nods with infinitely more patience than I have with that statement. "That's a start."

Donovan leads us through the warmly lit halls to his study, the contents of which have a haphazard quality similar to his hair. He sinks into the chair behind his desk, and Sylas and I take seats in the armchairs opposite, as if we're going to have a perfectly civil conversation about holding a fellow arch-lord hostage.

Wisely, Sylas begins with the main reason this whelp should be glad my brother *is* talking civilly and not cuffing him on his ears. "You trusted my judgment enough to take me into your confidence when Ambrose posed a threat, and to put me forward as arch-lord afterward. I don't believe I've done anything to damage that trust. And I can assure you that even if Arch-Lord Corwin weren't the soul-twined mate of one of my pack-kin, I'd disagree with this tactic."

Donovan's mouth twists. "You can't say that for sure, because he is. You wouldn't know his name or anything about him if it weren't for his connection to the human woman. I know you value her—and she's given much to the Seelie—but how can her accounts of his intentions be anything but skewed? She *is* his soul-twined mate; she's compelled by the Heart to see the best in him."

"He was willing to risk himself by coming to us and showing how much the cooperation between our realms meant to him," Sylas says. "He fulfilled his oaths and returned Talia and her companion as agreed with no harm done to either. He has stated clearly that he was the one who warned us about the impending attack two moons past—he couldn't have gotten away with a lie that bald so close to the Heart. Those are all objective facts."

"Even so, he hasn't been able to stop the attacks so far, has he?"

I lean back in my chair, studying the other arch-lord through narrowed eyes. "I'd say that's more of a point *against* this plan. His colleagues haven't valued his opinion enough to cater to it. Why would they back down simply because his life is under threat? It seems much more likely to me that they'll use this offense as a new excuse to come at us even harder. There's no pretending that the kidnapping of one of their rulers isn't an act of war. If you don't care about that, what did you have to argue with Ambrose about?"

Donovan glowers back at me. "Ambrose wanted to stage a full-out assault—as much manpower as possible, with undoubtedly hundreds if not thousands of lives lost on both sides. We simply wish to force a cease-fire."

"But my strategist is right," Sylas says. "Holding Arch-Lord Corwin gives us no power if the other Unseelie arch-lords would be willing to sacrifice him for the sake of carrying out their war. We're lucky they haven't already noted his absence and stormed across the border right into our domains."

Donovan shifts his weight, clearly uncomfortable with that thought. "We've already summoned warriors from the nearby packs. We didn't take this step unprepared. But surely even those feather-brains value their oaths to the Heart enough not to choose bloodshed when we're perfectly willing to return their colleague to them for a simple promise of peace."

I shrug. "It'd be nice to think that. You may even be right. But it hardly seems worth the gamble when they've already proven themselves bloodthirsty many times over. And what kind of peace would we really receive if it's agreed to under duress rather than through a real truce? They'll begrudge us this violation until they find some way to pay us back. Whatever agreement we reach, they'll be brainstorming ways to circumvent it the moment it's set."

"Then we ensure there is no circumventing it," Donovan says stubbornly.

Sylas shakes his head. "The greatest minds have never managed to strike a bargain neither party could wriggle their way out of. If we free Corwin and atone for this transgression now, he may yet speak up for the peace you want. We'll prove we can be reasonable, even if our baser instincts got the better of some of us today. But that window of opportunity is closing. If we're going to change anything, we have to do so before Celia alerts the winter realm tomorrow."

The younger arch-lord's gaze slides away from us, his eyes hazing with thought. A furrow creases his forehead. When he returns his attention to us, I can tell from the strain in his voice that we've gotten as far as we can with him.

"Perhaps I should have consulted with you before we proceeded with this course of action. I can see I might have decided differently then. On the other hand, when we had to make the decision, we didn't yet know how the human's return would play out."

"I still would have said—"

"I understand your position," Donovan cuts in, quiet but firm. "Please understand this: I can't become dependent on your judgment while I'm arch-lord in my own right. I was convinced by the points Celia laid out… and now I feel we've come too far to truly backtrack. What peace could our prisoner want with us no matter how we proceed? If we set him free, we'll suffer all the negative consequences of the attempt and none of the good. I'm sorry, Sylas."

Sylas inclines his head, accepting the impasse. "Let us hope we can avoid the worst of those possible consequences, then."

We remain silent for most of the long walk back to the new castle. My limbs itch to free my wolf, to run through the forest so swiftly the world narrows down to the thunder of my paws against the earth and the panting of my breath. But Sylas doesn't shift, so I remain beside him, waiting for him to indicate he's ready to start planning our next moves.

"Do we have any grounds for delaying Celia's overture to the Unseelie tomorrow?" he asks as the castle comes into view, a few windows still glowing with amber light.

"I'm sure I could stitch together an excuse that sounds halfway plausible, but I'm not sure she'd accept anything less than undeniable."

"That's true." He exhales slowly. "What are my options here, Whitt? I have an even greater responsibility to uphold the decisions of the arch-lords now that I *am* one. I can't imagine what chaos would result if I made a move against Celia and Donovan. But this plan of hers—I can't picture any way it ends well."

I appreciate his faith in me. If only I had more helpful advice to give. "I can't either, but your hands *are* rather tied. Perhaps there is some way Talia could press the advantage of her blood's boon with the full moon so close?"

Sylas makes a dismissive sound. "Celia doesn't care much for her beyond her blood. She'd order it taken by force if Talia attempted to put any conditions on her contribution. Then we'd have a different sort of war between the arch-lords."

I roll my shoulders, soaking in the warmth of the breeze before we head into the castle. I foresee a sleepless night ahead of me. "I'll dig through every record I can get my hands on. If there's a viable solution, you'll have it from me as soon as I've come across it."

As we cross the entrance room, Talia herself appears in the archway at the other end, luminous as always with her vibrant hair falling around her pale, pretty face and that new green dress following her lithe curves. The hope in her expression fades at the sight of us. "He wouldn't change his mind?"

The frustration in Sylas's expression deepens. "He didn't deny the points we raised, but he's afraid that even if we altered course now, the Unseelie will be so affronted that we'll have war on our hands either way."

She frowns, folding her arms over her chest. "They don't even know he's been captured yet, do they?"

"I expect someone will have wondered at his absence by now, but Celia won't be making a formal proclamation until tomorrow." Sylas grimaces. "I supposed we should be glad she granted us that much amnesty to make our own case, as poorly as it's gone. Donovan assumes that even if she doesn't get the chance to reveal her plot, Corwin won't hesitate to after how she's treated him."

"He doesn't want war either. No matter what happened today."

"I know. But I can understand why my colleagues would find it hard to believe."

Sylas walks over to Talia, checking that none of our

pack-kin are nearby, and enfolds her in an embrace. Any jealousy I might have felt watching her hug him back so tightly is long gone now. I only wish we had better news to comfort her with.

The three of us will stand together around her, whether she's bound in soul to that blighted bird shifter arch-lord or not.

"We haven't given up," Sylas assures her as he releases her. "There's still a little time."

Talia turns her bright, worried gaze on me. "You're going to look for answers—some policy or precedent that might convince Donovan or stop Celia? Can I help?"

I think of the boxes of parchment records recently carted over from Hearthshire that clutter my new office. I'm not sure she'd be able to make much of even the archaic fae handwriting many of our ancestors and peers documented their thoughts in. But the need to do *something* practically vibrates off of her. I don't know how to deny this sweet, fierce spirit I've come to love so much that it's been a constant ache inside me these last ten days.

It might do *me* some good, having her by my side for what little time she can stay there.

I beckon her over. "More eyes on the task can't hurt anything."

She falls into step beside me as we climb the stairs, slipping her hand into mine as easily as if she never left. As if she doesn't technically belong to another man in a way I can never hope to match. I squeeze her fingers, and she tightens her grip in return.

"So," I find myself saying lightly, "your wintery arch-lord didn't turn out to be quite as horrifying as we feared?"

"No, not at all. Just… different. It took a while for us to understand each other properly. And we still have a ways to go." Talia looks up at me. "That hasn't changed anything. I don't—I don't love you, or Sylas or August, any less than I did before."

I can't stop a smile from spreading across my lips. "And he doesn't mind knowing that?"

"I think he can't help minding a little. He didn't seem to think that we could compromise. But he's willing to be patient while I figure things out."

"Perhaps less patient now that our kind have collared him like a mongrel." Celia's scheme may have damaged not just our chances of real peace with the Unseelie but any hope of Talia's soul-twined mate accepting our place in her life as well, damn her. I resist the urge to grit my teeth.

"He knows that's not your fault," Talia says with so much confidence I envy her. She touches my face and draws me to her, and Heart help me, even if that soul-twined mate of hers is aware of this through her bond, I can't bring myself to care. I'm not going to deny her one bit of the passion I'm longing to pour into our kiss.

Talia's fingers curl against the back of my neck. I revel in the soft heat of her mouth, coaxing a whimper from her with a flick of my tongue. She's his, but for now, she's also *mine*.

And I'd be hers in every possible way I could be if so much wasn't at stake. She eases back down, her hand lingering by my neck and her head tipped close to mine. "It's not safe for me to know your true name yet, but I still hope someday it will be. If you still want to offer it by then."

I press another kiss to her temple. "I'll never not want you, mighty one." The desire to show her just how much I want her winds through me in a scorching current, but I rein it in. Our chances of ever reaching that day depend a great deal on us occupying ourselves in more productive ways tonight. "Come, let's see if we can't divert tomorrow's catastrophe."

"We'll figure something out," Talia says as we continue up the stairs. "There has to be something." But she sounds as if she's trying to convince herself as much as me.

Talia

When I step outside, the darkness closes in around me with the cooling night air. Only one window still shines with light overhead—the one in Whitt's study. It didn't take long for me to figure out that most of the fae records were more likely to give me a headache than let me solve our current problems, but I got the impression Whitt planned to stay up through the night if that's what it took.

I told him to let me know if he found anything that could help Corwin, even if he had to wake me up. But after I left the study, I discovered I was too restless to go to bed yet. I came downstairs instead, hoping the fresh air and the stillness of the night would help put my nerves a little more at ease.

Corwin has managed to drift off himself, as far as I can tell from the definite but formless sense of his presence on the other end of our bond. At least he's getting some rest.

My heart squeezes at the thought of him slumped in the stone-walled prison room I caught glimpses of through his awareness. Celia isn't treating him with any more dignity than a basic criminal.

Of course, for all I know she'd be even worse with any fae who *wasn't* an arch-lord.

A slim figure emerges from one of the pack village houses, which my pack-kin have started to expand to their full size. Harper pauses when she sees me and then walks over to join me, her mouth tightening. "No news about Corwin?"

I shake my head. "Not so far." And tomorrow morning, Celia will be informing the Unseelie arch-lords of his imprisonment and her demands. Once she does that, I don't know how there'll be any coming back.

I rub my arms, chilled from within, and Harper sidles closer. "It isn't right, what she did. I know she's an arch-lord, and I don't love the ravens or anything—but I don't think she's being fair to him at all."

"The trouble is getting *her* to see that." I sigh. "The Seelie and Unseelie have never really gotten along, right? And it's been almost thirty years of attacks from the winter side. It makes sense that she's fed up. I have no idea how you can change someone's mind in a situation like that."

Harper drops her gaze and then looks at me again. "I did something horrible to you, and you've been able to forgive me. If that's possible... there's got to be some way to make her see he's not a bad person."

"Or at least make Donovan see it. But Sylas and Whitt already talked to him and couldn't convince him. They know fae politics—if *they* couldn't get through to him..."

My friend offers me a soft smile. "Was it politics that convinced you to give me another chance? From what I've seen, you've been able to convince a lot of fae to change their minds about how much they should respect *you*. Maybe you can do that for your soul-twined mate too."

An ache comes into my chest. I wish it were that easy. "Yeah." Exhaustion rolls up over me, and I rub my eyes. "I guess I'll hope that sleeping on it will give me some answers."

"I'll see you tomorrow." Harper gives my forearm a comforting squeeze, and I shoot her a quick smile in return before heading back inside.

But once I've burrowed under the covers on my bed, I don't fall asleep right away. Harper's words keep running through my mind.

It's true—I *didn't* forgive her because it made sense to or out of some political strategy. It wasn't even her proving over and over how dedicated she was to making up for her mistake, although that made it easier to trust her.

No, when I really started thinking about her as my friend again—it was that evening in Corwin's palace when she sat with me and admitted how she'd envied me and how much she admired me. When we really talked like two people who wanted to understand each other, and it felt like we were more the same than the differences of being fae or human could come between us.

Has Donovan even talked to Corwin? Does he have any idea who the enemy he's condemning really is? Before I got to know the Unseelie arch-lord, *I* saw all of the winter fae as cruel villains.

Maybe there is something I can bring to Donovan that

my men couldn't. I can make it personal instead of political.

That thought chases me into an uneasy sleep. I wake up with the dawn, my nerves prickling.

There isn't much more time. If I'm going to talk to the youngest arch-lord, I have to do it now.

I dress and wash quickly, debating asking one of my men to accompany me. But if they haven't come to tell me they've found a fix, then they're still working on the problem or getting much-needed rest of their own.

Besides, I want Donovan to know that I'm speaking totally for myself, not acting as a mouthpiece for Sylas. I've never really talked with him before. He has to see me as a person in my own right, a person with valid viewpoints he might not have considered.

As I head out of the castle, my heart thumps faster. The daylight is still thin, the sun not yet risen to where it's visible in the sky. I'm not sure Donovan will even be awake himself yet.

Oh well. I can't wait for him to have a leisurely morning. I'll drag him out of bed to hear me out if I have to.

I've never walked from our new domain to Donovan's before. Even with the castles set fairly close to the central Bastion, it's a bit of a hike. By the time the glossy clay walls come into sight up ahead, my warped foot is throbbing in the braced boot, my limp becoming more pronounced.

My jaw clenches, and I force myself onward as quickly and steadily as I can. I don't need him thinking of me as weak.

Corwin's voice travels to me from within. *What are you doing, Talia?* The words come with a sense of resignation and fatigue, as if the sleep didn't do him much good.

Whatever I can to get you free, I reply firmly. *I'm not giving up without trying everything.*

A flicker of fear licks through me. *Don't put yourself in any danger on my account.*

I don't think this will be dangerous. The worse that'll happen is I'll embarrass myself. At least, I think so. Sylas has always said Donovan has the kindest views toward humans out of all the original arch-lords, and I'm still the source of their cure. He's not likely to allow me to get hurt even if he's annoyed by the intrusion, right?

Although even if I thought he might, I'd still be doing this.

The aches of Corwin's body from lying on the hard floor echo into me. He must catch my flare of anger on his behalf. *I'll survive this. I've been through worse.*

I'd like to aim for something a little higher than you simply surviving, I say.

As I wobble the last few steps to the castle door, uncomfortably conscious of the sun rising ever higher, a couple of guards materialize on the front steps. I raise my chin to stare at one and then the other. "I need to talk to Arch-Lord Donovan."

They eye me with some skepticism. My pink hair combined with my human attributes must make me immediately identifiable, but to most of the fae I'm still more a blood dispenser than a being with my own will. They wouldn't be expecting me to come calling on their lord by myself.

"On what matter?" one asks.

"That's for me to discuss with him." I frown at her. "You know I'm with Arch-Lord Sylas's pack. You know there's no way I could be a threat to any fae, let alone an arch-lord, anyway." I hold up my hands in a gesture of helplessness. I didn't even put on my belt with my dagger and my pouch of salt. Better that they see me as harmless.

The guards step closer together to mutter to each other, and I resist the urge to shift impatiently on my feet. Finally, the woman beckons me to follow her inside. "Come with me. I'll check whether he's willing to see you."

I hustle after her through the halls, past the ballroom where we gathered for a banquet what feels like years ago, into a tighter network of passages. The guard motions for me to stop at one bend and marches off alone. I stand there, hugging myself and tuning out the pain in my foot as well as I can.

If she comes back and tries to send me away, I'll have to make a scene. Yell at the top of my lungs, hope Donovan hears me and that I can say something that'll catch his attention. What would do that?

Thankfully, I don't need to find out. A minute later, the guard reappears and gestures for me to follow her with a jerk of her hand. The set of her mouth suggests that she's not pleased with the situation. She leads me around another corner to a door that's slightly ajar.

"She's here," she announces through the gap.

"Send her in," Donovan says in his warm tenor.

I slip past the door and find myself in a room that's clearly his office, though a lot messier than Sylas's, let alone Corwin's. Donovan is leaning rather casually against the front of his desk, but he watches me enter with wary attention as well as curiosity. His light brown eyes gleam with alertness, nearly as bright as his flame-like hair. At least it doesn't look as if my visit called him out of bed.

"You've come alone?" he says, even though the guard must have told him that. There's a click as she shuts the study door for us.

I'd like to sit down to rest my foot, but while he's standing, I draw myself up as straight as I can instead. "You've already talked to Sylas and Whitt. I'm here to make my own case. Would having someone fae with me make you more likely to listen?"

Donovan blinks at me as if he's startled that I've drawn attention so directly to my humanity and the prejudices that come with it. It takes him a moment to recover. "No. I'm willing to hear what you've come to say, although I must tell you it's unlikely you'll change my mind."

"Maybe you should wait until you've actually heard me before you decide that," I say with more tartness than I'd usually allow myself. But I'm getting tired of constantly having fae assume I'm not just harmless but hopeless as well, and at least my boldness brings a sharper intentness into Donovan's gaze.

He flicks his hand toward me. "By all means, begin."

I inhale deeply, my pulse kicking up another notch. Corwin's presence in the back of my mind both bolsters my resolve and justifies it. "I've come to speak for my soul-twined mate. To ask you to side with Sylas and insist that Celia let him go rather than continuing with her plan."

"And that's what Sylas and I have already spoken

about. I was clear in my feelings on the matter. Nothing you say could change the facts of the situation."

"I don't want to change the facts. I just think there are a lot of them that you don't know and probably haven't considered. You don't believe that Corwin will forgive what Celia's done to him. I *know* he will. I know that if he's released, he'll still work to stop the attacks on the Seelie."

Donovan's expression takes on a pitying cast that I don't like at all. "I can understand you feel close to him given your bond, but of course he'd portray himself in that light if he thinks it'll get him out of the prison."

I have to restrain a glare. "Do you think I can't tell the difference between a direct statement and the way fae like to talk around a subject so they don't have to lie? The problem isn't that I don't know what to believe—it's that you assume there's no way you can trust him. But you have a lot more in common with him than you've bothered to find out. I bet you're more like him than you're like Celia."

The arch-lord coughs a guffaw at that idea. "I hardly think one of the Unseelie and I—"

I cut in, with a quick whiff of apology to Corwin for revealing any of his history myself. "Did you know he found himself in the arch-lord position unexpectedly because his father died before his time? Like what happened with your mother. He's had to prove himself and deal with older colleagues who think they know better than him just as you have."

Donovan's face darkens. "Don't bring my mother into this."

"I'm not. I'm only saying that you've experienced a lot of the same struggles." I grope for a less fraught example. "You love music, don't you? You have that famous harp that everyone wanted to see during your banquet. Corwin's family named their domain after the music the castle they built creates. Heart's Cadence. He has a gorgeous harp—he plays it well too."

"I don't see what any of this has to do with the potential of war between our peoples."

Oh, for God's sake. I glower at him. "Do *you* want there to be full-out war? Even after all the attacks and the deaths that've already happened?"

"Of course not," Donovan says. "But it isn't my decision. As soon as word gets back to the Unseelie arch-lords about what we've done, they'll be even more up in arms. That's why we need some leverage."

"No, that's why you need to let Corwin go before Celia tells them. That's the only way they won't find out."

"You expect me to believe that after being captured and imprisoned—"

"Yes," I snap. "If you can get over thirty years of raids and killings and still want to find a way to make peace, then you should be able to imagine that he could get over one night in a prison cell. Maybe even for the exact same reasons it matters to you."

I flinch afterward even though Donovan hasn't moved, aware of how hostile my tone sounded. That's definitely not how anyone is supposed to speak to an arch-lord.

Donovan stares at me. My obvious fear of his reaction might even make him stop and think a little longer.

"Please," I say, willing my tone to soften. "I thought

the winter fae must all be horrible too. I don't know why they've been attacking the Seelie, but I know they're still *fae*, not mindless monsters. I promise you, I can tell the difference there too. The worst fae I've dealt with so far were right here in the realm of summer."

The corners of the arch-lord's mouth twitch downward—and so does his gaze, to my warped foot. To the way I'm standing with my weight mostly on the other to offset the ache. "You should sit down," he says abruptly.

"I'm fine. *I'm* not the one you need to be concerned about right now."

He lifts his head to meet my gaze, his stance less tense now but his gaze penetrating. "And what will *you* do if we release your mate? Will you go back to the winter realm and make a home for yourself with those fae?"

"Are you worried that I'll forget about helping with your curse?" I let out a short laugh. "I've met the worst fae here, but also the best. The summer realm has my loyalty first."

"For now."

The idea comes to me with a prickling sensation that starts in my gut. But once it's occurred to me, I can't shake it. Maybe I'll regret this, but I need him to trust *me* before he's ever going to trust Corwin.

"I'll swear to it. That I'll never spend more than a week at a time with the Unseelie and that I'll always return for the full moon, as long as the curse still exists. You and the other arch-lords can decide on the exact wording of the vow and the consequences of breaking it, and I'll take it. This morning, if that's what you need. Then you'll have that guarantee. Anything that hurts me will hurt Corwin too. You'll still have your leverage if anyone tries to break my promise."

My stomach twists, but Corwin reaches out to me like a squeeze of my hand. *It's all right. If they need that commitment, I don't resent you making it. I already knew you weren't going to be mine alone.*

Donovan considers me for several seconds longer. Then he lets out a rough chuckle. "I'm starting to see how you've won so much of Sylas's respect. I appreciate your dedication and that you were brave enough to speak up. But it still comes down to this Unseelie arch-lord who's all but an unknown quantity and a soul-twined bond proves very little about his loyalties. I'm sure you believe what you're saying, but his truth is the only one that matters."

I swallow hard. *Corwin, I'm not sure you're going to like this, but it might be our only way out. Can* you *trust me?*

He replies without hesitation. *What do you need from me, Talia?*

I answer him and Donovan at the same time. "Then speak to Corwin. Let's go talk to him right now. He can tell you how much the peace matters to him, straight from his own mouth."

At least, I hope he can lower those walls of his enough to show Donovan how much he means it—before it's too late to make a difference.

Corwin

 brace myself against the stone walls of my prison cell, holding in the urge to tug at the ridiculous collar that chafes my neck. The searing sensation of the iron within it has dwindled to a dull burning, but it still spreads all through my body with every movement.

That's not what I'm bracing myself for, though. I'm preparing for the interrogation about to commence.

Talia has kept her side of our bond open since we arrived here. I can follow her now as she and the red-haired Seelie arch-lord stride up to the entrance of the same limestone castle I was escorted into yesterday. Her determination cuts through her anxiety, but she *is* nervous. She's afraid her gambit won't play out in our favor.

I'm not certain it will either, although I'll give it my best.

Before her eyes, the elderly Seelie arch-lord in charge

of the warriors who took me into custody appears. She and the other arch-lord exchange stern words back and forth. Talia watches it all with a knot in her stomach. I try to extend reassurance toward her, but it may not be all that convincing. My own gut has tightened into a ball.

What will this young arch-lord whose past is strikingly similar to mine want to ask me? How much will I even be able to answer? I still have my duty to my own people to consider. It doesn't do me any good getting released from this prison if I put all the winter fae at a disadvantage with what I reveal.

At least he seems reasonably well-spoken. When he points out to my captor that she has no reason to stop him from speaking to me, that if what I say would change his mind about her plan then it's all the more important that he has the chance to hear it, she sighs but backs down. With a tentative rush of relief, Talia follows him into the castle.

Her foot is hurting her. A twinge shoots from her to me with each limping step. My hands clench at my sides with the wish that I was in a position to sweep her right off those feet—the way that one of her men, August, did when she first rushed to them on our arrival.

The memory doesn't raise my hackles as it might have once. So much joy flowed through her just at seeing them. When I accept that those three are intertwined with her life nearly as much as I am—more, in some ways—and set the jealousy aside… that joy is mine too. I can accept it from her and make it my own.

I can't remember the last time I felt anywhere near the

level of happiness that she shared with me in those first few moments before the warriors descended on me.

There's very little to rejoice at this particular moment. My awareness through Talia and of the outer world start to merge with the tapping of footsteps my own ears can pick up from farther down the dim hall. Talia's nose wrinkles at the damp, muddy scent that my senses adjusted to many hours ago. Another jolt of anger races through her knowing this is where I've been locked away.

So fierce is my soul-twined mate. It seems absurd that in my first realizing what she was, I balked at the idea of her human failings. If anyone called her weak within my hearing now, I'd laugh in their face.

Even in this precarious situation with so much resting on the conversation ahead, the knowledge that her ferocity has come out on my behalf wraps warmth around my heart.

Then the door to the cell swings open, and I'm seeing her before me—my mate and the red-haired arch-lord beside her. In that first second, it's hard to focus on anything but her: her gaze taking in the dried blood from a blow to my temple that I haven't had the magic to seal, the bindings that truss my wrists and ankles to ensure I can't put up a physical fight much easier than a magical one. Even more anger flares behind her delicate features.

"Who hurt him?" she demands of the guard who must have unlocked the door.

The Seelie warrior's expression turns carefully blank, but he speaks with an audible growl. "The occasional wound is unavoidable when ensuring a prisoner is secured.

No magic can touch him to heal it while the iron-cored collar is on him."

"I can see to it," says the arch-lord—Donovan, I've heard him called in Talia's presence. He shoos the guard away before returning his wary gaze to me. "If you'll let me."

"It isn't bothering me so much that I'd trouble you," I say evenly. "But if it's important to you, I wouldn't argue about it."

He crouches down near me, confident enough in his strength and my bindings to show no fear of attack. "Whatever you might think of us right now, we aren't brutes."

I could argue that I didn't need this one incident to think of the hotheaded, wolf-shifting summer fae as brutes, but my predicament and the memory of Talia's chiding hold my tongue. It is true that in the past few decades, we Unseelie have played that role toward the Seelie much more than vice versa. Certainly most of the glimpses I've had of Talia's pack through her eyes have been unexpectedly civilized, even if she's faced plenty of viciousness elsewhere in this realm.

Donovan pulls a square of cloth from one pocket and a small flask from another, and pours a little liquid on to the cloth. When he dabs at the scrape, my skin stings, and Talia tenses.

Donovan straightens up and draws back a step. "That's the best I can do for now. It's at least clean."

Talia remains near the door, a longing radiating from her to come to me and offer whatever comfort she can with her embrace. She doesn't want to interfere with the conversation, though, or to emphasize my current helplessness. I extend a current of affection through our bond.

"Your soul-twined mate has spoken valiantly on your behalf," Donovan says, as if I wasn't privy to that conversation too. Perhaps he doesn't realize. "I'd like to hear from your own mouth, with the Heart watching over us, your current feelings on relations between our peoples."

I'm well-practiced at speaking under pressure, at stripping away any emotions nagging at me to present the sort of crystalline practicality expected of an arch-lord. I aim for the words that'll express my thoughts most directly, without room for debate.

"I believe, as I have from the beginning, that the violence the Unseelie have perpetrated along the summer border was unnecessary, and that we would have been better served by reaching out to address our concerns peacefully. My current situation hasn't altered that opinion."

"What would your intentions be if you were freed without repercussions?"

"I would return to my domain and make no mention of this misstep to my colleagues. And I would continue to press them to open a dialogue with you and the other Seelie arch-lords, even more emphatically now that I have a stake in the lives of those in the summer realm." My gaze slides to Talia for a moment before returning to Donovan.

The Seelie arch-lord eyes me as if he's trying to work out some way my words can be a lie. Well, that likely *is* what he's thinking—that I'm twisting my statements to hide my true intent. But I'm not sure I could have been more baldly honest.

I'm almost starting to relax when he crosses his arms and shoots his next question at me. "And what can you tell us about your people's reasons for launching all those assaults on us in the first place?"

My breath catches at the base of my throat. I haven't even spoken to Talia about this. As she well knows. My noble mate leaps in before I have to say anything at all. "He can't talk about that without permission from the other Unseelie arch-lords."

That's true, but not quite as thoroughly as I let her believe. I smother my awareness of that fact and force a tight smile at Donovan. "All I can say is that while I highly disagree with their methods, I understand why they felt the need to take some kind of action. It wasn't out of malice."

I can't blame him for looking skeptical. "Then why do you disagree with them?" he asks. "Why not support them in their aggression against us, if you don't see it as unjustified?"

I roll my answer around in my mouth, every part of me balking at having to answer at all. There's no easy way to talk about this without giving away more than I trust this man who belongs to summer to know.

His eyes narrow with each passing second before I speak. I push myself to get on with it. "I can believe there's an urgent need for *some* sort of action without agreeing with the specific methods. I was willing to think better of the Seelie than my colleagues. I felt we should be able to reach a compromise that didn't require any violence. They were unwilling to take the risk of a true parlay."

Donovan scoffs, anger flashing in his eyes. "You talk about compromise and thinking better of us, and yet you won't even tell us why your people have been *murdering* ours for tens of years. How am I supposed to believe you're being fully honest? Why should you care what happens to any of us in the summer realm, especially after how you've been treated in the past day?"

I don't know how to answer that at all. My chest constricts, and a flicker of panic washes from Talia into me. She bites her lip, and I know she can tell as well as I can that the Seelie arch-lord is moments from walking away and leaving me here.

What does he want from me? I've told him what I can as plainly as I can. What more is there—

Talia's voice breaks through my thoughts, taut with worry. *He doesn't see how much it matters to you. He can't feel how you feel about it the way I can. He isn't going to think less of you if you show him you do care, I promise you. They're not like the Unseelie that way.*

No, they're not. As I gaze back at Donovan, meeting his glare, understanding hits me like a smack of fiery heat.

That's exactly what we've always scorned about the summer fae, isn't it? Their tempers and passions that they let overrun logic and good sense. But the Seelie arch-lord isn't seeing earnest practicality in my words any more than Talia did when I tried to wipe her longing for her lovers from her mind.

My colleagues would have applauded my self-control —if they were feeling generous—but to him I must sound cold. Unfeeling. And the matter to him is clearly one of intense emotion.

Why *should* he believe that I'm dedicated to peace if I only talk about it so dispassionately?

I open my mouth, and the constricting sensation crawls up to my throat. In the back of my mind, the memories rise up of my mother's sobs wrenching from her bedroom, of her scream as she stabbed a knife into her chest just shy of a fatal blood. The horrified faces of the folk of my flock. Other faces, frozen in deathly agony. My colleagues' sneering voices.

Shameful, the way we carried on. All that emotion whipping us this way and that. A crack of instability running straight through the family line…

Bad enough that my own people saw it. To let what I'm feeling show through now, to admit my hopes and fears, I might as well be tearing off my clothes in front of this man who's both a stranger and, at the moment, my enemy.

A flare of my own anger rises up. If he'd just listen to reason—if he didn't insist on doubting everything I say—

But then, wouldn't I be furious if the Seelie had been slaughtering the fae of my flock without any explanation, no matter how I might try to suppress that rage? Haven't I distrusted Talia's companions every step of the way?

I close my eyes against the clash of impulses inside me.

I spoke of compromise. Donovan's coming to me, asking me these questions, is his version of practicality. No doubt his emotions would dictate that he toss me to whatever fate his harsher colleague has in mind without concern for the larger consequences.

All Talia is asking is that I meet him halfway.

I can do this. I can let my guard down for her, for my people, for the future I've been arguing for all these years. If it backfires, if I go too far or reveal too much, then at least I tried instead of hiding away behind borders and walls both inside and out like the other winter arch-lords have insisted on for so long.

Inhaling sharply, I meet Donovan's eyes again. "I apologize. I've been speaking to you as an arch-lord, as I've spent decades teaching myself to act to fill that role. But you deserve an answer from one man to another. I've seen too much death in this lifetime to welcome it regardless of which sort of fae are meeting it. I've felt sick to my stomach with each new assault—and horrified with myself that I haven't been able to convince my colleagues of another approach. We've treated you horribly, and I can't tell you how sorry I am for that."

The strain of admitting so much to him and of the fraught emotions themselves brings a rasp into my voice. The Seelie arch-lord blinks, surprise softening the hostility in his face. "But in the end, you'll side with your kind ahead of ours as you have before," he says. "Has all that much really changed? If your soul-twined mate joins you in the winter realm—"

"She's already offered to swear to return here regularly," I break in, not seeing any point in pretending I wasn't watching when she made that promise. "And besides that..." I look at Talia again, an unmistakable swell of longing and affection squeezing around my lungs. Sensing it, she offers me a small but encouraging smile that just about kills me.

This isn't how I'd have wanted her to hear these words first, but if I don't give the conversation everything I have, I might not get a chance to do it properly. And all the ways she's defended me in the past day have only made me certain of how true they are, after only suspecting it before.

I drag my gaze back to Donovan. "I love her. More than I knew I could love anyone. But her soul is tied to the Seelie in ways even the Heart's will can't sever—and having seen her here among you, I wouldn't wish it to. Your people matter to her, and so they'll always matter to me as well."

Corwin… Talia's inner voice sounds both shaken and moved. She doesn't seem to know what else to say. I keep my gaze fixed on Donovan's, but I send all the warmth I have in me her way. I don't expect her to be able to match my devotion just yet. It'll be an honor to earn it in as much time as it takes me. Simply remembering her calling me her mate lights me up inside all over again and bolsters my next words.

"Give me the chance to take up the cause myself," I tell the Seelie arch-lord, "and I promise I won't rest until I've gotten my fellow arch-lords' agreement to have a proper negotiation with you so we can resolve this conflict peacefully. Before, I didn't know anything about the people we were attacking. Now I do, and that makes all the difference."

A tremor runs through me as I finish. It's been a long, hard day, and I've let loose more emotion in the past few minutes than I have for years before.

It's drained me, but in a strange way there's a relief to

that fatigue. The constant swallowing down and bottling up left a weight in my gut that's been partially lifted.

It takes a little while before Donovan recovers his own voice. He dips his head with more respect than he showed me on his arrival. "All right," he says. "I apologize for misjudging you and assuming all the Unseelie saw the situation the same way. Let me talk to my colleagues before it's too late to change course, and I'll see that you get out of here."

Talia

"I'm glad that we can say our farewells on friendlier terms than appeared possible earlier, and hopefully for only a short time," Sylas says, with the slightest of bows to Corwin as he holds out his hand.

The Unseelie arch-lord offers a hesitant smile and a firm shake in return. "As am I." His gaze slips from Sylas to Whitt and August flanking him. "I look forward to getting to know you all better face to face as much as I have through Talia."

There's no suppressing the giddy rush of seeing all of my men—and Corwin *is* mine, I can't deny it now—accepting each other and taking these first steps toward some kind of alliance.

Even more affection sweeps through my chest when Sylas steps back with a nod toward me. "We'll give you your privacy to say your goodbyes to your mate."

I shoot him a quick smile in thanks. The three of them

draw back to where Astrid was watching from the outskirts of the field, and together they meander into the sparse stretch of trees between here and the open area around the new castle.

I turn back to Corwin where he's standing just a few steps shy of the border's haze, almost the exact same spot as when he brought me back here yesterday.

The iron-cored collar has left a reddish ring around his neck that Sylas's healer couldn't completely erase. The sight of it sends a jab of distress through me. I go to him, rising up on my toes to gently touch that spot.

Corwin shows no pain from the contact through the sharper awareness that snaps into place with the brush of my skin to his, only a flicker of eager heat. "I'll just have to wear shirts with high collars for a few days until it fully heals," he says, with a trace of amusement as if he'll enjoy pulling one over on his colleagues. Considering what jerks they've been to him, maybe he will.

I let my hand drop to his chest. "You don't think the other arch-lords will suspect something went wrong here?"

He shakes his head. "I'll tell my staff that I was… encouraged to stay the night in honor of our bond. It's true enough in a way. If any of my colleagues have bothered to notice I was gone longer than expected, they'll hear the same."

"How long do you think it'll take to persuade them to agree to a proper meeting with the summer arch-lords?"

"I don't know, but I'm not going to be put off this time. They were already vaguely considering other options when we arrived for Sylas's coronation. The idea was to test out the Seelie's hostility to us and the success of the retaliatory spell… Our soul-twined bond complicated matters."

I remember the hostile faces I saw through his eyes around the marble table in their Hall of the Heart. "They're even less happy about that than they were before."

"They'll come to terms with it. I can tell them now that the Seelie arch-lords have vowed to allow us peaceful entrance into their space to speak with them, and that they're also willing to take the vows to cross the border and meet us on our territory if we'll swear the same. It'll be easier to persuade them." Corwin's mouth twists. "After that last battle during the full moon, I think it became undeniably clear that our current approach wasn't accomplishing our goals."

As long as the Unseelie don't decide to try some approach that's even more aggressive, I guess any kind of meeting will be a win. "You'll let me know as soon as anything's settled?"

"Of course." He strokes a careful hand over my hair, his expression its usual cool mask but a gleam of fondness in his eyes. "Perhaps it'll give me the chance to see you again sooner than your next visit."

I give him a crooked smile. "It's not as if I'll ever be completely out of reach."

"No. But I won't intrude on your time here. I know you wouldn't have rejoined me right away regardless."

That's true, and not just because of the Seelie curse and the three other men I've been apart from for too long. The only way we could convince Celia to agree to the terms of assembling with the Unseelie arch-lords was for me to take the oath I suggested to Donovan.

As long as the full-moon curse exists, I'm now bound to stay in the summer realm for the week around the full moon, and not to remain in the winter realm for more than a week at any other time without at least a day here in between. But Corwin hasn't shown any animosity over that promise. If anything, he's seemed almost pleased that I've solidified my loyalties to the Seelie.

I still don't know how we'll balance my conflicting affections in the long run, but we've reached a tentative, temporary understanding. I'll be mates in all but name to my Seelie men while I'm here, and continue to see how I might settle into the role of soul-twined mate to Corwin while I'm with him, with no resentment on either side. For now I think they're all just glad that I still want each of *them* in my life as well as the others.

I lean my head against Corwin's chest, and after a moment's hesitation, his arms rise to wrap around me. His embrace floods me with the tender joy that came with his words to Donovan this morning.

I love her.

Will I be able to say that in return sometime in the future? Everything still feels so precarious. But I'll miss him, even though he'll still be with me no matter how far apart we are. I want to know him better so I can find out just how deep my feelings for him will run.

You can take all the time you need, he says quietly through the bond, hugging me tighter. *I've waited centuries to meet my soul-twined mate. Patience is not a problem.*

My smile turns bittersweet. That line of thinking has

stirred up one difficult subject I have to touch on before he goes.

I ease back so I can gaze up at him. "Corwin—I know there are restrictions around what you can say about the Unseelie's political decisions and the rest. But I'm going to need to understand why all that fighting happened. Why you thought it was justified enough that you didn't interfere with the other arch-lords' plans. I get that you can't talk about it right now; I just—"

He quiets me with a graze of his fingers along my jaw. His dark eyes go intent and yet distant, as if he's focused on something a long way from here. Through the quiver of physical contact, I pick up on a tumultuous whirl of emotions he's sorting through. So much goes on inside this man, hidden beneath his cool exterior.

"I can tell you the basics of it now," he says in a low voice. "I just ask that you don't share it with any of the Seelie, that you let us bring the matter to them. My responsibilities allow me to speak up when I trust that it'll help my people more than harm them. If you say you can hold to that, I'll trust that you mean it."

My pulse hiccups. "It isn't anything that could hurt the Seelie, is it?"

"No, I can't see that it affects them in any way other than how we've reacted in the past. If my efforts fail and my colleagues strike out with more violence, then I won't fault you for betraying the secret."

"Okay." I drag in a breath. "Unless it comes to that, I can keep it to myself."

He's silent for a moment as he seems to gather his

words. Then he lifts his other hand to my face, cupping it gently between his palms.

"A different curse is spreading across the winter realm. One that has stolen too many lives already, including my father's. And I can't help but think that whatever it is in you that heals the Seelie's curse may give us the answer to ours as well."

ABOUT THE AUTHOR

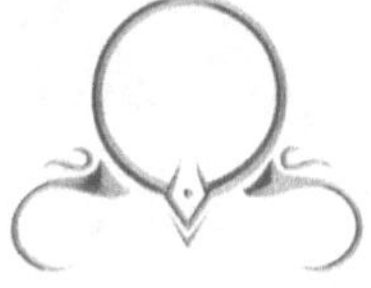

Eva Chase lives in Canada with her family. She loves stories both swoony and supernatural, and strong women and the men who appreciate them. Along with the Bound to the Fae series, she is the author of the Flirting with Monsters series, the Cursed Studies trilogy, the Royals of Villain Academy series, the Moriarty's Men series, the Looking Glass Curse trilogy, the Their Dark Valkyrie series, the Witch's Consorts series, the Dragon Shifter's Mates series, the Demons of Fame Romance series, the Legends Reborn trilogy, and the Alpha Project Psychic Romance series.

Connect with Eva online:
www.evachase.com
eva@evachase.com

www.ingramcontent.com/pod-product-compliance
Lightning Source LLC
Chambersburg PA
CBHW030556170726
48283CB00002B/355